Henry Sumner Maine

Popular Government

four essays - I. Prospects of popular government; II. Nature of democracy; III. Age

of progress; IV. Constitution of the United States

Henry Sumner Maine

Popular Government
four essays - I. Prospects of popular government; II. Nature of democracy; III. Age of progress; IV. Constitution of the United States

ISBN/EAN: 9783337423841

Printed in Europe, USA, Canada, Australia, Japan

Cover: Foto ©Andreas Hilbeck / pixelio.de

More available books at **www.hansebooks.com**

POPULAR GOVERNMENT

FOUR ESSAYS

I. PROSPECTS OF POPULAR GOVERNMENT
II. NATURE OF DEMOCRACY
III. AGE OF PROGRESS
IV. CONSTITUTION OF THE UNITED STATES

By SIR HENRY SUMNER MAINE, F.R.S.

FOREIGN ASSOCIATE MEMBER OF THE INSTITUTE OF FRANCE

NEW EDITION

LONDON
JOHN MURRAY, ALBEMARLE STREET
1890

PRINTED BY
SPOTTISWOODE AND CO., NEW-STREET SQUARE
LONDON

PREFACE.

THE four Essays which follow are connected with studies to which, during much of my life, I have devoted such leisure as I have been able to command. Many years ago I made the attempt, in a work on " Ancient Law," to apply the so-called Historical Method of inquiry to the private laws and institutions of Mankind. But, at the outset of this undertaking, I found the path obstructed by a number of *à priori* theories which, in all minds but a few, satisfied curiosity as to the Past and paralysed speculation as to the Future. They had for their basis the hypothesis of a Law and State of Nature antecedent to all positive institutions, and a hypothetical system of Rights and Duties appropriate to the natural condition. The gradual recovery of the natural condition was assumed to be the same thing as the progressive improvement of human institutions. Upon the examination, which was indispensable, of the true

origin and real history of these theories, I found them
to rest upon a very slender philosophical foundation,
but at the same time they might be shown to have
been extremely powerful both for good and for evil.
One of the characteristics most definitely associated
with Nature and her Law was simplicity, and thus
the theories of which I am speaking brought about
(though less in England than in other countries)
many valuable reforms of private law, by simplifying
it and clearing it from barbarous technicalities. They
had, further, a large share in the parentage of International Law, and they thus helped to mitigate in
some small degree the sanguinary quarrelsomeness
which has accompanied the human race through the
whole course of its history.   But, on the other hand,
they in my judgment unnerved the human intellect,
and thus made it capable of the extravagances into
which it fell at the close of the eighteenth century.
And they certainly gave a false bias to all historical
inquiry into the growth of society and the development of law.

    It had always been my desire and hope to apply
the Historical Method to the political institutions of
men.   But, here again, the inquiry into the history of
these institutions, and the attempt to estimate their true
value by the results of such an inquiry, are seriously

embarrassed by a mass of ideas and beliefs which have grown up in our day on the subject of one particular form of government, that extreme form of popular government which is called Democracy. A portion of the notions which prevail in Europe concerning Popular Government are derived (and these are worthy of all respect) from observation of its practical work-ing; a larger portion merely reproduce technical rules of the British or American Constitutions in an altered or disguised form ; but a multitude of ideas on this subject, ideas which are steadily absorb-ing or displacing all others, appear to me, like the theories of jurisprudence of which I have spoken, to have been conceived *à priori*. They are, in fact, another set of deductions from the assumption of a State of Nature. Their true source has never been forgotten on the Continent of Europe, where they are well known to have sprung from the teaching of Jean-Jacques Rousseau, who believed that men emerged from the primitive natural condition by a process which made every form of government, except Demo-cracy, illegitimate. In this country they are not often explicitly, or even consciously, referred to their real origin, which is, nevertheless, constantly betrayed by the language in which they are expressed. Demo-cracy is commonly described as having an inherent

superiority over every other form of government. It
is supposed to advance with an irresistible and pre-
ordained movement. It is thought to be full of the
promise of blessings to mankind ; yet if it fails to
bring with it these blessings, or even proves to be
prolific of the heaviest calamities, it is not held to
deserve condemnation. These are the familiar marks
of a theory which claims to be independent of experience and observation on the plea that it bears
the credentials of a golden age, non-historical and
unverifiable.

During the half-century in which an *à priori*
political theory has been making way among all the
civilised societies of the West, a set of political facts
have disclosed themselves by its side which appear
to me to deserve much more consideration than they
have received. Sixty or seventy years ago, it was
inevitable that an inquirer into political science should
mainly employ the deductive method of investigation.
Jeremy Bentham, who was careless of remote history,
had little before him beyond the phenomena of the
British Constitution, which he saw in the special light
of his own philosophy and from the point of view of
a reformer of private law. Besides these he had a
few facts supplied by the short American Constitutional experience, and he had the brief and most

unsuccessful experiments of the French in democratic
government. But since 1815, and especially since
1830, Popular Government has been introduced into
nearly all Continental Europe and into all Spanish
America, North, Central, and South ; and the working
of these new institutions has furnished us with a number of facts of the highest interest. Meantime, the
ancient British Constitution has been modifying itself
with a rapidity which could not be foreseen in Bentham's day. I suspect that there were few observant
Englishmen who, in presence of the agitation which
filled the summer and autumn of 1884, were not aston-
ished to discover the extent to which the Constitution
of their country had altered, under cover of old language
and old forms. And, all the while, the great strength
of some of the securities which the American Federal
Constitution has provided against the infirmities of
popular government has been proving itself in a
most remarkable way. Thus, in nearly all the
civilised world, a large body of new facts has been
formed by which I endeavour, in these Essays, to
test the value of the opinions which are gaining
currency in our day concerning Popular Government
as it verges on Democracy.

It would argue ignorance or bad faith to deny the
benefits for which, amid some calamities, mankind is

indebted to Popular Government. Nevertheless, if there be even an approximation to truth in the con clusions which I have reached in the three papers first printed in this volume, some assumptions commonly made on the subject must be discarded. In the Essay on the " Prospects of Popular Government " I have shown that, as a matter of fact, Popular Government, since its reintroduction into the world, has proved itself to be extremely fragile. In the Essay on the " Nature of Democracy " I have given some reasons for thinking that, in the extreme form to which it tends, it is, of all kinds of government, by far the most difficult. In the "Age of Progress " I have argued that the perpetual change which, as understood in modern times, it appears to demand, is not in harmony with the normal forces ruling human nature, and is apt therefore to lead to cruel disappoint- ment or serious disaster. If I am in any degree right, Popular Government, especially as it approaches the democratic form, will tax to the utmost all the political sagacity and statesmanship of the world to keep it from misfortune. Happily, if there are some facts which augur ill for its duration and success, there are others which suggest that it is not beyond the powers of human reason to discover remedies for its infirmities. For the purpose of bringing out a certain number of these latter facts, and at the same time of indicating the quarter in which the political student (once set free from *à priori* assumptions) may seek materials for a reconstruction of his science, I have examined and analysed the Constitution of the United States, a topic on which much misconception seems to be abroad. There are some who appear to suppose that it sprang at once from the brain like the Goddess of Wisdom, an idea very much in harmony with modern Continental fancies respecting the origin of Democracy. I have tried to show that its birth was in reality natural, from ordinary historical antecedents ; and that its connection with wisdom lay in the skill with which sagacious men, conscious that certain weaknesses which it had inherited would be aggravated by the new circumstances in which it would be placed, provided it with appliances calculated to minimise them or to neutralise them altogether. Its success, and the success of such American institutions as have succeeded, appears to me to have arisen rather from skilfully applying the curb to popular impulses than from giving them the rein. While the British Constitution has been insensibly transforming itself into a popular government surrounded on all sides by difficulties, the American Federal Constitution has proved that, nearly a century ago, several expedients were discovered by which some of these difficulties may be greatly miti-gated and some altogether overcome.

The publication of the substance of these Essays in the " Quarterly Review," besides giving me a larger audience than could be expected for a dissertation on abstract and general Politics which had little direct bearing on the eager controversies of Party, has gained for me the further advantage of a number of criticisms which reached me before this volume took its final shape. At the head of these I must place a series of observations with which Lord Acton has favoured me. I have freely availed myself of these results of his great learning and profound thought.

H. S. MAINE.

London : 1885.

CONTENTS.

ESSAY I.

THE PROSPECTS OF POPULAR GOVERNMENT.

THE blindness of the privileged classes in France to the Revolution which was about to overwhelm them furnishes some of the best-worn commonplaces of modern history. There was no doubt much in it to surprise us. What King, Noble, and Priest could not see, had been easily visible to the foreign observer. " In short," runs the famous passage in Chesterfield's letter of December 25, 1753, " all the symptoms which I ever met with in history previous to great changes and revolutions in government now exist and daily increase in France." A large number of writers of our day, manifesting the wisdom which comes after the event, have pointed out that the signs of a terrible time ought not to have been mistaken. The Court, the Aristocracy, and the Clergy should have understood that, in face of the irreligion which was daily becoming more fashionable, the belief in privilege conferred by birth could not be long maintained. They should have noted the portents of imminent

B

political disturbance in the intense jealousy of classes. They should have been prepared for a tremendous social upheaval by the squalor and misery of the peasants. They should have observed the immediate causes of revolution in the disorder of the finances and in the gross inequality of taxation. They should have been wise enough to know that the entire structure, of which the keystone was a stately and scandalous Court, was undermined on all sides. " Beautiful Armida Palace, where the inmates live enchanted lives ; lapped in soft music of adulation ; waited on by the splendours of the world ; which nevertheless hangs wondrously as by a single hair."[1]

But although Chesterfield appeals to history, the careful modern student of history will perhaps think the blindness of the French nobility and clergy eminently pardonable. The Monarchy, under whose broad shelter all privilege grew and seemed to thrive, appeared to have its roots deeper in the past than any existing European institution. The countries which now made up France had enjoyed no experience of popular government since the rude Gaulish freedom. From this, they had passed into the condition of a strictly administered, strongly governed, highly taxed, Roman province. The investigations of the young and learned school of historians rising in France leave it questionable

[1] Carlyle, *French Revolution*, i. 4.

whether the Germans, who are sometimes supposed
to have redeemed their own barbarism by reviving
liberty, brought anything like freedom to Gaul.
There was little more than a succession of German to
Roman privileged classes. German captains shared
the great estates, and assumed the rank, of the half-
official, half-hereditary nobility, who abounded in the
province. A German King, who was in reality only a
Roman general bearing a barbarous title, reigned over
much of Gaul and much of Central Europe. When his
race was supplanted by another in its kingship, the
new power got itself decorated with the old Roman
Imperial style ; and when at length a third dynasty
arose, the monarchy associated with it gradually
developed more vigour and vitality than any other
political institution in Europe. From the accession
of Hugh Capet to the French Revolution, there had
been as nearly as possible 800 years. During all
this time, the French Royal House had steadily
gained in power. It had wearied out and beaten
back the victorious armies of England. It had
emerged stronger than ever from the wars of religion
which humbled English kingship in the dust, dealing
it a blow from which it never thoroughly recovered.
It had grown in strength, authority, and splendour,
till it dazzled all eyes. It had become the model for
all princes. Nor had its government and its relation
to its subjects struck all men as they seem to have

struck Chesterfield. Eleven years before Chesterfield wrote, David Hume, a careful observer of
France, had thus written in 1742, " Though all kinds
of government be improved in modern times, yet
monarchical government seems to have made the
greatest advance to perfection.   It may now be
affirmed of civilised monarchies, what was formerly
said of republics alone, that they are a government of
laws, not of men.   They are found susceptible of
order, method, and constancy, to a surprising degree.
Property is there secure ; industry is encouraged ;
the arts flourish ; and the Prince lives among his
subjects like a father among his children."   And
Hume expressly adds that he saw more " sources of
degeneracy " in free governments like England than
in France, " the most perfect model of pure monarchy." [2]

Nevertheless, Hume was unquestionably wrong
in his conclusion, and Chesterfield was as unquestionably right.   The French privileged classes might
conceivably have foreseen the great Revolution, simply because it happened.   The time, however, which
is expended in wondering at their blindness, or in
pitying it with an air of superior wisdom, is as
nearly as possible wasted.   Next to what a modern
satirist has called " Hypothetics "— the science of that
which might have happened but did not—there is no

[2] Hume, Essay XII. " Of Civil Liberty."

more unprofitable study than the investigation of the possibly predictable, which was never predicted. It is of far higher advantage to note the mental condition of the French upper classes as one of the most remarkable facts in history, and to ask ourselves whether it conveys a caution to other generations than theirs. This line of speculation is at the least interesting. We too, who belong to Western Europe towards the end of the nineteenth century, live under a set of institutions which all, except a small minority, regard as likely to be perpetual. Nine men out of ten, some hoping, some fearing, look upon the popular government which, ever widening its basis, has spread and is still spreading over the world, as destined to last for ever, or, if it changes its form, to change it in one single direction. The democratic principle has gone forth conquering and to conquer, and its gainsayers are few and feeble. Some Catholics, from whose minds the diplomacy of the present Pope has not banished the Syllabus of the last, a fairly large body of French and Spanish Legitimists, and a few aged courtiers in the small circles surrounding exiled German and Italian princes, may still believe that the cloud of democratic ascendency will pass away. Their hopes may be as vain as their regrets ; but nevertheless those who recollect the surprises which the future had in store for men equally confident in the perpetuity of the present, will ask themselves whether it is really true that the expectation of virtual permanence for governments of the modern type rests upon solid grounds of historical experience as regards the past, and of rational probability as regards the time to come. I endeavour in these pages to examine the question in a spirit different from that which animates most of those who view the advent of democracy either with enthusiasm or with despair.

Out of the many names commonly applied to the political system prevailing or tending to prevail in all the civilised portions of the world, I have chosen "popular government"[3] as the name which, on the whole, is least open to objection.　But what we are witnessing in West European politics is not so much the establishment of a definite system, as the continuance, at varying rates, of a process.　The truth is that, within two hundred years, the view taken of government, or (as the jurists say) of the relation of sovereign to subject, of political superior to political inferior, has been changing, sometimes partially and slowly, sometimes generally and rapidly.　The character of this change has been described by John Stuart Mill in the early pages of his "Essay on Liberty," and more recently by Mr. Justice Stephen,

---

[3] It will be seen that I endeavour to use the term "democracy," throughout this volume, in its proper and only consistent sense ; that is, for a particular form of government.

who in his " History of the Criminal Law of England"
very strikingly uses the contrast between the old and
the new view of government to illustrate the difference between two views of the law of seditious libel.
I will quote the latter passage as less coloured than
the language of Mill by the special preferences of the
writer :—

Two different views may be taken (says Sir James
Stephen) of the relation between rulers and their subjects.
If the ruler is regarded as the superior of the subject,
as being by the nature of his position presumably wise and
good, the rightful ruler and guide of the whole population, it
must necessarily follow that it is wrong to censure him
openly, and, even if he is mistaken, his mistakes should be
pointed out with the utmost respect, and that, whether
mistaken or not, no censure should be cast on him likely or
designed to diminish his authority. If, on the other hand,
the ruler is regarded as the agent and servant, and the
subject as the wise and good master, who is obliged to delegate his power to the so-called ruler because, being a
multitude, he cannot use it himself, it must be evident that
this sentiment must be reversed. Every member of the
public who censures the ruler for the time being exercises
in his own person the right which belongs to the whole of
which he forms a part. He is finding fault with his own
servant.[4]

The States of Europe are now regulated by political institutions answering to the various stages of

---

[4] Stephen's *History of the Criminal Law of England*, ii. 299.

the transition from the old view, that "rulers are presumably wise and good, the rightful rulers and guides of the whole population," to the newer view, that "the ruler is the agent and servant, and the subject the wise and good master, who is obliged to delegate his power to the so-called ruler because, being a multitude, he cannot use it himself." Russia and Turkey are the only European States which completely reject the theory that governments hold their powers by delegation from the community, the word " community " being somewhat vaguely understood, but tending more and more to mean at least the whole of the males of full age living within certain territorial limits. This theory, which is known on the Continent as the theory of national sovereignty, has been fully accepted in France, Italy, Spain, Portugal, Holland, Belgium, Greece, and the Scandinavian States. In Germany it has been repeatedly repudiated by the Emperor and his powerful Minister, but it is to a very great extent acted upon. England, as is not unusual with her, stands by herself. There is no country in which the newer view of government is more thoroughly applied to practice, but almost all the language of the law and constitution is still accommodated to the older ideas concerning the relation of ruler and subject.

But, although no such inference could be drawn from English legal phraseology, there is no doubt

that the modern popular government of our day is
of purely English origin. When it came into existence, there were Republics in Europe, but they
exercised no moral and little political influence.
Although in point of fact they were most of them
strict oligarchies, they were regarded as somewhat
plebeian governments, over which monarchies took
rightful precedence. " The Republics in Europe,"
writes Hume in 1742, " are at present noted for want
of politeness. The good manners of a Swiss civilised
in Holland is an expression for rusticity among the
French. The English in some degree fall under the
same censure, notwithstanding their learning and
genius. And if the Venetians be an exception, they
owe it perhaps to their communication with other
Italians." If a man then called himself a Republican,
he was thinking of the Athenian or Roman Republic,
one for a while in a certain sense a democracy, the
other from first to last an aristocracy, but both ruling
a dependent empire with the utmost severity. In
reality, the new principle of government was solely
established in England, which Hume always classes
with Republics rather than with Monarchies. After
tremendous civil struggles, the doctrine that governments serve the community was, in spirit if not in
words, affirmed in 1689. But it was long before
this doctrine was either fully carried out by the
nation or fully accepted by its rulers. William III.

was merely a foreign politician and general, who submitted to the eccentricities of his subjects for the
sake of using their wealth and arms in foreign
war. On this point the admissions of Macaulay are
curiously in harmony with the view of William taken
in the instructions of Louis XIV. to his diplomatists
which have lately been published. Anne certainly
believed in her own quasi-divine right ; and George I.
and George II. were humbler kings of the same type
as William, who thought that the proper and legitimate form of government was to be found, not in
England, but in Hanover. As soon as England had
in George III. a king who cared more for English
politics than for foreign war, he repudiated the
doctrine altogether ; nor can it be said that it was
really admitted by any English sovereign until,
possibly, the present reign. But even when the
horror of the French Revolution was at its highest,
the politician, who would have been in much danger of
prosecution if he had toasted the People as the " sole
legitimate source of power," could always save himself by drinking to " the principles which placed the
House of Hanover on the throne." These principles
in the meantime were more and more becoming the
actual rule of government, and before George III. died
they had begun their victorious march over Europe.

Popular government, as first known to the
English, began to command the interest of the Con-

tinent through the admiration with which it inspired
a certain set of French thinkers towards the middle
of the last century. At the outset, it was not English
Liberty which attracted them, but English Toleration
and also English Irreligion, the last one of the most
fugitive phases through which the mind of a portion
of the nation passed, but one which so struck the
foreign observer that, at the beginning of the present
century, we find Napoleon Bonaparte claiming the
assistance of the Pope as rightfully his because he
was the enemy of the British misbeliever. Gradually
the educated classes of France, at whose feet sat the
educated class of all Continental countries, came to
interest themselves in English political institutions ;
and then came two events, one of which greatly
encouraged, while the other in the end greatly dis-
couraged, the tendency of popular government to
diffuse itself. The first of them was the foundation
of the United States. The American Constitution is
distinctively English ; this might be proved alone, as
Mr. Freeman has acutely observed, by its taking two
Houses, instead of one, or three, or more, as the
normal structure of a legislative assembly. It is in
fact the English Constitution carefully adapted to a
body of Englishmen who had never had much to do
with an hereditary king and an aristocracy of birth,
and who had determined to dispense with them
altogether. The American Republic has greatly

influenced the favour into which popular government grew. It disproved the once universal assumptions, that no Republic could govern a large territory, and that no strictly Republican government could be stable. But at first the Republic became interesting for other reasons. It now became possible for Continental Europeans to admire popular government without submitting to the somewhat bitter necessity of admiring the English, who till lately had been the most unpopular of European nations. Frenchmen in particular, who had helped and perhaps enabled the Americans to obtain their independence, naturally admired institutions which were indirectly their own creation ; and Frenchmen who had not served in the American War saw the American freeman reflected in Franklin, who pleased the school of Voltaire because he believed nothing, and the school of Rousseau because he wore a Quaker coat. The other event strongly influencing the fortunes of popular government was the French Revolution, which in the long-run rendered it an object of horror. The French, in their new Constitutions, followed first the English and then the American model, but in both cases with large departures from the originals. The result in both cases was miserable miscarriage. Political liberty took long to recover from the discredit into which it had been plunged by the Reign of Terror. In England, detestation of the Revolution

did not cease to influence politics till 1830.   But,
abroad, there was a reaction to the older type of
popular government in 1814 and 1815 ; and it was
thought possible to combine freedom and order by
copying, with very slight changes, the British Constitution.   From a longing for liberty, combined
with a loathing of the French experiments in it, there
sprang the state of opinion in which the constitutional movements of the Continent had their birth.
The British political model was followed by France,
by Spain and Portugal, and by Holland and Belgium,
combined in the kingdom of the Netherlands ; and,
after a long interval, by Germany, Italy, and Austria.

The principle of modern popular government
was thus affirmed less than two centuries ago, and
the practical application of that principle outside these
islands and their dependencies is not quite a century
old.   What has been the political history of the
commonwealths in which this principle has been
carried out in various degrees?   The inquiry is
obviously one of much importance and interest ; but,
though the materials for it are easily obtained, and
indeed are to a large extent within the memory of
living men, it is very seldom or very imperfectly
prosecuted.   I undertake it solely with the view of
ascertaining, within reasonable limits of space, how
far actual experience countenances the common
assumption of our day, that popular government is

likely to be of indefinitely long duration. I will first take France, which began with the imitation of the English, and has ended with the adoption of the American model. Since the introduction of political freedom into France, the existing government, nominally clothed with all the powers of the State, has been three times overturned by the mob of Paris, in 1792, in 1830, and in 1848. It has been three times overthrown by the Army ; first in 1797, on the 4th of September (18 Fructidor), when the majority of the Directors with the help of the soldiery annulled the elections of forty-eight departments, and deported fifty-six members of the two Assemblies, condemning also to deportation two of their own colleagues. The second military revolution was effected by the elder Bonaparte on the 9th of November (18 Brumaire), 1799 ; and the third by the younger Bonaparte, on December 2, 1851. The French Government has also been three times destroyed by foreign invasion, in 1814, 1815, and 1870 ; the invasion having been in each case provoked by French aggression, sympathised in by the bulk of the French people. In all, putting aside the anomalous period from 1870 to 1885, France, since she began her political experiments, has had forty-four years of liberty and thirty-seven of stern dictatorship.[5] But it has to be

---

[5] I include in the thirty-seven years the interval between September 1797 and November 1799.

remembered, and it is one of the curiosities of this period of history, that the elder Bourbons, who in practice gave very wide room to political freedom, did not expressly admit the modern theory of popular government ; while the Bonapartes, who proclaimed the theory without qualification, maintained in practice a rigid despotism.

Popular government was introduced into Spain just when the fortune of war was declaring itself decisively in favour of Wellington and the English army. The Extraordinary Cortes signed at Cadiz a Constitution, since then famous in Spanish politics as the Constitution of 1812, which proclaimed in its first article that sovereignty resided in the nation. Ferdinand VII., on re-entering Spain from France, repudiated this Constitution, denouncing it as Jacobinical ; and for about six years he reigned as absolutely as any of his forefathers. But in 1820 General Riego, who was in command of a large force stationed near Cadiz, headed a military insurrection in which the mob joined ; and the King submitted to the Constitution of 1812. In 1823 the foreign invader appeared ; the French armies entered Spain at the instigation of the Holy Alliance, and re-established Ferdinand's despotism, which lasted till his death. Popular government was, however, reintroduced by his widow as Regent for his daughter, no doubt for the purpose of strengthening Isabella's title to the

throne against her uncle, Don Carlos. It is probably
unnecessary to give the subsequent political history
of Spain in any detail. There are some places in
South America where the people date events, not
from the great earthquakes, but from the years in
which, by a rare intermission, there is no earthquake
at all. On the same principle we may note that
during the nine years following 1845, and the nine
years following 1857, there was comparative, though
not complete, freedom from military insurrection in
Spain. As to the residue of her political history, my
calculation is that between the first establishment of
popular government in 1812 and the accession of the
present King, there have been forty military risings
of a serious nature, in most of which the mob took
part. Nine of them were perfectly successful, either
overthrowing the Constitution for the time being, or
reversing the principles on which it was administered.
I need hardly say that both the Queen Regent,
Christina, and her daughter Isabella, were driven out
of Spain by the army or the fleet, with the help of
the mob ; and that the present King, Alfonso, was
placed on the throne through a military *pronuncia-
miento* at the end of 1874. It is generally thought
that he owes his retention of it since 1875 to statesmanship of a novel kind. As soon as he has assured
himself that the army is in earnest, he changes his
ministers.

The real beginning of popular or parliamentary government in Germany and the Austrian dominions, other than Hungary, cannot be placed earlier than 1848. The interest of German politics from 1815 to that year consists in the complaints, ever growing fainter, of the German communities who sought to compel the Princes to redeem their promises of Constitutions made during the War of Independence, and of the efforts of the Princes to escape or evade their pledges. Francis the Second expressed the prevailing feeling in his own way when he said to the Hungarian Diet, ' totus mundus stultizat, et vult habere novas constitutiones.' With some exceptions in the smaller States there were no parliamentary institutions in Germany till the King of Prussia conceded, just before 1848, the singular form of constitutional government which did not survive that year. But as soon as the mob of Paris had torn up the French Constitutional Charter, and expelled the Constitutional King, mobs, with their usual accompaniment the army, began to influence German and even Austrian politics. National Assemblies, on the French pattern, were called together at Berlin, at Vienna, and at Frankfort. All of them were dispersed in about a year, and directly or indirectly by the army. The more recent German and Austrian Constitutions are all of royal origin. Taking Europe as a whole, the most durably successful experiments in popular

C

government have been made either in small States, too weak for foreign war, such as Holland and Belgium, or in countries, like the Scandinavian States, where there was an old tradition of political freedom. The ancient Hungarian Constitution has been too much affected by civil war for any assertion about it to be safe. Portugal, for a while scarcely less troubled than Spain by military insurrection, has been free from it of late ; and Greece has had the dynasty of her kings once changed by revolution.

If we look outside Europe and beyond the circle of British dependencies, the phenomena are much the same. The civil war of 1861–65, in the United States, was as much a war of revolution as the war of 1775–1782. It was a war carried on by the adherents of one set of principles and one construction of the Constitution against the adherents of another body of principles and another Constitutional doctrine. It would be absurd, however, to deny the relative stability of the Government of the United States, which is a political fact of the first importance ; but the inferences which might be drawn from it are much weakened, if not destroyed, by the remarkable spectacle furnished by the numerous republics set up from the Mexican border-line to the Straits of Magellan. It would take many of these pages even to summarise the whole political history of the Spanish-American communities. There have

been entire periods of years during which some of
them have been disputed between the multitude and
the military, and again when tyrants, as brutal as
Caligula or Commodus, reigned over them like a
Roman Emperor in the name of the Roman people.
It may be enough to say of one of them, Bolivia,
which was recently heard of through her part in the
war on the Pacific coast, that out of fourteen Presidents of the Bolivian Republic thirteen have died
assassinated or in exile.[6]   There is one partial explanation of the inattention of English and European
politicians to a most striking, instructive, and uniform
body of facts : Spanish—though, next to English, it
is the most widely diffused language of the civilised
world—is little read or spoken in England, France,
or Germany.   There are, however, other theories to
account for the universal and scarcely intermitted
political confusion which at times has reigned in all
Central and South America, save Chili and the Bra-
zilian Empire.   It is said that the people are to a
great extent of Indian blood, and that they have been
trained in Roman Catholicism.   Such arguments
would be intelligible if they were used by persons
who maintained that a highly special and exceptional
political education is essential to the successful practice of popular government ; but they proceed from
those who believe that there is at least a strong pre-

[6] Arana, *Guerre du Pacifique*, i. 33.

sumption in favour of democratic institutions everywhere. And as regards the Roman Catholic Church,
it should at least be remembered that, whatever else
it may be, it is a great school of equality.

I have now given shortly the actual history of
popular government since it was introduced, in its
modern shape, into the civilised world. I state the
facts, as matter neither for congratulation nor for
lamentation, but simply as materials for opinion. It
is manifest that, so far as they go, they do little to
support the assumption that popular government has
an indefinitely long future before it. Experience
rather tends to show that it is characterised by great
fragility, and that, since its appearance, all forms of
government have become more insecure than they
were before. The true reason why the extremely
accessible facts which I have noticed are so seldom
observed and put together is that the enthusiasts for
popular government, particularly when it reposes on
a wide basis of suffrage, are actuated by much the
same spirit as the zealots of Legitimism. They assume their principle to have a sanction antecedent to
fact. It is not thought to be in any way invalidated
by practical violations of it, which merely constitute
so many sins the more against imprescriptible right.
The convinced partisans of democracy care little for
instances which show democratic governments to be
unstable. These are merely isolated triumphs of the

principle of evil.   But the conclusion of the sober
student of history will not be of this kind.   He will
rather note it as a fact, to be considered in the most
serious spirit, that since the century during which the
Roman Emperors were at the mercy of the Prætorian
soldiery, there has been no such insecurity of government as the world has seen since rulers became
delegates of the community.

Is it possible to assign any reasons for this
singular modern loss of political equilibrium ?   I
think that it is possible to a certain extent.   It may
be observed that two separate national sentiments
have been acting on Western Europe since the beginning of the present century.   To call them by
names given to them by those who dislike them, one
is Imperialism and the other is Radicalism.   They
are not in the least purely British forms of opinion,
but are coextensive with civilisation.   Almost all
men in our day are anxious that their country should
be respected of all and dependent on none, that it
should enjoy greatness and perhaps ascendency ; and
this passion for national dignity has gone hand in
hand with the desire of the many, ever more and
more acquiesced in by the few, to have a share of
political power under the name of liberty, and to
govern by rulers who are their delegates.   The two
newest and most striking of political creations in
Europe, the German Empire, and the Italian King-

dom, are joint products of these forces. But for the first of these coveted objects, Imperial rank, great armies and fleets are indispensable, and it becomes ever more a necessity that the men under arms should be nearly coextensive with the whole of the males in the flower of life. It has yet to be seen how far great armies are consistent with popular government resting on a wide suffrage. No two organisations can be more opposed to one another than an army scientifically disciplined and equipped, and a nation democratically governed. The great military virtue is obedience; the great military sin is slackness in obeying. It is forbidden to decline to carry out orders, even with the clearest conviction of their inexpediency. But the chief democratic right is the right to censure superiors ; public opinion, which means censure as well as praise, is the motive force of democratic societies. The maxims of the two systems flatly contradict one another, and the man who would loyally obey both finds his moral constitution cut into two halves. It has been found by recent experience that the more popular the civil institutions, the harder it is to keep the army from meddling with politics. Military insurrections are made by officers, but not before every soldier has discovered that the share of power which belongs to him as a unit in a regiment is more valuable than his fragment of power as a unit in a constituency.

Military revolts are of universal occurrence ; but far
the largest number have occurred in Spain and the
Spanish-speaking countries.   There have been ingenious explanations of the phenomenon, but the
manifest explanation is Habit.   An army which has
once interfered with politics is under a strong temptation to interfere again.   It is a far easier and far
more effective way of causing an opinion to prevail
than going to a ballot-box, and far more profitable
to the leaders.   I may add that, violent as is the
improbability of military interference in some countries, there is probably no country except the United
States in which the army could not control the
government, if it were of one mind and if it retained
its military material.

Popular governments have been repeatedly overturned by the Army and the Mob in combination;
but on the whole the violent destruction of these
governments in their more extreme forms has been
effected by the army, while in their more moderate
shapes they have had the mob for their principal
assailant.   It is to be observed that in recent times
mobs have materially changed both their character
and their method of attack.   A mob was once a
portion of society in a state of dissolution, a collection of people who for the time had broken loose
from the ties which bind society together.   It may
have had a vague preference for some political or

religious cause, but the spirit which animated it was mainly one of mischief, or of disorder, or of panic. But mobs have now come more and more to be the organs of definite opinions. Spanish mobs have impartially worn all colours ; but the French mob which overthrew the government of the elder Bourbons in 1830, while it had a distinct political object in its wish to defeat the aggressive measures of the King, had a further bias towards Ultra-Radicalism or Republicanism, which showed itself strongly in the insurrectionary movements that followed the accession of Louis Philippe to the throne. The mob, which in 1848 overturned the government of the younger Bourbons, aimed at establishing a Republic, but it had also a leaning to Socialism ; and the frightful popular insurrection of June 1848 was entirely Socialistic. At present, whenever in Europe there is a disturbance like those created by the old mobs, it is in the interest of the parties which style themselves Irreconcileable, and which refuse to submit their opinions to the arbitration of any governments, however wide be the popular suffrage on which they are based. But besides their character, mobs have changed their armament. They formerly wrought destruction by the undisciplined force of sheer numbers ; but the mob of Paris, the most successful of all mobs, owed its success to the Barricade. It has now lost this advantage ; and a generation is coming to maturity, which perhaps will never have learned that the Paris of to-day has been entirely constructed with the view of rendering for ever impossible the old barricade of paving-stones in the narrow streets of the demolished city. Still more recently, however, the mob has obtained new arms. During the last quarter of a century, a great part, perhaps the greatest part, of the inventive faculties of mankind has been given to the arts of destruction; and among the newly discovered modes of putting an end to human life on a large scale, the most effective and terrible is a manipulation of explosive compounds quite unknown till the other day. The bomb of nitro-glycerine and the parcel of dynamite are as characteristic of the new enemies of government as their Irreconcileable opinions.

There can be no more formidable symptom of our time, and none more menacing to popular government, than the growth of Irreconcileable bodies within the mass of the population. Church and State are alike convulsed by them; but, in civil life, Irreconcileables are associations of men who hold political opinions as men once held religious opinions. They cling to their creed with the same intensity of belief, the same immunity from doubt, the same confident expectation of blessedness to come quickly, which characterises the disciples of an infant faith. They are doubtless a product of democratic senti-

ment ; they have borrowed from it its promise of a
new and good time at hand, but they insist on the
immediate redemption of the pledge, and they utterly
refuse to wait until a popular majority gives effect to
their opinions. Nor would the vote of such a majority have the least authority with them, if it sanc-
tioned any departure from their principles. It is
possible, and indeed likely, that if the Russians voted
by universal suffrage to-morrow, they would confirm
the Imperial authority by enormous majorities ; but
not a bomb nor an ounce of dynamite would be
spared to the reigning Emperor by the Nihilists.
The Irreconcileables are of course at feud with
governments of the older type, but these governments make no claim to their support ; on the other
hand, they are a portion of the governing body of
democratic commonwealths, and from this vantage
ground they are able to inflict deadly injury on
popular government. There is in reality no closer
analogy than between these infant political creeds
and the belligerent religions which are constantly
springing up even now in parts of the world ; for
instance, that of the Tae-pings in China. Even in
our own country we may observe that the earliest
political Irreconcileables were religious or semi-
religious zealots.   Such were both the Independents
and the Jacobites. Cromwell, who for many striking
reasons might have been a personage of a much later

age, was an Irreconcileable at the head of an army ;
and we all know what he thought of the Parliament
which anticipated the democratic assemblies of our
day.

Of all modern Irreconcileables, the Nationalists
appear to be the most impracticable, and of all
governments, popular governments seem least likely
to cope with them successfully. Nobody can say
exactly what Nationalism is, and indeed the dan-
gerousness of the theory arises from its vagueness.
It seems full of the seeds of future civil convulsion.
As it is sometimes put, it appears to assume that
men of one particular race suffer injustice if they are
placed under the same political institutions with men
of another race. But Race is quite as ambiguous a
term as Nationality. The earlier philologists had
certainly supposed that the branches of mankind
speaking languages of the same stock were somehow
connected by blood ; but no scholar now believes
that this is more than approximately true, for conquest, contact, and the ascendency of a particular
literate class, have quite as much to do with community of language as common descent. Moreover,
several of the communities claiming the benefit of the
new theory are certainly not entitled to it. The
Irish are an extremely mixed race, and it is only by
a perversion of language that the Italians can be
called a race at all. The fact is that any portion of a

political society, which has had a somewhat different history from the rest of the parts, can take advantage of the theory and claim independence, and can thus threaten the entire society with dismemberment. Where royal authority survives in any vigour, it can to a certain extent deal with these demands. Almost all the civilised States derive their national unity from common subjection, past or present, to royal power ; the Americans of the United States, for example, are a nation because they once obeyed a king. Hence too it is that such a miscellany of races as those which make up the Austro-Hungarian Monarchy can be held together, at all events temporarily, by the authority of the Emperor-King. But democracies are quite paralysed by the plea of Nationality. There is no more effective way of attacking them than by admitting the right of the majority to govern, but denying that the majority so entitled is the particular majority which claims the right.

The difficulties of popular government, which arise from the modern military spirit and from the modern growth of Irreconcileable parties, could not perhaps have been determined without actual experience. But there are other difficulties which might have been divined, because they proceed from the inherent nature of democracy. In stating some of them, I will endeavour to avoid those which are suggested by mere dislike or alarm : those which I propose to specify were in reality noted more than two centuries ago by the powerful intellect of Hobbes, and it will be seen what light is thrown on some political phenomena of our day by his searching analysis.

Political liberty, said Hobbes, is political power. When a man burns to be free, he is not longing for the " desolate freedom of the wild ass " ; what he wants is a share of political government. But, in wide democracies, political power is minced into morsels, and each man's portion of it is almost infinitesimally small. One of the first results of this political comminution is described by Mr. Justice Stephen in a work [7] of earlier date than that which I have quoted above. It is that two of the historical watchwords of Democracy exclude one another, and that, where there is political Liberty, there can be no Equality.

The man who can sweep the greatest number of fragments of political power into one heap will govern the rest. The strongest man in one form or another will always rule. If the government is a military one, the qualities which make a man a great soldier will make him a ruler. If the government is a monarchy, the qualities which kings value in counsellors, in administrators, in generals, will give power. In a pure democracy, the ruling men will be the Wire-pullers and

[7] *Liberty, Fraternity, and Equality.* By Sir James Stephen. 1873. P. 239.

their friends; but they will be no more on an equality with
the people than soldiers or Ministers of State are on an
equality with the subjects of a Monarchy. . . . In some ages,
a powerful character, in others cunning, in others power of
transacting business, in others eloquence, in others a good
hold upon commonplaces and a facility in applying them to
practical purposes, will enable a man to climb on his neigh-
bours' shoulders and direct them this way or that ; but under
all circumstances the rank and file are directed by leaders of
one kind or another who get the command of their collective
force.

There is no doubt that, in popular governments
resting on a wide suffrage, either without an army or
having little reason to fear it, the leader, whether or
not he be cunning, or eloquent, or well provided with
commonplaces, will be the Wire-puller. The process of cutting up political power into petty fragments has in him its most remarkable product. The
morsels of power are so small that men, if left to
themselves, would not care to employ them. In
England, they would be largely sold, if the law permitted it ; in the United States they are extensively
sold in spite of the law ; and in France, and to a less
extent in England, the number of " abstentions "
shows the small value attributed to votes. But the
political *chiffonnier* who collects and utilises the fragments is the Wire-puller. I think, however, that it
is too much the habit in this country to describe him
as a mere organiser, contriver, and manager. The

particular mechanism which he constructs is no doubt of much importance. The form of this mechanism recently erected in this country has a close resemblance to the system of the Wesleyan Methodists ; one system, however, exists for the purpose of keeping the spirit of Grace a-flame, the other for maintaining the spirit of Party at a white heat. The Wire-puller is not intelligible unless we take into account one of the strongest forces acting on human nature—Party feeling. Party feeling is probably far more a survival of the primitive combativeness of mankind than a consequence of conscious intellectual differences between man and man. It is essentially the same sentiment which in certain states of society leads to civil, intertribal, or international war ; and it is as universal as humanity. It is better studied in its more irrational manifestations than in those to which we are accustomed. It is said that Australian savages will travel half over the Australian continent to take in a fight the side of combatants who wear the same Totem as themselves. Two Irish factions who broke one another's heads over the whole island are said to have originated in a quarrel about the colour of a cow. In Southern India, a series of dangerous riots are constantly arising through the rivalry of parties who know no more of one another than that some of them belong to the party of the right hand and others to that of the left hand. Once

a year, large numbers of English ladies and gentlemen, who have no serious reason for preferring one
University to the other, wear dark or light blue
colours to signify good wishes for the success of
Oxford or Cambridge in a cricket-match or boat-race.
Party differences, properly so called, are supposed to
indicate intellectual, or moral, or historical preferences; but these go a very little way down into the
population, and by the bulk of partisans they are
hardly understood and soon forgotten. "Guelf" and
"Ghibelline" had once a meaning, but men were
under perpetual banishment from their native land
for belonging to one or other of these parties long
after nobody knew in what the difference consisted.
Some men are Tories or Whigs by conviction; but
thousands upon thousands of electors vote simply for
yellow, blue, or purple, caught at most by the appeals
of some popular orator.

It is through this great natural tendency to take
sides that the Wire-puller works. Without it he
would be powerless. His business is to fan its flame;
to keep it constantly acting upon the man who has
once declared himself a partisan; to make escape from
it difficult and distasteful. His art is that of the
Nonconformist preacher, who gave importance to a
body of commonplace religionists by persuading them
to wear a uniform and take a military title, or of the
man who made the success of a Temperance Society

by prevailing on its members to wear always and openly a blue ribbon. In the long-run, these contrivances cannot be confined to any one party, and their effects on all parties and their leaders, and on the whole ruling democracy, must be in the highest degree serious and lasting. The first of these effects will be, I think, to make all parties very like one another, and indeed in the end almost indistinguishable, however leaders may quarrel and partisan hate partisan. In the next place, each party will probably become more and more homogeneous ; and the opinions it professes, and the policy which is the outcome of those opinions, will less and less reflect the individual mind of any leader, but only the ideas which seem to that mind to be most likely to win favour with the greatest number of supporters. Lastly, the wire-pulling system, when fully developed, will infallibly lead to the constant enlargement of the area of suffrage. What is called universal suffrage has greatly declined in the estimation, not only of philosophers who follow Bentham, but of the *à priori* theorists who assumed that it was the inseparable accompaniment of a Republic, but who found that in practice it was the natural basis of a tyranny. But extensions of the suffrage, though no longer believed to be good in themselves, have now a permanent place in the armoury of parties, and are sure to be a favourite weapon of the Wire-puller. The Athenian statesmen who, worsted in a quarrel of aristocratic cliques, " took the people into partnership," have a close parallel in the modern politicians who introduce household suffrage into towns to " dish " one side, and into counties to " dish " the other.

Let us now suppose the competition of Parties, stimulated to the utmost by the modern contrivances of the Wire-puller, to have produced an electoral system under which every adult male has a vote, and perhaps every adult female. Let us assume that the new machinery has extracted a vote from every one of these electors. How is the result to be expressed? It is, that the average opinion of a great multitude has been obtained, and that this average opinion becomes the basis and standard of all government and law. There is hardly any experience of the way in which such a system would work, except in the eyes of those who believe that history began since their own birth. The universal suffrage of white males in the United States is about fifty years old ; that of white and black is less than twenty. The French threw away universal suffrage after the Reign of Terror ; it was twice revived in France, that the Napoleonic tyranny might be founded on it ; and it was introduced into Germany, that the personal power of Prince Bismarck might be confirmed. But one of the strangest of vulgar ideas is that a very wide suffrage could or would promote progress, new

ideas, new discoveries and inventions, new arts of
life. Such a suffrage is commonly associated with
Radicalism ; and no doubt amid its most certain
effects would be the extensive destruction of existing
institutions ; but the chances are that, in the long-
run, it would produce a mischievous form of Conservatism, and drug society with a potion compared
with which Eldonine would be a salutary draught.
For to what end, towards what ideal state, is the
process of stamping upon law the average opinion of
an entire community directed? The end arrived at
is identical with that of the Roman Catholic Church,
which attributes a similar sacredness to the average
opinion of the Christian world.   " Quod semper, quod
ubique, quod ab omnibus," was the canon of Vincent
of Lerins.   " Securus judicat orbis terrarum," were
the words which rang in the ears of Newman and
produced such marvellous effects on him.   But did
any one in his senses ever suppose that these were
maxims of progress? The principles of legislation
at which they point would probably put an end to all
social and political activities, and arrest everything
which has ever been associated with Liberalism.   A
moment's reflection will satisfy any competently
instructed person that this is not too broad a proposition.   Let him turn over in his mind the great
epochs of scientific invention and social change during
the last two centuries, and consider what would have

occurred if universal suffrage had been established at any one of them. Universal suffrage, which to-day excludes Free Trade from the United States, would certainly have prohibited the spinning-jenny and the power-loom. It would certainly have forbidden the threshing-machine. It would have prevented the adoption of the Gregorian. Calendar ; and it would have restored the Stuarts. It would have proscribed the Roman Catholics with the mob which burned Lord Mansfield's house and library in 1780, and it would have proscribed the Dissenters with the mob which burned Dr. Priestley's house and library in 1791.

There are possibly many persons who, without denying these conclusions in the past, tacitly assume that no such mistakes will be committed in the future, because the community is already too enlightened for them, and will become more enlightened through popular education. But without questioning the advantages of popular education under certain aspects, its manifest tendency is to diffuse popular commonplaces, to fasten them on the mind at the time when it is most easily impressed, and thus to stereotype average opinion. It is of course possible that universal suffrage would not now force on governments the same legislation which it would infallibly have dictated a hundred years ago ; but then we are necessarily ignorant what germs of social and material improvement there may be in the womb of time, and how far they may conflict with the popular prejudice which hereafter will be omnipotent. There is in fact just enough evidence to show that even now there is a marked antagonism between democratic opinion and scientific truth as applied to human societies. The central seat in all Political Economy was from the first occupied by the theory of Population. This theory has now been generalised by Mr. Darwin and his followers, and, stated as the principle of the survival of the fittest, it has become the central truth of all biological science. Yet it is evidently disliked by the multitude, and thrust into the background by those whom the multitude permits to lead it. It has long been intensely unpopular in France and the continent of Europe ; and, among ourselves, proposals for recognising it through the relief of distress by emigration are visibly being supplanted by schemes founded on the assumption that, through legislative experiments on society, a given space of land may always be made to support in comfort the population which from historical causes has come to be settled on it.

It is perhaps hoped that this opposition between democracy and science, which certainly does not promise much for the longevity of popular government, may be neutralised by the ascendency of instructed leaders. Possibly the proposition would not be very unsafe, that he who calls himself a friend of democracy because he believes that it will be always under wise guidance is in reality, whether he knows it or not, an enemy of democracy. But at all events the signs of our time are not at all of favourable augury for the future direction of great multitudes by statesmen wiser than themselves. The relation of political leaders to political followers seems to me to be undergoing a twofold change. The leaders may be as able and eloquent as ever, and some of them certainly appear to have an unprecedentedly "good hold upon commonplaces, and a facility in applying them ;" but they are manifestly listening nervously at one end of a speaking-tube which receives at its other end the suggestions of a lower intelligence. On the other hand, the followers, who are really the rulers, are manifestly becoming impatient of the hesitations of their nominal chiefs, and the wrangling of their representatives. I am very desirous of keeping aloof from questions disputed between the two great English parties ; but it certainly seems to me that all over Continental Europe, and to some extent in the United States, parliamentary debates are becoming ever more formal and perfunctory, they are more and more liable to being peremptorily cut short, and the true springs of policy are more and more limited to clubs and associations deep below the level of the highest education and experience. There

is one State or group of States, whose political condition deserves particular attention.   This is Switzerland, a country to which the student of politics may
always look with advantage for the latest forms and
results of democratic experiment.   About forty years
ago, just when Mr. Grote was giving to the world
the earliest volumes of his " History of Greece," he
published " Seven Letters on the recent Politics of
Switzerland," explaining that his interest in the Swiss
Cantons arose from their presenting "a certain analogy
nowhere else to be found in Europe " to the ancient
Greek States.   Now, if Grote had one object more
than another at heart in writing his History, it was to
show, by the example of the Athenian democracy,
that wide popular governments, so far from meriting
the reproach of fickleness, are sometimes characterised
by the utmost tenacity of attachment, and will follow
the counsels of a wise leader, like Pericles, at the cost
of any amount of suffering, and may even be led by
an unwise leader, like Nicias, to the very verge of
destruction.   But he had the acuteness to discern in
Switzerland the particular democratic institution,
which was likely to tempt democracies into dispensing
with prudent and independent direction.   He speaks
with the strongest disapproval of a provision in the
Constitution of Lucerne, by which all laws, passed
by the Legislative Council, were to be submitted for
veto or sanction to the vote of the people throughout

the Canton. This was originally a contrivance
of the ultra-Catholic party, and was intended to
neutralise the opinions of the Catholic Liberals, by
bringing to bear on them the average opinion of the
whole Cantonal population. A year after Mr. Grote
had published his " Seven Letters," the French Revolution of 1848 occurred, and, three years later, the
violent overthrow of the democratic institutions
established by the French National Assembly was
consecrated by the very method of voting which he
had condemned, under the name of the Plébiscite.
The arguments of the French Liberal party against
the Plébiscite, during the twenty years of stern
despotism which it entailed upon France, have always
appeared to me to be arguments in reality against the
very principle of democracy. After the misfortunes
of 1870, the Bonapartes and the Plébiscite were alike
involved in the deepest unpopularity ; but it seems
impossible to doubt that Gambetta, by his agitation
for the *scrutin de liste*, was attempting to recover as
much as he could of the plebiscitary system of voting.
Meantime, it has become, in various shapes, one of
the most characteristic of Swiss institutions. One
article of the Federal Constitution provides that, if
fifty thousand Swiss citizens, entitled to vote, demand
the revision of the Constitution, the question whether
the Constitution be revised shall be put to the vote of
the people of Switzerland, " aye " or " no." Another

enacts that, on the petition of thirty thousand citizens, every Federal law and every Federal decree, which is not urgent, shall be subject to the *referendum* ; that is, it shall be put to the popular vote. These provisions, that when a certain number of voters demand a particular measure, or require a further sanction for a particular enactment, it shall be put to the vote of the whole country, seems to me to have a considerable future before them in democratically governed societies. When Mr. Labouchere told the House of Commons in 1882 that the people were tired of the deluge of debate, and would some day substitute for it the direct consultation of the constituencies, he had more facts to support his opinion than his auditors were perhaps aware of.

Here then we have one great inherent infirmity of popular governments, an infirmity deducible from the principle of Hobbes, that liberty is power cut into fragments. Popular governments can only be worked by a process which incidentally entails the further subdivision of the morsels of political power ; and thus the tendency of these governments, as they widen their electoral basis, is towards a dead level of commonplace opinion, which they are forced to adopt as the standard of legislation and policy. The evils likely to be thus produced are rather those vulgarly associated with Ultra-Conservatism than those of Ultra-Radicalism. So far indeed as the human race has experience, it is not by political societies in any way resembling those now called democracies that human improvement has been carried on. History, said Strauss—and, considering his actual part in life, this is perhaps the last opinion which might have been expected from him—History is a sound aristocrat.[8] There may be oligarchies close enough and jealous enough to stifle thought as completely as an Oriental despot who is at the same time the pontiff of a religion ; but the progress of mankind has hitherto been effected by the rise and fall of aristocracies, by the formation of one aristocracy within another, or by the succession of one aristocracy to another. There have been so-called democracies, which have rendered services beyond price to civilisation, but they were only peculiar forms of aristocracy. The short-lived Athenian democracy, under whose shelter art, science, and philosophy shot so wonderfully upwards, was only an aristocracy which rose on the ruins of one much narrower. The splendour which attracted the original genius of the then civilised world to Athens was provided by the severe taxation of a thousand subject cities ; and the skilled labourers who worked

---

[8] The opinion of Strauss appears to be shared by M. Ernest Renan. It occurs twice in the singular piece which he calls *Caliban.* "Toute civilisation est d'origine aristocratique" (p. 77). "Toute civilisation est l'œuvre des aristocrates" (p. 91).

under Phidias, and who built the Parthenon, were slaves.

The infirmities of popular government, which consist in its occasional wanton destructiveness, have been frequently dwelt upon and require less attention. In the long-run, the most interesting question which they suggest is, to what social results does the progressive overthrow of existing institutions promise to conduct mankind ?   I will again quote Mr. Labouchere, who is not the less instructive because he may perhaps be suspected of taking a certain malicious pleasure in stating roundly what many persons who employ the same political watchwords as himself are reluctant to say in public, and possibly shrink from admitting to themselves in their own minds.

Democrats are told that they are dreamers, and why? Because they assert that, if power be placed in the hands of the many, the many will exercise it for their own benefit. Is it not a still wilder dream to suppose that the many will in future possess power, and use it not to secure what they consider to be their interests, but to serve those of others? . . . Is it imagined that artisans in our great manufacturing towns are so satisfied with their present position that they will hurry to the polls, to register their votes in favour of a system which divides us socially, politically, and economically, into classes, and places them at the bottom with hardly a possibility of rising? . . . Is the lot (of the agricultural labourer) so happy a one that he will humbly and cheerfully affix his cross to the name of the man who tells him that it can never be changed for the better? . . . We know that

artisans and agricultural labourers will approach the consideration of political and social problems with fresh and
vigorous minds. . . . For the moment, we demand the
equalisation of the franchise. . . . Our next demands will be
electoral districts, cheap elections, payment of members, and
abolition of hereditary legislators. When our demands are
complied with, we shall be thankful, but we shall not rest.
On the contrary, having forged an instrument for democratic
legislation, we shall use it.[9]

The persons who charged Mr. Labouchere with
dreaming because he thus predicted the probable
course, and defined the natural principles, of future
democratic legislation, seem to me to have done him
much injustice. His forecast of political events is
extremely rational ; and I cannot but agree with him
in thinking it absurd to suppose that, if the hard-
toiled and the needy, the artisan and the agricultural
labourer, become the depositaries of power, and if
they can find agents through whom it becomes
possible for them to exercise it, they will not employ
it for what they may be led to believe are their own
interests. But in an inquiry whether, independently
of the alarm or enthusiasm which they excite in
certain persons or classes, democratic institutions
contain any seed of dissolution or extinction, Mr.
Labouchere's speculation becomes most interesting
just where it stops. What is to be the nature of the
legislation by which the lot of the artisan and of the

agricultural labourer is to be not merely altered for
the better, but exchanged for whatever station and
fortune they may think it possible to confer on themselves by their own supreme authority ? Mr. Labouchere's language, in the above passage and in
other parts of his paper, like that of many persons
who agree with him in the belief that government
can indefinitely increase human happiness, undoubtedly suggests the opinion, that the stock of
good things in the world is practically unlimited in
quantity, that it is (so to speak) contained in a vast
storehouse or granary, and that out of this it is now
doled in unequal shares and unfair proportions. It
is this unfairness and inequality which democratic
law will some day correct. Now I am not concerned
to deny that, at various times during the history of
mankind, narrow oligarchies have kept too much of
the wealth of the world to themselves, or that false
economical systems have occasionally diminished the
total supply of wealth, and, by their indirect operation, have caused it to be irrationally distributed.
Yet nothing is more certain, than that the mental
picture which enchains the enthusiasts for benevolent
democratic government is altogether false, and that,
if the mass of mankind were to make an attempt at
redividing the common stock of good things, they
would resemble, not a number of claimants insisting
on the fair division of a fund, but a mutinous crew,

feasting on a ship's provisions, gorging themselves on the meat and intoxicating themselves with the liquors, but refusing to navigate the vessel to port. It is among the simplest of economical truths, that far the largest part of the wealth of the world is constantly perishing by consumption, and that, if it be not renewed by perpetual toil and adventure, either the human race, or the particular community making the experiment of resting without being thankful, will be extinguished or brought to the very verge of extinction.

This position, although it depends in part on a truth of which, according to John Stuart Mill,[1] nobody is habitually aware who has not bestowed some thought on the matter, admits of very simple illustration. It used to be a question hotly debated among Economists how it was that countries recovered with such surprising rapidity from the effects of the most destructive and desolating wars. "An enemy lays waste a country by fire and sword, and destroys or carries away nearly all the movable wealth existing in it, and yet, in a few years after, everything is much as it was before." Mill,[2] following Chalmers, gives the convincing explanation that nothing in such a case has happened which would not have occurred in any circumstances. "What the

[1] Mill, *Principles of Political Economy*, i. 5. 5.
[2] Ibid. i. 5. 7.

enemy has destroyed would have been destroyed in a
little time by the inhabitants themselves ; the wealth
which they so rapidly reproduce would have needed
to be reproduced and would have been reproduced in
any case, and probably in as short an interval." In
fact, the fund by which the life of the human race
and of each particular society is sustained, is never
in a statical condition. It is no more in that condition than is a cloud in the sky, which is perpetually
dissolving and perpetually renewing itself. " Everything which is produced is consumed ; both what is
saved and what is said to be spent ; and the former
quite as rapidly as the latter." The wealth of mankind is the result of a continuing process, everywhere
complex and delicate, and nowhere of such complexity
and delicacy as in the British Islands. So long as
this process goes on under existing influences, it is
not, as we have seen, interrupted by earthquake,
flood, or war ; and, at each of its steps, the wealth
which perishes and revives has a tendency to
increase. But if we alter the character or diminish
the force of these influences, are we sure that wealth,
instead of increasing, will not dwindle and perhaps
disappear? Mill notes an exception to the revival of
a country after war. It may be depopulated, and if
there are not men to carry it on, the process of reproduction will stop. But may it not be arrested by
any means short of exterminating the population?

An experience, happily now rare in the world, shows that wealth may come very near to perishing through diminished energy in the motives of the men who reproduce it. You may, so to speak, take the heart and spirit out of the labourers to such an extent that they do not care to work. Jeremy Bentham observed about a century ago that the Turkish Government had in his day impoverished some of the richest countries in the world far more by its action on motives than by its positive exactions ; and it has always appeared to me that the destruction of the vast wealth accumulated under the Roman Empire, one of the most orderly and efficient of governments, and the decline of Western Europe into the squalor and poverty of the Middle Ages, can only be accounted for on the same principle. The failure of reproduction through relaxation of motives was once an everyday phenomenon in the East ; and this ex-plains to students of Oriental history why it is that throughout its course a reputation for statesmanship was always a reputation for financial statesmanship. In the early days of the East India Company, villages " broken by a severe settlement " were constantly calling for the attention of the Government ; the assessment on them did not appear to be excessive on English fiscal principles, but it had been heavy enough to press down the motives to labour, so that they could barely recover themselves. The pheno-

menon, however, is not confined to the East, where
no doubt the motives to toil are more easily affected
than in Western societies. No later than the end of
the last century, large portions of the French pea-
santry ceased to cultivate their land, and large
numbers of French artisans declined to work, in despair at the vast requisitions of the Revolutionary
Government during the Reign of Terror; and, as might
be expected, the penal law had to be called in to
compel their return to their ordinary occupations.[3]

It is perfectly possible, I think, as Mr. Herbert
Spencer has shown in a recent admirable volume,[4] to
revive even in our day the fiscal tyranny which once
left even European populations in doubt whether it
was worth while preserving life by thrift and toil.
You have only to tempt a portion of the population
into temporary idleness by promising them a share
in a fictitious hoard lying (as Mill puts it) in an
imaginary strong-box which is supposed to contain
all human wealth. You have only to take the
heart out of those who would willingly labour and
save, by taxing them *ad misericordiam* for the most
laudable philanthropic objects. For it makes not the
smallest difference to the motives of the thrifty and

---

[3] Taine, *Origines de la France Contemporaine*, tom. iii., 'La
Révolution.' See, as to artisans, p. 75 (note), and as to cultiva-
tors, p. 511.

[4] *The Man versus the State*, by Herbert Spencer. London,
1884

industrious part of mankind whether their fiscal
oppressor be an Eastern despot, or a feudal baron, or
a democratic legislature, and whether they are taxed
for the benefit of a Corporation called Society, or for
the advantage of an individual styled King or Lord.
Here then is the great question about democratic
legislation, when carried to more than a moderate
length. How will it affect human motives ? What
motives will it substitute for those now acting on
men ? The motives, which at present impel mankind to the labour and pain which produce the
resuscitation of wealth in ever-increasing quantities,
are such as infallibly to entail inequality in the dis-
tribution of wealth. They are the springs of action
called into activity by the strenuous and never-ending
struggle for existence, the beneficent private war
which makes one man strive to climb on the shoulders
of another and remain there through the law of the
survival of the fittest.

These truths are best exemplified in the part of
the world to which the superficial thinker would perhaps look for the triumph of the opposite principle.
The United States have justly been called the home
of the disinherited of the earth ; but, if those vanquished under one sky in the struggle for existence
had not continued under another the same battle in
which they had been once worsted, there would have
been no such exploit performed as the cultivation of

the vast American territory from end to end and from side to side.   There could be no grosser delusion than to suppose this result to have been attained by democratic legislation.   It has really been obtained through the sifting out of the strongest by natural selection.   The Government of the United States, which I examine in another part of this volume, now rests on universal suffrage, but then it is only a political government.   It is a government under which coercive restraint, except in politics, is reduced to a minimum.   There has hardly ever before been a community in which the weak have been pushed so pitilessly to the wall, in which those who have succeeded have so uniformly been the strong, and in which in so short a time there has arisen so great an inequality of private fortune and domestic luxury.   And at the same time, there has never been a country in which, on the whole, the persons distanced in the race have suffered so little from their ill-success.   All this beneficent prosperity is the fruit of recognising the principle of population, and the one remedy for its excess in perpetual emigration.   It all reposes on the sacredness of contract and the stability of private property, the first the implement, and the last the reward, of success in the universal competition. These, however, are all principles and institutions which the British friends of the 'artisan' and 'agricultural labourer' seem not a little inclined to treat as their ancestors did agricultural and industrial machinery. The Americans are still of opinion that more is to be got for human happiness by private energy than by public legislation. The Irish, however, even in the United States, are of another opinion, and the Irish opinion is manifestly rising into favour here. But on the question, whether future democratic legislation will follow the new opinion, the prospects of popular government to a great extent depend. There are two sets of motives, and two only, by which the great bulk of the materials of human subsistence and comfort have hitherto been produced and reproduced. One has led to the cultivation of the territory of the Northern States of the American Union, from the Atlantic to the Pacific. The other had a considerable share in bringing about the industrial and agricultural progress of the Southern States, and in old days it produced the wonderful prosperity of Peru under the Incas. One system is economical competition ; the other consists in the daily task, perhaps fairly and kindly allotted, but enforced by the prison or the scourge. So far as we have any experience to teach us, we are driven to the conclusion, that every society of men must adopt one system or the other, or it will pass through penury to starvation.

I have thus shown that popular governments of the modern type have not hitherto proved stable as

compared with other forms of political rule, and that
they include certain sources of weakness which do
not promise security for them in the near or remote
future. My chief conclusion can only be stated
negatively. There is not at present sufficient evidence
to warrant the common belief, that these governments
are likely to be of indefinitely long duration. There
is, however, one positive conclusion from which no
one can escape who bases a forecast of the prospects
of popular government, not on moral preference or
à priori assumption, but on actual experience as
witnessed to by history. If there be any reason for
thinking that constitutional freedom will last, it is
a reason furnished by a particular set of facts, with
which Englishmen ought to be familiar, but of which
many of them, under the empire of prevailing ideas,
are exceedingly apt to miss the significance. The
British Constitution has existed for a considerable
length of time, and therefore free institutions generally
may continue to exist. I am quite aware that this
will seem to some a commonplace conclusion, perhaps
as commonplace as the conclusion of M. Taine, who,
after describing the conquest of all France by the
Jacobin Club, declares that his inference is so simple,
that he hardly ventures to state it. " Jusqu'à présent,
je n'ai guère trouvé qu'un (principe) si simple qu'il
semblera puéril et que j'ose à peine l'énoncer. Il
consiste tout entier dans cette remarque, qu'une

société humaine, surtout une société moderne, est une chose vaste et compliquée." This observation, that "a human society, and particularly a modern society, is a vast and complicated thing," is in fact the very proposition which Burke enforced with all the splendour of his eloquence and all the power of his argument ; but, as M. Taine says, it may now seem to some too simple and commonplace to be worth putting into words.   In the same way, many persons in whom familiarity has bred contempt, may think it a trivial observation that the British Constitution, if not (as some call it) a holy thing, is a thing unique and remarkable.   A series of undesigned changes brought it to such a condition, that satisfaction and impatience, the two great sources of political conduct, were both reasonably gratified under it.   In this condition it became, not metaphorically but literally, the envy of the world, and the world took on all sides to copying it.   The imitations have not been generally happy.   One nation alone, consisting of Englishmen, has practised a modification of it successfully, amidst abounding material plenty.   It is not too much to say, that the only evidence worth mentioning for the duration of popular government is to be found in the success of the British Constitution during two centuries under special conditions, and in the success of the American Constitution during one century under conditions still more peculiar and more unlikely to recur. Yet, so far as our own Constitution is concerned, that nice balance of attractions, which caused it to move evenly on its stately path, is perhaps destined to be disturbed. One of the forces governing it may gain dangerously at the expense of the other; and the British political system, with the national greatness and material prosperity attendant on it, may yet be launched into space and find its last affinities in silence and cold.

ESSAY II.

THE NATURE OF DEMOCRACY.

JOHN AUSTIN, a name honoured in the annals of English jurisprudence, published shortly before his death a pamphlet called a " Plea for the Constitution." In this publication,[1] which marks the farthest re-bound of a powerful mind from the peculiar philo-sophical Radicalism of the immediate pupils of Jeremy Bentham, Austin applies the analytical power, on which his fame rests, to a number of ex-pressions which entered in his day, as they do in ours, into every political discussion. Among them, he examines the terms Aristocracy and Democracy, and of the latter he says :—

Democracy is still more ambiguous than Aristocracy. It signifies properly a form of government, that is, any govern-ment in which the governing body is a comparatively large fraction of the entire nation. As used loosely, and par-ticularly by French writers, it signifies the body of the

---

[1] *A Plea for the Constitution*, by John Austin. London, 1859.

nation, or the lower part of the nation, or a way of thinking and feeling favourable to democratical government. It not unfrequently bears the meaning which is often given to the word "people," or the words "sovereign people," that is, some large portion of the nation which is not actually sovereign, but to which, in the opinion of the speaker, the sovereignty ought to be transferred.

The same definition of Democracy, in its only proper and consistent sense, is given by M. Edmond Scherer, in his powerful and widely circulated pamphlet, named " La Démocratie et la France." [2] I shall have to refer presently to M. Scherer's account of the methods by which the existing French political system is made to discharge the duties of government ; but, meantime, the greatest merit of his publication does not seem to me to lie in its exposure of the servility of the deputies to the electoral committees, or of the public extravagance by which their support is purchased. It lies rather in M. Scherer's examination of certain vague abstract propositions, which are commonly accepted without question by the Republican politicians of France, and indeed of the whole Continent. In our day, when the extension of popular government is throwing all the older political ideas into utter confusion, a man of ability can hardly render a higher service to his country, than by the

[2] *La Démocratie et la France.* Études par Edmond Scherer. Paris, 1883.

analysis and correction of the assumptions which pass from mind to mind in the multitude, without inspiring a doubt of their truth and genuineness. Some part of this intellectual circulating medium was base from the first ; another was once good coin, but it is clipped and worn on all sides ; another consists of mere tokens, which are called by an old name, because there is a conventional understanding that it shall still be used. It is urgently necessary to rate all this currency at its true value ; and, as regards a part of it, this was done once for all by Sir J. F. Stephen, in his admirable volume on " Liberty, Fraternity, and Equality." But the political smashers are constantly at work, and their dupes are perpetually multiplying, while there is by no means a corresponding activity in applying the proper tests to all this spurious manufacture. We Englishmen pass on the Continent as masters of the art of government ; yet it may be doubted whether, even among us, the science, which corresponds to the art, is not very much in the condition of Political Economy before Adam Smith took it in hand. In France the condition of political thought is even worse. Englishmen abandon a political dogma when it has led to practical disaster. But it has been the lot of Frenchmen to have their attention fastened on the last eleven years of the last century and on the first fifteen of the present, almost to the exclusion of the rest of their history ; and the political ideas which grew up during this period have hardly relaxed their hold on the French intellect at all, after seventy years of further experience.

M. Scherer, so far as my knowledge extends, has been the first French writer to bring into clear light the simple truth stated by Austin, that Democracy means properly a particular form of government.[3] This truth, in modern Continental politics, is the beginning of wisdom. There is no word about which a denser mist of vague language, and a larger heap of loose metaphors, has collected. Yet, although Democracy does signify something indeterminate, there is nothing vague about it. It is simply and solely a form of government. It is the government of the State by the Many, as opposed, according to the old Greek analysis, to its government by the Few, and to its government by One. The border between the Few and the Many, and again between the varieties of the Many, is necessarily indeterminate ; but Democracy not the less remains a mere form of government ; and, inasmuch as of these forms the most definite and determinate is Monarchy—the government of the State by one person—Democracy is most accurately described as inverted Monarchy. And this description answers to the actual historical process by which the great modern Republics have been formed.

[3] Scherer, p. 3.

Villari [4] has shown that the modern State of the
Continental type, with distinctly defined administrative departments as its organs, was first constituted
in Italy. It grew, not out of the mediæval Republican
municipalities, which had nothing in common with
modern government, but out of that most ill-famed
of all political systems, the Italian tyranny or Prince-
dom. The celebrated Italian state-craft, spread all
over Europe by Italian statesmen, who were generally
ecclesiastics, was applied to France by Louis XIV.
and Colbert, the pupils of Cardinal Mazarin ; and
out of the contact of this new science with an administrative system in complete disorder, there sprang
Monarchical France. The successive French Republics have been nothing but the later French Monarchy,
upside down. Similarly, the Constitutions and the
legal systems of the several North American States,
and of the United States, would be wholly unintel-
ligible to anybody who did not know that the ancestors of the Anglo-Americans had once lived under
a King, himself the representative of older Kings
infinitely more autocratic, and who had not observed
that throughout these bodies of law and plans of
government the People had simply been put into the
King's seat, occasionally filling it with some awk-
wardness. The advanced Radical politician of our
day would seem to have an impression that Demo-

[4] Villari, *Machiavelli*, i. 15, 36, 37.

cracy differs from Monarchy in essence. There can be no grosser mistake than this, and none more fertile of further delusions. Democracy, the government of the commonwealth by a numerous but indeterminate portion of the community taking the place of the Monarch, has exactly the same conditions to satisfy as Monarchy ; it has the same functions to discharge, though it discharges them through different organs. The tests of success in the performance of the necessary and natural duties of a government are precisely the same in both cases.

Thus in the very first place, Democracy, like Monarchy, like Aristocracy, like any other government, must preserve the national existence. The first necessity of a State is that it should be durable. Among mankind regarded as assemblages of individuals, the gods are said to love those who die young ; but nobody has ventured to make such an assertion of States. The prayers of nations to Heaven have been, from the earliest ages, for long national life, life from generation to generation, life prolonged far beyond that of children's children, life like that of the everlasting hills. The historian will sometimes speak of governments distinguished for the loftiness of their aims, and the brilliancy of the talents which they called forth, but doomed to an existence all too brief. The compliment is in reality a paradox, for in matters of government all objects are vain and all

talents wasted, when they fail to secure national dur-
ability.   One might as well eulogise a physician for
the assiduity of his attendance and the scientific
beauty of his treatment, when the patient has died
under his care.   Next perhaps to the paramount
duty of maintaining national existence, comes the
obligation incumbent on Democracies, as on all
governments, of securing the national greatness and
dignity.   Loss of territory, loss of authority, loss of
general respect, loss of self-respect, may be unavoidable evils, but they are terrible evils, judged by the
pains they inflict and the elevation of the minds by
which these pains are felt ; and the Government
which fails to provide a sufficient supply of generals
and statesmen, of soldiers and administrators, for the
prevention and cure of these evils, is a government
which has miscarried.   It will also have miscarried,
if it cannot command certain qualities which are
essential to the success of national action.   In all
their relations with one another (and this is a fundamental assumption of International law) States must
act as individual men.   The defects which are defects
in individual men, and perhaps venial defects, are
faults in States, and generally faults of the extremest
gravity.   In all war and all diplomacy, in every part
of foreign policy, caprice, wilfulness, loss of self-
command, timidity, temerity, inconsistency, inde-
cency, and coarseness, are weaknesses which rise to the

level of destructive vices ; and if Democracy is more
liable to them than are other forms of government,
it is to that extent inferior to them. It is better for
a nation, according to an English prelate, to be free
than to be sober. If the choice has to be made,
and if there is any real connection between Democracy and liberty, it is better to remain a nation
capable of displaying the virtues of a nation than
even to be free.

If we turn from the foreign to the domestic duties
of a nation, we shall find the greatest of them to be,
that its government should compel obedience to the
law, criminal and civil. The vulgar impression no
doubt is, that laws enforce themselves. Some communities are supposed to be naturally law-abiding,
and some are not. But the truth is (and this is a
commonplace of the modern jurist) that it is always
the State which causes laws to be obeyed. It is quite
true that this obedience is rendered by the great bulk
of all civilised societies without an effort and quite
unconsciously. But that is only because, in the
course of countless ages, the stern discharge of their
chief duty by States has created habits and sentiments which save the necessity for penal interference,
because nearly everybody shares them. The venerable legal formulas, which make laws to be administered in the name of the King, formulas which modern
Republics have borrowed, are a monument of the

grandest service which governments have rendered,
and continue to render, to mankind. If any government should be tempted to neglect, even for a moment,
its function of compelling obedience to law—if a
Democracy, for example, were to allow a portion of
the multitude of which it consists to set some law
at defiance which it happens to dislike—it would be
guilty of a crime which hardly any other virtue could
redeem, and which century upon century might fail
to repair.

On the whole, the dispassionate student of politics,
who has once got into his head that Democracy is
only a form of government, who has some idea of
what the primary duties of government are, and who
sees the main question, in choosing between them, to
be which of them in the long-run best discharges these
duties, has a right to be somewhat surprised at the
feelings which the advent of Democracy excites.
The problem which this event, if it be near at hand,
suggests, is not sentimental but practical ; and one
might have expected less malediction on one side, and
less shouting and throwing up of caps on the other.
The fact, however, is that, when the current of human
political tastes, which in the long course of ages has
been running in all sorts of directions, sets strongly
towards one particular point, there is always an out-
burst of terror or enthusiasm ; and the explanation
of the feelings roused on such occasions, which is true

for our day and of a tendency towards Democracy, is probably true also for all time. The great virtue of Democracies in some men's eyes, their great vice in the eyes of others, is that they are thought to be more active than other forms of government in the discharge of one particular function. This is the alteration and transformation of law and custom—the process known to us as reforming legislation. As a matter of fact, this process—which is an indispensable, though in the long-run a very subordinate, province of a good modern government—is not at all peculiar to Democracies. If the whole of the known history of the human race be examined, we shall see that the great authors of legislative change have been powerful Monarchies. The long wail at the iniquit'es of Nineveh and Babylon, which runs through the latter part of the Old Testament, is the expression of Jewish resentment at the " big legislation " with which the nations that most study the Old Testament are supposed to have fallen in love. The trituration of old usage was carried infinitely further by the Roman Emperors, ever increasing in thoroughness as the despotism grew more stringent. The Emperor was in fact the symbolic beast which the Prophet saw devouring, breaking to pieces and stamping the residue with its feet. We ourselves live in the dust of Roman Imperialism, and by far the largest part of modern law is nothing more than a sedimentary formation left

F

by the Roman legal reforms. The rule holds good
through all subsequent history. The one wholesale
legal reformer of the Middle Ages was Charles the
Great. It was the French Empire of the Bonapartes
that gave real practical currency to the new French
jurisprudence which has overrun the civilised world,
for the governments immediately arising out of the
Revolution left little behind them beyond projects of
law or laws which were practically inapplicable from
the contradictions which they contained.

The truth seems to be that the extreme forms of
government, Monarchy and Democracy, have a pecu-
liarity which is absent from the more tempered political systems founded on compromise, Constitutional
Kingship and Aristocracy. When they are first
established in absolute completeness, they are highly
destructive. There is a general, sometimes chaotic,
upheaval, while the *nouvelles couches* are settling into
their place in the transformed commonwealth. The
new rulers sternly insist, that everything shall be
brought into strict conformity with the central
principle of the system over which they preside ; and
they are aided by numbers of persons to whom the
old principles were hateful, from their fancy for ideal
reforms, from impatience of a monotonous stability, or
from a natural destructiveness of temperament. What
the old monarchies, established in the valleys of the
great Eastern rivers, had to contend against was reli-

gious tenacity and tribal obstinacy; and they transported whole populations in order that these might be
destroyed. What a modern Democracy fights with is
privilege; and it knows no rest till this is trampled
out. But the legislation of absolutism, democratic
or otherwise, is transitory. Before the Jews had
taken home their harps from Babylon, they found
themselves the subjects of another mighty conquering
Monarchy, of which they observed with wonder that
the law of the Medes and Persians altereth not.
There is no belief less warranted by actual experience,
than that a democratic republic is, after the first and
in the long-run, given to reforming legislation. As
is well known to scholars, the ancient republics
hardly legislated at all; their democratic energy was
expended upon war, diplomacy, and justice; but they
put nearly insuperable obstacles in the way of a
change of law. The Americans of the United States
have hedged themselves round in exactly the same
way. They only make laws within the limits of their
Constitutions, and especially of the Federal Constitution; and, judged by what has become the English
standard, their legislation within these limits is
almost trivial. As I attempted to show in my first
essay, the legislative infertility of democracies springs
from permanent causes. The prejudices of the people
are far stronger than those of the privileged classes;

F 2

they are far more vulgar ; and they are far more
dangerous, because they are apt to run counter to
scientific conclusions.   This assertion is curiously
confirmed by the political phenomena of the moment.
The most recent of democratic inventions is the
" Referendum " of the Swiss Federal Constitution,
and of certain Cantonal Constitutions.   On the
demand of a certain number of citizens, a law voted
by the Legislature is put to the vote of the entire
population, lest by any chance its " mandate " should
have been exceeded.   But to the confusion and dis-
may of the Radical leaders in the Legislature, the
measures which they most prized, when so put, have
been negatived.

Democracy being what it is, the language used of
it in our day, under its various disguises of Freedom,
the " Revolution," the " Republic," Popular Government, the Reign of the People, is exceedingly remarkable.   Every sort of metaphor, signifying irresistible
force, and conveying admiration or dread, has been
applied to it by its friends or its enemies.   A great
English orator once compared it to the Grave, which
takes everything and gives nothing back.   The most
widely read American historian altogether loses himself in figures of speech.   " The change which Divine
wisdom ordained, and which no human policy or force
could hold back, proceeded as uniformly and majestically as the laws of being, and was as certain as the

decrees of eternity."[5]   And again, " The idea of freedom had never been wholly unknown ; . . . the rising
light flashed joy across the darkest centuries, and its
growing energy can be traced in the tendency of the
ages."[6] These hopes have even found room for themselves among the commonplaces of after-dinner oratory. " The great tide of Democracy is rolling on,
and no hand can stay its majestic course," said Sir
Wilfrid Lawson of the Franchise Bill.[7] But the
strongest evidence of the state of excitement into which
some minds are thrown by an experiment in government, which is very old and has never been particularly successful, is afforded by a little volume with
the title " Towards Democracy." The writer is not
destitute of poetical force, but the smallest conception
of what Democracy really is makes his rhapsodies
about it astonishing. " Freedom ! " sings this disciple
of Walt Whitman—

And among the far nations there is a stir like the stir of
the leaves of the forest.

Joy, joy, arising on earth.

[5] Bancroft, *History of the United States*, "The American
Revolution," vol. i. p. 1. Mr. Bancroft was almost verbally anticipated in this sentence by a person whom he resembles in nothing
except in his love of phrases. " Français républicains," said Maxi-
milian Robespierre, in his speech at the festival of the Supreme
Being, " n'est-ce pas l'Être Suprême qui, dès le commencement
des temps, décréta la République ? "

[6] Bancroft, *ubi supra*, p. 2.

[7] On April 15, 1884.

And lo! the banners lifted from point to point, and the
spirits of the ancient races looking abroad—the divinely
beautiful daughters of God calling to their children.

.   .   .   .   .   .

Lo! the divine East from ages and ages back intact her
priceless jewel of thought—the germ of Democracy—bringing
down!

.   .   .   .   .   .

O glancing eyes! O leaping shining waters! Do I not
know that thou, Democracy, dost control and inspire; that
thou too hast relations to them,
    As surely as Niagara has relations to Erie and Ontario?

Towards the close of the poem this line occurs—
' I heard a voice say, What is Freedom ? " It is impossible that the voice could ask a more pertinent
question. If the author of " Towards Democracy "
had ever heard the answer of Hobbes, that Freedom
is " political power divided into small fragments," or
the dictum of John Austin and M. Scherer, that " Democracy is a form of government," his poetical vein
might have been drowned, but his mind would have
been invigorated by the healthful douche of cold
water.

The opinion that Democracy was irresistible and
inevitable, and probably perpetual, would, only a
century ago, have appeared a wild paradox. There
had been more than 2,000 years of tolerably well-
ascertained political history, and at its outset,

ESSAY II.   THE NATURE OF DEMOCRACY.   71

Monarchy, Aristocracy, and Democracy, were all plainly discernible. The result of a long experience was, that some Monarchies and some Aristocracies had shown themselves extremely tenacious of life. The French monarchy and the Venetian oligarchy were in particular of great antiquity, and the Roman empire was not even then quite dead. But the democracies which had risen and perished, or had fallen into extreme insignificance, seemed to show that this form of government was of rare occurrence in political history, and was characterised by an extreme fragility. This was the opinion of the fathers of the American Federal Republic, who over and over again betray their regret that the only government which it was possible for them to establish was one which promised so little stability. It became very shortly the opinion of the French Revolutionists, for no sooner has the Constitutional Monarchy fallen than the belief that a new era has begun for the human race gives signs of rapidly fading; and the language of the Revolutionary writers becomes stained with a dark and ever-growing suspiciousness, manifestly inspired by genuine fear that Democracy must perish, unless saved by unflagging energy and unsparing severity. Nevertheless, the view that Democracy is irresistible is of French origin, like almost all other sweeping political generalisations. It may be first detected about fifty years ago, and it was mainly spread over the world by the

book of De Tocqueville on Democracy in America.
Some of the younger speculative minds in France were
deeply struck by the revival of democratic ideas in
France at the Revolution of 1830, and among them
was Alexis de Tocqueville, born a noble and educated
in Legitimism. The whole fabric of French Revolutionary belief had apparently been ruined beyond hope
of recovery, ruined by the crimes and usurpations of
the Convention, by military habits and ideas, by the
tyranny of Napoleon Bonaparte, by the return of the
Bourbons with a large part of the system of the older
monarchy, by the hard repression of the Holy Alliance.
Yet so slight a provocation as the attempt of Charles
X. to do what his brother had done [8] without serious
resistance, brought back the whole torrent of revolutionary sentiment and dogma, which at once overran
the entire European continent. No doubt it seemed
as if there were something in Democracy which made
it resistless ; and yet, as M. Scherer has shown in one
of the most valuable parts of his pamphlet, the Frenchmen of that idea did not mean the same thing as the
modern French Extremist or the English Radical
when they spoke of Democracy. If their view be put
affirmatively, they meant the ascendency of the middle
classes ; if negatively, they meant the non-revival of
the old feudal society. The French people were very
long in shaking off their fear that the material advan-

[8] By his Ordinance of September 1816.

tages, secured to them by the first French Revolution, were not safe ; and this fear it was which, as we perceive from the letters of Mallet du Pan,[9] reconciled them to the tyranny of the Jacobins and caused them to look with the deepest suspicion on the plans of the Sovereigns allied against the Republic. Democracy, however, gradually took a new sense, chiefly under the influence of wonder at the success of the American Federation, in which most of the States had now adopted universal suffrage; and by 1848 the word had come to be used very much with its ancient meaning, the government of the commonwealth by the Many. It is perhaps the scientific tinge which thought is assuming among us that causes so many Englishmen to take for granted that Democracy is inevitable, because many considerable approaches to it have been made in our country. No doubt, if adequate causes are at work, the effect will always follow ; but, in politics, the most powerful of all causes are the timidity, the listlessness, and the superficiality, of the gene-

[9] The newly published correspondence of Mallet du Pan with the Court of Vienna, between 1794 and 1798, is of the highest interest and value. M. Taine, who contributes the Preface, has several times affirmed that Mallet was one of the very few persons who understood the French Revolution. It seems clear that, while these letters were being written, the Republic was falling into the deepest unpopularity, mitigated only by the fears of which we have spoken above. It was undoubtedly saved by the military genius of Napoleon Bonaparte. The one serious mistake of Mallet was his blindness to that genius. He thought General Bonaparte a charlatan.

rality of minds. If a large number of Englishmen,
belonging to classes which are powerful if they exert
themselves, continue saying to themselves and others
that Democracy is irresistible and must come, beyond
all doubt it will come.

The enthusiasm for Democracy, which is conveyed
by the figures of speech applied to it, is equally
modern with the impression of its inevitableness. In
reality, considering the brilliant stages in the history
of a certain number of commonwealths with which
Democracy has been associated, nothing is more remarkable than the small amount of respect for it
professed by actual observers, who had the opportunity and the capacity for forming a judgment on
it. Mr. Grote did his best to explain away the poor
opinion of the Athenian Democracy entertained by
the philosophers who filled the schools of Athens ;
but the fact remains that the founders of political
philosophy found themselves in presence of Democracy, in its pristine vigour, and thought it a bad
form of government. The panegyrics of which it is
now the object are, again, of French origin. They
come to us from the oratory and literature of the
first French Revolution, which, however, soon exchanged glorification of the new birth of the human
race for a strain of gloomy suspicion and homicidal
denunciation. The language of admiration which
prevailed for a while had still remoter sources ; and

it may be observed, as an odd circumstance, that, while the Jacobins generally borrowed their phraseology from the legendary history of the early Roman Republic, the Girondins preferred resorting for metaphors to the literature which sprang from Rousseau. On the whole, I think that the historical ignorance which made heroes of Brutus and Scævola was less abjectly nonsensical than the philosophical silliness which dwelt on the virtues of mankind in a state of natural democracy. If anybody wishes to know what was the influence of Rousseau in diffusing the belief in a golden age, when men lived, like brothers, in freedom and equality, he should read, not so much the writings of the sage, as the countless essays printed in France by his disciples just before 1789. They furnish very disagreeable proof that the intellectual flower of a cultivated nation may be brought, by fanatical admiration of a social and political theory, into a condition of downright mental imbecility.[1]

---

[1] Brissot, the Girondin leader, while still a young man and an enthusiastic Royalist, had argued, long before Proudhon, that Property is Theft. There is, he said, a natural right to correct the injustice of the institution, by stealing. But he held the still more remarkable opinion, that cannibalism is natural and justifiable. Since, he argued, under the reign of Nature the sheep does not spare the insects on the grass, and the wolf and the man eat the sheep, why have not all these creatures a natural right to eat creatures of their own kind? (*Recherches philosophiques sur le droit de propriété et sur le vol considéré dans sa nature.* Par Brissot de Warville.)

The language of the Jacobins and the language of the Girondins might be thought to have perished amid ridicule and disgust ; but, in fact, it underwent a rehabilitation, like that which has fallen to the lot of Catiline, of Nero, and of Richard III. Tocqueville thought Democracy was inevitable, but he looked on its approach with distrust and dread. In the course, however, of the succeeding fifteen years two books were published, which, whatever their popularity, might fairly be compared with the writings of which we have spoken above, for a total abnegation of common sense. Louis Blanc[2] took the homicidal pedant, Robespierre, for his hero ; Lamartine, the feeble and ephemeral sect of Girondins ; and from the works of these two writers has proceeded much the largest part of the language eulogistic of Democracy, which pervades the humbler political literature of the Continent, and now of Great Britain also.

There is indeed one kind of praise which Democracy has received, and continues to receive, in the greatest abundance. This is praise addressed to the governing Demos by those who fear it, or desire to conciliate it, or hope to use it. When it has once

---

[2] The *Histoire des Girondins* of Lamartine was published in 1847. The publication of the *Histoire de la Révolution Française* of Louis Blanc began in 1847, and went on till 1862 ; the *Histoire de Dix Ans* of the same writer had been published in 1841–44. The first part of De Tocqueville's work was published in 1835, the second in 1839.

become clear that Democracy is a form of government, it will be easily understood what panegyrics of the multitude amount to. Democracy is Monarchy inverted, and the modes of addressing the multitude are the same as the modes of addressing kings. The more powerful and jealous the sovereign, the more unbounded is the eulogy, the more extravagant is the tribute. " O King, live for ever," was the ordinary formula of beginning an address to the Babylonian or Median king, drunk or sober. " Your ascent to power proceeded as uniformly and majestically as the laws of being and was as certain as the decrees of eternity," says Mr. Bancroft to the American people. Such flattery proceeds frequently from the ignobler parts of human nature, but not always. What seems to us baseness, passed two hundred years ago at Versailles for gentleness, and courtliness ; and many people have every day before them a monument of what was once thought suitable language to use of a King of England, in the Dedication of the English Bible to James I. There is no reason to suppose that this generation will feel any particular shame at flattery, though the flattery will be addressed to the people and not to the King. It may even become commoner, through the growth of scientific modes of thought. Dean Church, in his recent volume on " Bacon," has made the original remark that Bacon behaved himself to powerful men as he behaved him-

self to Nature. *Parendo vinces.* If you resist Nature,
she will crush you ; but if you humour her, she will
place her tremendous forces at your disposal.   It is
madness to offer direct resistance to a royal virago or
a royal pedant, but by subservience you may command
either of them.   There is much of this feeling in the
state of mind of intelligent and highly educated Radicals, when they are in presence of a mob.   They make
their choice, according to the composition of their
audience, between two wonderful alternative theories
of our day—one, that the artisan of the towns knows
everything, because his work is so monotonous, and
because he has so much time on his hands ; the
other, that the labourer of the country districts knows
everything, because his work is so various and his
faculties so constantly active through this variety.
Thus it comes to pass that an audience composed of
roughs or clowns is boldly told by an educated man
that it has more political information than an equal
number of scholars.   This is not the opinion of the
speaker ; but it may be made, he thinks, the opinion
of the mob, and he knows that the mob could not
act as if it were true, unless it worked through
scholarly instruments.

The best safeguard against the various delusions
and extravagances which I have been examining is
a little better knowledge of the true lines of movement which the political affairs of mankind have

followed. In the opinion of a number of English gentlemen, whose authority is now somewhat on the decline, political history began in 1688. Mr. Bright seems to me to express himself often as if he thought that it began with the commencement of the Anti-Corn-Law agitation, and might be considered as having been practically arrested when the Corn-Law was repealed in 1846. There are younger men who are persuaded that it commenced with a certain crisis in the municipal history of Birmingham. The truth, however, is, that we live in a day in which a strand is unwinding itself, which was steadily knitting itself up during long ages. It is difficult to imagine a more baseless historical generalisation than that which Mr. Bancroft addresses to his American readers. During all the period when a change was proceeding " which no human policy could hold back," the movement of political affairs—what Mr. Bancroft calls the " tendency of the ages "—was as distinctly towards Monarchy as it now is towards Democracy. Mankind appear to have begun that stage in their history, which is more or less visible to our eyes, with the germs in each society of all the three definite forms of government—Monarchy, Aristocracy, and Democracy. Everywhere the King and Popular Assembly are seen side by side, the first a priestly and judicial, but primarily a fighting, personage ; the last sometimes under the control of an aristocratic Senate, and itself

varying from a small oligarchy to something like the
entirety of the free male population.   At the dawn of
history, Aristocracy seems to be gaining on Monarchy,
and Democracy on Aristocracy.   And this passage of
political development is especially well known to us
through the accidents which have preserved to us a
portion of the records of two famous societies, the
Athenian Republic, the cradle of philosophy and art,
and the Roman Republic, which began the conquests
destined to embrace a great part of the world.   This
last Republic was always more or less of an Aristocracy ; but from the time of its fall, and the establishment of the Roman Empire, there was on the whole,
for seventeen centuries, an all but universal movement
towards kingship.   There were, no doubt, evanescent
revivals of popular government. The barbarian races,
when they broke into the central Roman territory,
brought with them very generally some amount of the
ancient tribal liberty which, reintroduced into Mediterranean Europe, seemed again for a while likely to prove
the seed of political freedom.   The Roman municipal
system, left to work unchecked within the walled
cities of Northern Italy, reproduced a form of democracy   But Italian Commonwealths, and feudal
Estates and Parliaments, all sank, with one memorable exception. before the ever-growing power and
prestige of military despotic governments.   The historian of our day is apt to moralise and lament over

the change, but it was everywhere in the highest degree popular, and it called forth an enthusiasm quite as genuine as that of the modern Radical for the coming Democracy. The Roman Empire, the Italian tyrannies, the English Tudor Monarchy, the French centralised Kingship, the Napoleonic despotism, were all hailed with acclamation, most of it perfectly sincere, either because anarchy had been subdued, or because petty local and domestic oppressions were kept under, or because new energy was infused into national policy. In our own country, the popular government, born of tribal freedom, revived sooner than elsewhere; protected by the insularity of its home, it managed to live ; and thus the British Constitution became the one important exception to the "tendency of the ages," and through its remote influence this tendency was reversed, and the movement to Democracy began again. Nevertheless, even with us, though the King might be feared or disliked, the King's office never lost its popularity. The Commonwealth and the Protectorate were never for a moment in real favour with the nation. The true enthusiasm was reserved for the Restoration. Thus, from the reign of Augustus Cæsar to the establishment of the United States, it was Democracy which was always, as a rule, on the decline, nor was the decline arrested till the American Federal Government was founded, itself the offspring of the British Constitution   At

G

this moment, Democracy is receiving the same unqualified eulogy which was once poured on Monarchy; and though in its modern shape it is the product of a whole series of accidents, it is regarded by
some as propelled in a continuous progress by an
irresistible force.

Independently of the historical question, how the
fashion of bowing profoundly before Democracy grew
up, it has to be considered how far the inverted Monarchy, which bears this name, deserves the reverence
paid to it. The great philosophical writer who had
the best opinion of it was Jeremy Bentham. His
authority had to do with the broad extension of the
suffrage in most of the States of the American Union,
and he was the intellectual father of the masculine
school of English Radicals which died out with Mr.
Grote. He claimed for governments having the essential characteristics of Democracy, that they were much
more free than other governments from what he called
" sinister " influences. He meant by a sinister influence, a motive leading a government to prefer the
interest of small portions of a community to the interest of the whole. I certainly think that, with an
all-important qualification to be mentioned presently,
this credit was justly claimed for Democracy by Bentham, and with especial justice in relation to the circumstances of his own time. During the most active
period of his long life the French Revolution had

stopped all progress, and amid the relaxation of public watchfulness which followed, all sorts of small interests had found themselves niches in the English Budget, like the robber barons of mediæval Italy and Germany on every precipitous hill. Bentham thought it natural that they should do this. The lords of life, he said, are pleasure and pain. Every man follows his own interest as he understands it, and the part of the community which has political power will use it for its own objects. The remedy is to transfer political power to the entire community. It is impossible that they should abuse it, for the interest which they will try to promote is the interest of all, and the interest of all is the proper end and object of all legislation.

On this apparently irresistible reasoning, one or two remarks have to be made. In the first place, the praise here claimed for Democracy is shared by it with Monarchy, particularly in its most absolute forms. There is no doubt that the Roman Emperor cared more for the general good of the vast group of societies subject to him, than the aristocratic Roman Republic had done. The popularity of the great kings who broke up European feudalism, arose from their showing to all their vassals a far more even impartiality than could be obtained from petty feudal rulers ; and in our own day, vague and shadowy as are the recommendations of what is called a Nationality, a State founded on this principle has generally one real

G 2

practical advantage through its obliteration of small tyrannies and local oppressions. It has further to be observed, that a very serious weakness in Bentham's argument has been disclosed by the experience of half a century, an experience which might be carried much farther back with the help of that historical inquiry which Bentham neglected and perhaps despised. Democratic governments no doubt attempt to legislate and administer in the interests of Democracy, provided only the words are taken to mean the interests which Democracy supposes to be its own. For purposes of actual government, the standard of interest is not any which Bentham would have approved, but merely popular opinion. Nobody would have acknowledged this more readily than Bentham, if his marvellously long life could have been prolonged to this day. He was the ancestor of the advanced Liberals or Radicals who now carry everything before them. All their favourite political machinery came from his intellectual workshop. Household suffrage (which he faintly preferred to universal suffrage), vote by ballot, and the short Parliaments once in favour, received his energetic advocacy; and he detested the House of Lords. Yet there is no political writer whose strongest and most fundamental opinions are so directly at variance with the Radical ideas of the moment. One has only to turn over his pages for abundant evidence of this assertion. Over and over

again, you come upon demonstration that all the
mechanism of human society depends on the satisfaction of reasonable expectations, and therefore on the
strict maintenance of proprietary right, and the in-
violability of contract. You find earnest cautions
against the hasty acquisition of private property by
the State for public advantage, and vehement protests
against the removal of abuses without full compensation to those interested in them. Amid his denunciation of these capital vices of the legislator, it is
amusing to read his outbreaks[3] of enthusiasm for the
inclosure of commons, now sometimes described as
stealing the inheritance of the poor. The very vices
of political argument which he was thought to have
disposed of for ever have gained a new vitality among
the political school he founded. The "Anarchical
Sophisms" which he exposed have migrated from
France to England, and may be read in the literature
of Advanced Liberalism side by side with the Parliamentary Fallacies which he laughed at in the
debates of a Tory House of Commons.

The name of Jeremy Bentham, one of the few who

[3] "In England, one of the greatest and best understood im-
provements is the inclosure of commons. When we pass over
the lands which have undergone this happy change, we are
enchanted as with the appearance of a new colony; harvests,
flocks, and smiling habitations, have now succeeded to the sad-
ness and sterility of the desert. Happy conquests of peaceful
industry ! Noble aggrandisements which inspire no alarms and
provoke no enemies !"—Bentham's *Works*, i. 342.

have wholly lived for what they held to be the good of
the human race, has become even among educated men
a byword for what is called his "low view" of human
nature. The fact is that, under its most important
aspect, he greatly overrated human nature. He over-
estimated its intelligence. He wrongly supposed that
the truths which he saw, clearly cut and distinct, in
the dry light of his intellect, could be seen by all
other men or by many of them. He did not understand that they were visible only to the Few—to the
intellectual aristocracy. His delusion was the greater
from his inattention to facts which lay little beyond
the sphere of his vision. Knowing little of history,
and caring little for it, he neglected one easy method
of assuring himself of the extreme falseness of the
conceptions of their interest, which a multitude of
men may entertain. "The world," said Machiavelli,
"is made up of the vulgar" Thus Bentham's fundamental proposition turns against himself. It is that,
if you place power in men's hands, they will use it
for their interest. Applying the rule to the whole of
a political community, we ought to have a perfect
system of government ; but, taking it in connection
with the fact that multitudes include too much ignorance to be capable of understanding their interest, it
furnishes the principal argument against Democracy.

The immunity from sinister influences, the freedom from temptation to prefer the smaller interest to

the greater, which Bentham claimed for Democracy,
should thus have been extended by him to the more
absolute forms of Monarchy.   If indeed this sugges-
tion had been made to him, he would probably have
replied that Monarchy has a tendency to show unjust
favours to the military, the official, and the courtly
classes, the classes nearest to itself.   Monarchy, however, had had a very long history in Bentham's day,
and Democracy a very short one ; and it is only
as the political history of the American Union has
developed itself, that we are able to detect in wide
popular governments the same infirmities that characterised the kingly governments, of which they are
the inverted reproductions.   Under the shelter of one
government as of the other, all sorts of selfish interests breed and multiply, speculating on its weaknesses
and pretending to be its servants, agents, and delegates.   Nevertheless, after making all due qualifications, I do not at all deny to Democracies some portion of the advantage which so masculine a thinker
as Bentham claimed for them.   But, putting this
advantage at the highest, it is more than compensated
by one great disadvantage.   Of all the forms of
government, Democracy is by far the most difficult.
Little as the governing multitude is conscious of this
difficulty, prone as the masses are to aggravate it by
their avidity for taking more and more powers into
their direct management, it is a fact which experience

has placed beyond all dispute. It is the difficulty of democratic government that mainly accounts for its ephemeral duration.

The greatest, most permanent, and most fundamental of all the difficulties of Democracy, lies deep in the constitution of human nature. Democracy is a form of government, and in all governments acts of State are determined by an exertion of will. But in what sense can a multitude exercise volition ? The student of politics can put to himself no more pertinent question than this. No doubt the vulgar opinion is, that the multitude makes up its mind as the individual makes up his mind ; the Demos determines like the Monarch. A host of popular phrases testify to this belief. The "will of the People," "public opinion," the "sovereign pleasure of the nation," "Vox Populi, Vox Dei," belong to this class, which indeed constitutes a great part of the common stock of the platform and the press But what do such expressions mean ? They must mean that a great number of people, on a great number of questions, can come to an identical conclusion, and found an identical determination upon it. But this is manifestly true only of the simplest questions. A very slight addition of difficulty at once sensibly diminishes the chance of agreement, and, if the difficulty be considerable, an identical opinion can only be reached by trained minds assisting themselves by demonstration

more or less rigorous. On the complex questions of
politics, which are calculated in themselves to task to
the utmost all the powers of the strongest minds, but
are in fact vaguely conceived, vaguely stated, dealt
with for the most part in the most haphazard manner
by the most experienced statesmen, the common determination of a multitude is a chimerical assumption;
and indeed, if it were really possible to extract an
opinion upon them from a great mass of men, and
to shape the administrative and legislative acts of a
State upon this opinion as a sovereign command, it is
probable that the most ruinous blunders would be
committed, and all social progress would be arrested.
The truth is, that the modern enthusiasts for Democracy make one fundamental confusion. They mix
up the theory, that the Demos is capable of volition,
with the fact, that it is capable of adopting the opinions
of one man or of a limited number of men, and of
founding directions to its instruments upon them.

The fact, that what is called the will of the people
really consists in their adopting the opinion of one
person or a few persons, admits of a very convincing
illustration from experience. Popular Government
and Popular Justice were originally the same thing.
The ancient democracies devoted much more time and
attention to the exercise of civil and criminal jurisdiction than to the administration of their public
affairs ; and, as a matter of fact, popular justice has

lasted longer, has had a more continuous history, and
has received much more observation and cultivation,
than popular government. Over much of the world
it gave way to Royal Justice, which was of at least
equal antiquity, but it did not give way as universally
or as completely as popular government di l to monarchy. We have in England a relic of the ancient
Popular Justice in the functions of the Jury. The
Jury—technically known as the " country "—is the
old adjudicating Democracy, limited, modified, and
improved, in accordance with the principles suggested
by the experience of centuries, so as to bring it into
harmony with modern ideas of judicial efficiency.[4]
The change which has had to be made in it is in the
highest degree instructive. The Jurors are twelve,
instead of a multitude. Their main business is to
say " Aye " or " No " on questions which are doubtless
important, but which turn on facts arising in the
transactions of everyday life. In order that they may
reach a conclusion, they are assisted by a system of
contrivances and rules of the highest artificiality and
elaboration. An expert presides over their investigations—the Judge, the representative of the rival
and royal justice—and an entire literature is concerned with the conditions under which evidence on

---

[4] This intricate subject is discussed by Stephen (*History of
Criminal Law*, i. 254); Stubbs (*Constitutional History*, i. 685,
especially Note 3) ; Maine (*Early Law and Custom*, p. 160).

the facts in dispute may be laid before them. There
is a rigid exclusion of all testimony which has a tendency to bias them unfairly. They are addressed, as
of old, by the litigants or their advocates, but their
inquiry concludes with a security unknown to
antiquity, the summing-up of the expert President,
who is bound by all the rules of his profession to the
sternest impartiality. If he errs, or if they flagrantly
err, the proceedings may be quashed by a superior
Court of experts. Such is Popular Justice, after ages
of cultivation. Now it happens that the oldest Greek
poet has left us a picture, certainly copied from reality,
of what Popular Justice was in its infancy. The
primitive Court is sitting ; the question is " guilty "
or " not guilty." The old men of the community
give their opinions in turn ; the adjudicating Democracy, the commons standing round about, applaud
the opinion which strikes them most, and the applause
determines the decision. The Popular Justice of the
ancient republics was essentially of the same character. The adjudicating Democracy simply followed
the opinion which most impressed them in the speech
of the advocate or litigant. Nor is it in the least
doubtful that, but for the sternly repressive authority
of the presiding Judge, the modern English Jury
would, in the majority of cases, blindly surrender its
verdict to the persuasiveness of one or other of the
counsel who have been retained to address it.

A. modern governing democracy is the old adjudicating democracy very slightly changed. It cannot
indeed be said that no attempt has been made to
introduce into the multitudinous government modifications resembling those which have turned the
multitudinous tribunal into the Jury, for a variety
of expedients for mitigating the difficulty of popular
government have been invented and applied in England and the United States. But in our day a
movement appears to have very distinctly set in
towards unmodified democracy, the government of a
great multitude of men striving to take the bulk of
their own public affairs into their own hands. Such
a government can only decide the questions submitted
to it, as the old popular Courts of Justice decided
them, by applauding somebody who speaks to it.
The ruling multitude will only form an opinion by
following the opinion of somebody—it may be of a
great party leader—it may be, of a small local politician—it may be, of an organised association—it
may be, of an impersonal newspaper. The process
of deciding in accordance with plausibilities (in the
strict sense of this last word) goes on over an enormous area, growing ever more confused and capricious,
and giving results even more ambiguous or inarticu-
late, as the numbers to be consulted are multiplied.

The most interesting, and on the whole the most
successful, experiments in popular government, are

those which have frankly recognised the difficulty
under which it labours. At the head of these we
must place the virtually English discovery of government by Representation, which caused Parliamentary
institutions to be preserved in these islands from the
destruction which overtook them everywhere else, and
to devolve as an inheritance upon the United States.
Under this system, when it was in its prime, an electoral body, never in this country extraordinari'y large,
chose a number of persons to represent it in Parliament, leaving them unfettered by express instructions, but having with them at most a general
understanding, that they would strive to give a particular direction to public policy. The effect was to
diminish the difficulties of popular government, in
exact proportion to the diminution in the number of
persons who had to decide public questions. But
this famous system is evidently in decay, through
the ascendency over it which is being gradually obtained by the vulgar assumption that great masses of
men can directly decide all necessary questions for
themselves. The agency, by which the representative is sought to be turned into the mere mouthpiece
of opinions collected in the locality which sent him
to the House of Commons, is, we need hardly say,
that which is generally supposed to have been introduced from the United States under the name of the
Caucus, but which had very possibly a domestic

exemplar in the ecclesiastical organisation of the
Wesleyan Methodists. The old Italian toxicologists
are said to have always arranged their discoveries in a
series of three terms—first the poison, next the antidote, thirdly the drug which neutralised the antidote.
The antidote to the fundamental infirmities of democracy was Representation, but the drug which defeats
it has now been found in the Caucus. And, by an
unhappy mischance, the rapid conversion of the unfettered representative into the instructed delegate
has occurred just at the time when the House of
Commons itself is beginning to feel the inevitable
difficulties produced by its numerousness. Jeremy
Bentham used to denounce the non-attendance of
Members of Parliament at all sittings as a grave
abuse; but it now appears that the scanty attendance of members, and the still scantier participation
of most of them in debate, were essential to the conduct of business by the House of Commons, which
was then, as it is still, the most numerous deliberative
Assembly in the world. The Obstruction spoken of
by politicians of experience with lamentation and surprise is nothing more than a symptom of the familiar
disease of large governing bodies; it arises from the
numbers of the House of Commons, and from the
variety of opinions struggling in it for utterance.
The remedies hitherto tried for the cure of Obstruction will prove, in my judgment, to be merely pal-

liatives. No multitudinous assembly which seeks really to govern can possibly be free from it ; and it will probably lead to a constitutional revolution, the House of Commons abandoning the greatest part of its legislative authority to a Cabinet of Executive Ministers.

Another experiment, which, like the system of Representation, is founded on the acknowledgment of fundamental difficulties, has been attempted several times in our generation, though not in our country. In one of its forms it has been known as the Plébis-cite. A question, or a series of questions, is simplified as much as possible, and the entire enfranchised por-tion of the community is asked to say "Aye" or "No" to it. The zealots of democracy are beginning to forget, or conveniently to put aside, the enormous majorities by which the French nation, now supposed to be governing itself as a democracy, gave only the other day to a military despot any answer which he desired ; but it may be conceded to them that the question put to the voters was not honestly framed, however much it was simplified in form. Whether Louis Napoleon Bonaparte should be President for life with large legislative powers ? whether he should be an hereditary Emperor ? whether he should be allowed to divest himself of a portion of the autho-rity he had assumed ? were not simple, but highly complex questions, incapable of being replied to by

a naked " Yes " or " No." But the principle of the
Plébiscite has been engrafted on the Swiss Federal
Constitution ; and in some of the Cantonal Constitutions the " Referendum," as it is called, had existed
from an earlier date.   Here there is no ground for a
charge of dishonesty.   A new law is first thoroughly
debated, voted upon, and amended, by the Legislature ; and the debates are carried by the newspapers
to every corner of Swiss territory.   But it does not
come at once into force.   If a certain number of citizens so desire, the entire electoral body is called upon
to say " Aye " or " No " to the question whether the
law shall become operative.   I do not undertake to
say that the expedient has failed, but it can only be
considered thoroughly successful by those who wish
that there should be as little legislation as possible.
Contrary to all expectations,[5] to the bitter disappointment of the authors of the Referendum, laws of the

[5] What these expectations were, may be gathered from the
language of M. Numa Droz. M. Droz calls the Referendum
"l'essai le plus grandiose qu'une République ait jamais tenté."
The effect, however, has been that, since the commencement of the
experiment in 1874 there have been vetoed, among other laws
passed by the Federal Legislature, an Electoral Law (twice over),
a Law on Currency, a Law creating a Department of Education,
a Law creating a Department of Justice, a Law providing a salary
for a Secretary of Legation at Washington, and a Law permitting
the venue to be changed to the Federal Court when there is reason
to suspect the fairness of a Cantonal tribunal.   It is remarkable
that, under a Cantonal Referendum, a Law establishing a progressive Income Tax was negatived.

highest importance. some of them openly framed for
popularity, have been vetoed by the People after they
had been adopted by the Federal or Cantonal Legislature. This result is sufficiently intelligible. It is
possible, by agitation and exhortation, to produce in
the mind of the average citizen a vague impression
that he desires a particular change. But, when the
agitation has settled down on the dregs, when the
excitement has died away, when the subject has been
threshed out, when the law is before him with all its
detail, he is sure to find in it much that is likely to
disturb his habits, his ideas, his prejudices, or his interests; and so, in the long-run, he votes " No " to
every proposal. The delusion that Democracy, when
it has once had all things put under its feet, is a progressive form of government, lies deep in the convic-
tions of a particular political school; but there can
be no delusion grosser. It receives no countenance
either from experience or from probability. Englishmen in the East come into contact with vast populations of high natural intelligence, to which the very
notion of innovation is loathsome ; and the very fact
that such populations exist should suggest that the
true difference between the East and the West lies
merely in this, that in Western countries there is a
larger minority of exceptional persons who, for good
reasons or bad, have a real desire for change. All
that has made England famous, and all that has made

II

England wealthy, has been the work of minorities, sometimes very small ones. It seems to me quite certain that, if for four centuries there had been a very widely extended franchise and a very large electoral body in this country, there would have been no reformation of religion, no change of dynasty, no toleration of Dissent, not even an accurate Calendar. The threshing-machine, the power-loom, the spinning-jenny, and possibly the steam-engine, would have been prohibited. Even in our day, vaccination is in the utmost danger, and we may say generally that the gradual establishment of the masses in power is of the blackest omen for all legislation founded on scientific opinion, which requires tension of mind to understand it and self-denial to submit to it.

The truth is, that the inherent difficulties of democratic government are so manifold and enormous that, in large and complex modern societies, it could neither last nor work if it were not aided by certain forces which are not exclusively associated with it, but of which it greatly stimulates the energy. Of these forces, the one to which it owes most is unquestionably Party.

No force acting on mankind has been less carefully examined than Party, and yet none better deserves examination. The difficulty which Englishmen in particular feel about it is very like that which men once experienced when they were told

that the air had weight. It enveloped them so evenly
and pressed on them so equally, that the assertion
seemed incredible. Nevertheless it is not hard to
show that Party and Party Government are very
extraordinary things. Let us suppose it to be still
the fashion to write the apologues so dear to the last
century, in which some stranger from the East or
West, some Persian full of intelligent curiosity, some
Huron still unspoilt by civilisation, or some unpre-
judiced Bonze from India or China, described the
beliefs and usages of European countries, just as they
struck him, to his kinsmen at the other end of the
world. Let us assume that in one of these trifles, by
a Voltaire or a Montesquieu, the traveller gave an
account of a cultivated and powerful European Commonwealth, in which the system of government consisted in half the cleverest men in the country taking
the utmost pains to prevent the other half from governing. Or let us imagine some modern writer, with
the unflinching perspicacity of a Machiavelli, analysing
the great Party Hero—leader or agitator—as the
famous Italian analysed the personage equally interesting and important in his day, the Tyrant or
Prince. Like Machiavelli, he would not stop to
praise or condemn on ethical grounds : " he would
follow the real truth of things rather than an imaginary view of them." [6] " Many Party Heroes," he

[6] *The Prince*, xv. (101).

would say, " have been imagined, who were never
seen or known to exist in reality." But he would
describe them as they really were. Allowing them
every sort of private virtue, he would deny that their
virtues had any effect on their public conduct, except
so far as they helped to make men believe their public
conduct virtuous. But this public conduct he would
find to be not so much immoral as non-moral. He
would infer, from actual observation, that the party
Hero was debarred by his position from the full practice of the great virtues of veracity, justice, and moral
intrepidity. He could seldom tell the full truth ; he
could never be fair to persons other than his followers
and associates ; he could rarely be bold except in the
interests of his faction. The picture drawn by him
would be one which few living men would deny to be
correct, though they might excuse its occurrence in
nature on the score of moral necessity. And then, a
century or two later, when Democracies were as much
forgotten as the Italian Princedoms, our modern Machiavelli would perhaps be infamous and his work a
proverb of immorality.

Party has many strong affinities with Religion.
Its devotees, like those of a religious creed, are apt to
substitute the fiction that they have adopted it upon
mature deliberation for the fact that they were born
into it or stumbled into it. But they are in the
highest degree reluctant to come to an open breach

with it ; they count it shame to speak of its weak
points, except to co-religionists ; and, whenever it is
in serious difficulty, they return to its assistance or
rescue. Their relation to those outside the pale—the
relation of Whig to Tory, of Conservative to Liberal
—is on the whole exceedingly like that of Jew to
Samaritan. But the closest resemblances are between
party discipline and military discipline ; and indeed,
historically speaking, Party is probably nothing more
than a survival and a consequence of the primitive
combativeness of mankind. It is war without the
city transmuted into war within the city, but mitigated in the process. The best historical justification
which can be offered for it is that it has often
enabled portions of the nation, who would otherwise
be armed enemies, to be only factions. Party strife,
like strife in arms, develops many high but imper-
fect and one-sided virtues ; it is fruitful of self-denial
and self-sacrifice. But wherever it prevails, a great
part of ordinary morality is unquestionably sus-
pended ; a number of maxims are received, which
are not those of religion or ethics ; and men do acts
which, except as between enemies, and except as
between political opponents, would be very generally
classed as either immoralities or sins.

Party disputes were originally the occupation of
aristocracies, which joined in them because they loved
the sport for its own sake : and the rest of the com-

munity followed one side or the other as its clients.
Now-a-days, Party has become a force acting with vast
energy on multitudinous democracies, and a number
of artificial contrivances have been invented for facili-
tating and stimulating its action.   Yet, in a democracy, the fragment of political power falling to each
man's share is so extremely small, that it would be
hardly possible, with all the aid of the Caucus, the
Stump, and the Campaign newspaper, to rouse the
interests of thousands or millions of men, if Party
were not coupled with another political force.   This,
to speak plainly, is Corruption.   A story is current
respecting a conversation of the great American,
Alexander Hamilton, with a friend who expressed
wonder at Hamilton's extreme admiration of so
corrupt a system as that covered by the name of
the British Constitution.   Hamilton is said to have,
in reply, expressed his belief that when the corruption came to an end the Constitution would fall to
pieces.   The corruption referred to was that which
had been openly practised by the Whig Ministers
of George I. and George II. through the bestowal
of places and the payment of sums of money, but
which in the reign of George III. had died down
to an obscurer set of malpractices, ill-understood,
but partially explained by the constant indebtedness
of the thrifty King.   Hamilton of course meant that,
amid the many difficulties of popular government,

he doubted whether, in its English form, it could be
carried on, unless support were purchased by governments ; and this opinion might very plausibly have
been held concerning the early governments of the
Hanoverian dynasty, so deeply unpopular did the
" Revolution Settlement" soon become with large
classes of Englishmen. What put an end to this
corruption was in reality not an English but a French
phenomenon—the Revolution begun in 1789, which,
through the violent repulsion with which it inspired
the greatest part of the nation, and the half-avowed
attraction which it had for the residue, supplied the
English parties with principles of action which did
not need the co-operation of any corrupt inducement
to partisanship. The corruption which we find denounced by Bentham after the close of the great war
was not bribery, but vested interest ; nor did the old
practices ever revive in England in their ancient
shape. Votes at elections continued to be bought
and sold, but not votes in Parliament.

Whether Hamilton looked forward to an era of
purity in his own country, cannot be certainly
known. He and his coadjutors undoubtedly were
unprepared for the rapid development of Party
which soon set in ; they evidently thought that their
country would be poor ; and they probably expected
to see all evil influences defeated by the elaborate
contrivances of the Federal Constitution. But the

United States became rapidly wealthy and rapidly populous ; and the universal suffrage of all white men, native-born or immigrant, was soon established by the legislation of the most powerful States. With wealth, population, and widely diffused electoral power, corruption sprang into vigorous life. President Andrew Jackson, proclaiming the principle of " to the victors the spoils," which all parties soon adopted, expelled from office all administrative servants of the United States who did not belong to his faction ; and the crowd of persons filling these offices, which are necessarily very numerous in so vast a territory, together with the groups of wealthy men interested in public lands and in the countless industries protected by the Customs tariff, formed an extensive body of contributors from whom great amounts of money were levied by a species of taxation, to be presently expended in wholesale bribery. A reaction against this system carried the present President of the United States into office ; but the opinion of almost all the politicians who the other day supported Mr. Blaine bore probably the closest resemblance to Hamilton's opinion about Great Britain. They were persuaded that the American Party system cannot continue without corruption. It is impossible to lay down M. Scherer's pamphlet[7] without a conviction, that the same opinion is held of France by the

[7] See especially pages 24, 25, 27, 29, 35.

public men who direct the public affairs of the French Republic. The account which this writer gives of the expedients by which all French Governments have sought to secure support, since the resignation of Marshal MacMahon, is most deplorable. There is a scale of public corruption, with an excessive and extravagant scheme of public works at one end of it, and at the other the open barter of votes by the electoral committees for the innumerable small places in the gift of the highly centralised French administration. The principle that the spoils belong to the victors has been borrowed from the United States, and receives a thoroughgoing application. Every branch of the public service—even, since M. Scherer wrote, the judicial bench—has been completely purged of functionaries not professing allegiance to the party in power for the time being.

We Englishmen, alone among popularly governed communities, have tried an expedient peculiar to ourselves. We have handed over all patronage to the Civil Service Commissioners, and we have adopted the Corrupt Practices Act. It is a most singular fact, that the only influences having an affinity for the old corruption, which still survive in Great Britain, are such as can be brought to bear on those exalted regions of society, in which stars, garters, ribands, titles, and lord-lieutenancies, still circulate. What will be the effect on British government of the heroic remedies we have administered to ourselves, has yet to be seen. What will come of borrowing the Caucus from the United States, and refusing to soil our fingers with the oil used in its native country to lubricate the wheels of the machine? Perhaps we are not at liberty to forget that there are two kinds of bribery. It can be carried on by promising or giving to expectant partisans places paid out of the taxes, or it may consist in the directer process of legislating away the property of one class and transferring it to another. It is this last which is likely to be the corruption of these latter days.

Party and Corruption, as influences which have shown themselves capable of bringing masses of men under civil discipline, are probably as old as the very beginning of political life. The savage ferocity of party strife in the Greek States has been described by the great Greek historian in some of his most impressive sentences; and nothing in modern times has approached the proportions of the corruption practised at the elections of the Roman Republic, in spite of all the impediments placed in its way by an earlier form of the Ballot. But in quite recent times a third expedient has been discovered for producing, not indeed agreement, but the semblance of agreement, in a multitude of men. This is generalisation, the trick of rapidly framing, and confidently uttering, general propositions on political

subjects. It was once supposed that the power
of appreciating general propositions was especially
characteristic of the highest minds, which it distinguished from those of a vulgar stamp always
immersed in detail and in particulars. Once or
twice, indeed, in the course of their intellectual
history, mankind have fallen on their knees to
worship generalisation; and indeed, without help
from it, it is probable that the strongest intellect
would not be able to bear the ever-accumulating
burden of particular facts. But, in these latter days,
a ready belief in generalities has shown itself to be
a characteristic, not indeed of wholly uneducated,
but of imperfectly educated minds. Meantime, men
ambitious of political authority have found out the
secret of manufacturing generalities in any number.
Nothing can be simpler. All generalisation is the
product of abstraction ; all abstraction consists in
dropping out of sight a certain number of particular
facts, and constructing a formula which will embrace
the remainder ; and the comparative value of general
propositions turns entirely on the relative importance
of the particular facts selected and of the particular
facts rejected. The modern facility of generalisation
is obtained by a curious precipitation and careless-
ness in this selection and rejection, which, when
properly carried out, is the only difficult part of
the entire process. General formulas, which can be

seen on examination to have been arrived at by attending only to particulars few, trivial, or irrelevant, are turned out in as much profusion as if they dropped from an intellectual machine ; and debates in the House of Commons may be constantly read, which consisted wholly in the exchange of weak generalities and strong personalities. On a pure Democracy this class of general formulas has a prodigious effect. Crowds of men can be got to assent to general statements, clothed in striking language, but unverified and perhaps incapable of verification ; and thus there is formed a sort of sham and pretence of concurrent opinion. There has been a loose acquiescence in a vague proposition, and then the People, whose voice is the voice of God, is assumed to have spoken. Useful as it is to democracies, this levity of assent is one of the most enervating of national habits of mind. It has seriously enfeebled the French intellect. It is most injuriously affecting the mind of England. It threatens little short of ruin to the awakening intellect of India, where political abstractions, founded exclusively upon English facts, and even here requiring qualification, are applied by the educated minority, and by their newspapers, to a society which, through nine-tenths of its structure, belongs to the thirteenth century of the West.

The points which I have attempted to establish

are these. Without denying to democratic governments some of the advantages which were claimed
for them by the one thinker of the first order who
has held Democracy to be in itself a good form of
government, I have pointed out that it has the signal
disadvantage of being the most difficult of all governments, and that the principal influences by which
this difficulty has hitherto been mitigated are in-
jurious either to the morality or to the intellect of
the governing multitude. If the government of the
Many be really inevitable, one would have thought
that the possibility of discovering some other and
newer means of enabling it to fulfil the ends for
which all governments exist, would have been a
question exercising all the highest powers of the
strongest minds, particularly in the community
which, through the success of its popular institutions,
has paved the way for all modern Democracy. Yet
hardly anything worth mentioning has been produced on the subject in England or on the Continent.
I ought, however, to notice a series of discussions
which have long been going on in the little State
of Belgium, ending in a remarkable experiment.
Alarmed by a reckless agitation for universal suffrage,
the best heads in the country have devised an
electoral law,[8] which is worthy of the most respectful

_____

[8] *Code Electoral Belge*, p. 289. Provincial and Communal
Law of August 24, 1883.

attention. Under its provisions, an attempt is made
to attach the franchise, not only to property, but to
proved capacity in all its manifestations, to confer it
not simply on the men who contribute a certain
amount to the revenue, but on every man who has
taken honours at a High School or at College, on
everybody who can pass an examination with credit,
on every foreman of a workshop or factory. The
idea is to confer power not on the Many, but on the
strongest among the Many. The experiment, however, is at present confined to Provincial and Communal Elections; and we have yet to see whether an
electoral system, which would be attended by peculiar difficulties in England, can be successfully carried
out even in Belgium. On the whole, there is only
one country in which the question of the safest and
most workable form of democratic government has
been adequately discussed, and the results of discussion tested by experiment. This is the United States
of America. American experience has, I think, shown
that, by wise Constitutional provisions thoroughly
thought out beforehand, Democracy may be made
tolerable. The public powers are carefully defined ;
the mode in which they are to be exercised is fixed ;
and the amplest securities are taken that none of the
more important Constitutional arrangements shall be
altered without every guarantee of caution and every
opportunity for deliberation. The expedient is not

conclusive, for the Americans, settled in a country of boundless unexhausted wealth, have never been tempted to engage in socialistic legislation; but, as far as it has gone, a large measure of success cannot be denied to it, success which has all but dispelled the old ill-fame of democracies.   The short history of the United States has, at the same time, established one momentous negative conclusion.   When a democracy governs, it is not safe to leave unsettled any important question concerning the exercise of public powers.   I might give many instances of this, but the most conclusive is the War of Secession, which was entirely owing to the omission of the "fathers" to provide beforehand for the solution of certain Constitutional problems, lest they should stir the topic of negro slavery.   It would seem that, by a wise Constitution, Democracy may be made nearly as calm as water in a great artificial reservoir; but if there is a weak point anywhere in the structure, the mighty force which it controls will burst through it and spread destruction far and near.

This warning deserves all the attention of Englishmen.   They are opening the way to Democracy on all sides.   Let them take heed that it be not admitted into a receptacle of loose earth and sand.   And, in laying this caution to heart, it would be well for them to consider what sort of a Constitution it is to which they must trust for the limitation of the powers, and the neutralisation of the weaknesses, of the two or three millions of voters who have been admitted to the suffrage, in addition to the multitude enfranchised in 1867. The events of the summer and autumn of 1884 were not reassuring. During all that time, the air was hot and thick with passionate assertions of contradictory opinions. The points on which the controversy turned were points in the construction of the Constitution, and the fact that the ablest men in the country took sides upon them proves them to be unsettled. Nor does there exist any acknowledged authority by which they can be adjudicated upon and decided. It is useless to appeal to the law, for the very charge against the House of Lords was, that the law had been put abusively into operation. It is useless to allege the authority of the electoral body, for the very charge against the House of Commons was, that it did not represent the constituencies. To describe such a dispute as serious, is hardly to do it justice : but, in order to bring into full light the scope and number of the doubtful questions which it proved to exist, I will mention in turn the principal depositaries of public authority in this country—the Crown, the Cabinet, the House of Lords, and the House of Commons—and I will note the various opinions which appear to be held as to the part which each of them should take in legislation by which the structure of the Constitution is altered.

The powers over legislation which the law recognises in the Crown are its power to veto Bills
which have passed both the House of Commons and
the House of Lords, and its power to dissolve Parliament. The first of these powers has probably been
lost through disuse. There is not, at the same time,
the smallest reason for supposing that it was abandoned through any inconsistency with popular government. It was not employed, because there was
no occasion for employing it. The reigns of the first
Hanoverian Sovereigns were periods of activity in
foreign policy, and the legislation of the time was
utterly insignificant ; the King's Government was,
moreover, steadily drawing to itself the initiative in
legislation, and for more than a century the Kings
succeeded on the whole in governing through what
Ministers they pleased. As to the right to dissolve
Parliament by an independent exercise of the royal
will, it cannot be quite confidently asserted to have
become obsolete. The question has been much discussed in the Colonies which attempt to follow the
British Constitutional procedure, and it seems to be
generally allowed that a representative of the Crown
cannot be blamed for insisting on a dissolution of the
Legislature, though his Ministers are opposed to it.
It is probable, however, that in this country the object
would be practically attained in a different way. The
Crown would appoint Ministers who were willing

I

to take the not very serious risks involved in appealing to the constituencies. The latest precedent in
this case is quite modern. William IV., her Majesty's
uncle and immediate predecessor, replaced Lord Mel-
bourne by Sir Robert Peel in 1834, and Sir Robert
Peel, as he afterwards told the House of Commons,
took upon himself the entire responsibility of dissolving Parliament.

The Cabinet, which through a series of Constitutional fictions has succeeded to all the powers of the
Crown, has drawn to itself all, and more than all, of
the royal power over legislation. It can dissolve
Parliament, and, if it were to advise the Crown to
veto a Bill which has been passed through both
Houses, there is no certainty that the proceeding
would be seriously objected to. That it can arrest a
measure at any stage of its progress through either
House of Parliament, is conceded on all hands ; and
indeed the exercise of this power was exemplified on
the largest scale at the end of the Session of 1884,
when a large number of Bills of the highest importance were abandoned in deference to a Cabinet decision. The Cabinet has further become the sole source
of all important legislation, and therefore, by the
necessity of the case, of all Constitutional legislation ;
and as a measure amending the Constitution passes
through the House of Commons, the modification or
maintenance of its details depends entirely on the fiat
of the Ministers of the day. Although the Cabinet,

as such, is quite unknown to the law, it is manifestly
the English institution which is ever more and more
growing in authority and influence ; and already,
besides wielding more than the legislative powers of
the Crown, it has taken to itself nearly all the legislative powers of Parliament, depriving it in particular
of the whole right of initiation.   The long familiarity
of Englishmen with this institution, and with the
copies of it made in the European countries which
possess Constitutions, has blinded them to its extreme
singularity.   There is a fashion among historians of
expressing wonder, not unmixed with dislike, at the
secret bodies and councils which they occasionally
find invested with authority in famous States.   In
ancient history, the Spartan Ephors—in modern
history, the Venetian Council of Ten—are criticised
in this spirit.   Many of these writers are Englishmen,
and yet they seem quite unconscious that their own
country is governed by a secret[9] Council.   There can
be very little doubt that the secrecy of the Cabinet
is its strength.   A great part of the weakness of

[9] No secret has been better kept than that of English Cabinet procedure.   Apart from Cabinet Ministers, past and present,
there are probably not a dozen men in the country who know
accurately how Cabinets conduct their deliberations, and how
they arrive at a conclusion.   Some information may, however, be
obtained from the published Diaries of the second Lord Ellenborough, from some printed, but unpublished, Memoirs left by
Lord Broughton (Sir J. Cam Hobhouse), and in some degree
from Lord Malmesbury's recent *Memoirs of an ex-Minister*.

Democracy springs from publicity of discussion ; and nobody who has had any share in public business can have failed to observe, that the chances of agreement among even a small number of persons increase in nearly exact proportion to the chances of privacy. If the growth in power of the Cabinet is checked, it will probably be from causes of very recent origin.   It is essentially a committee of the men who lead the party which has a majority in the House of Commons. But there are signs that its authority over its party is passing to other committees, selected less for eminence in debate and administration than for the adroit management of local political business.

The House of Lords, as a matter of strict law, has the right to reject or amend any measure which is submitted to it ; nor has this legal right in either of its forms been disused or abandoned, save as regards money-bills.   But it has lately become evident that, when the right is exerted over measures amending the Constitution, strong differences of opinion exist as to the mode and conditions of its exercise ; and, as is not uncommon in this country, it is very difficult to gather from the violent language of the disputants, whether they contend that the law should be altered, or that the exertion of power with which they are quarrelling is forbidden by usage, precedent, conventional understanding, or mere expediency. The varieties of doctrine are many and wide apart.

On the one hand, one extreme party compares the rejection of a Bill by the House of Lords to the veto
of a Bill by the Crown, and insists that the first
power should be abandoned as completely as the last
is believed to have been. Conversely, the most influential [1] members of the House of Lords allow that
it would act improperly in rejecting a constitutional
measure, of which the electoral body has signified
its approval by the result of a general election. Between these positions there appear to be several inter-
mediate opinions, most of them, however, stated in
language of the utmost uncertainty and vagueness.
Some persons appear to think that the House of
Lords ought not to reject or postpone a constitutional
measure which affects the powers of the House of
Commons, or its relation to the constituencies, or the
constituencies themselves. Others seem to consider
that the power of rejection might be exercised on
such a measure, if the majority by which it has
passed the House of Commons is small, but not if
it exceeds a certain number. Lastly, little can be
extracted from the language of a certain number of
controversialists, violent as it is, except an opinion
that the House of Lords ought not to do wrong, and
that it did wrong on one particular occasion.

[1] Lord Salisbury strongly urged this principle upon the House
of Lords when the Bill for disestablishing and disendowing the
Established Church of Ireland was before it. This speech probably secured the passing of the Bill.

The power of the House of Commons over legislation, including constitutional legislation, might seem at first sight to be complete and unqualified. Nevertheless, as I have pointed out, it some time ago surrendered the initiative in legislation, and it is now more and more surrendering the conduct of it, to the so-called Ministers of the Crown. It may further be observed from the language of those who, on the whole, contend for the widest extension of its powers, that a new theory has made its appearance, which raises a number of embarrassing questions as to the authority of the House of Commons in constitutional legislation. This is the theory of the Mandate. It seems to be conceded that the electoral body must supply the House of Commons with a Mandate to alter the Constitution. It has been asserted that a Mandate to introduce Household Suffrage into the counties was given to the House of Commons elected in 1880, but not a Mandate to confer the suffrage on Women. What is a Mandate? As used here, the word has not the meaning which belongs to it in English, French, or Latin. I conjecture that it is a fragment of a French phrase, *mandat impératif*, which means an express direction from a constituency which its representative is not permitted to disobey, and I imagine the mutilation to imply that the direction may be given in some loose and general manner. But in what manner? Is it meant

that, if a candidate in an election address declares
that he is in favour of household suffrage or woman
suffrage, and is afterwards elected, he has a mandate
to vote for it, but not otherwise ?   And, if so, how
many election addresses, containing such references,
and how many returns, constitute a Mandate to the
entire House of Commons ?   Again, assuming the
Mandate to have been obtained, how long is it in
force ?   The House of Commons may sit for seven
years under the Septennial Act ; but the strict law
has hardly ever prevailed, and in the great majority
of cases the House of Commons has not lasted for
nearly the whole period.   May it give effect to its
Mandate in its fourth, or fifth, or sixth Session, or
must an alteration of the Constitution be the earliest
measure to which a Parliament commissioned to deal
with it must address itself ?

These unsettled questions formed the staple of the
controversy which raged among us for months, but
the prominence which they obtained is not in the
very least arbitrary or accidental.   The question of
the amount and nature of the notice which the
electoral body shall receive of an intended change in
the Constitution ; the question whether anything
like a " Mandate " shall be given by that body to the
Legislature ; the question whether existing constituencies shall have full jurisdiction over proposed constitutional innovation ; the question of the majority

which shall be necessary for the decision of the
Legislature on a constitutional measure; all these
questions belong to the very essence of constitutional
doctrine.   There is no one of them which is peculiar
to this country ; what is peculiar to this country is
the extreme vagueness with which all of them are
conceived and stated.   The Americans of the United
States, feeling on all sides the strongest pressure of
Democracy, but equipped with a remarkable wealth
of constitutional knowledge inherited from their forefathers, have had to take up and solve every one
of them.   I will endeavour to show what have been
their methods of solution.   I will not at present go
for an example to the Constitution of the United
States, abounding as it does in the manifold restric-
tions thought necessary by its framers for the purpose of securing in a probably democratic society
the self-command without which it could not become
or remain a nation.   It will be sufficient for my object to quote the provisions respecting the procedure
to be followed on constitutional amendments, contained in the Constitutions of individual States,
which, I need not say, can only legislate within the
limits permitted to them by the Federal Constitution.
One of the subjects, however, on which the powers
of the several States were till lately exclusive and are
still most extensive, is the Franchise ; and this gives
a peculiar value and interest to the provisions which

I will proceed to extract from the Constitution of the great State of New York.

Article 13 of the Constitution of New York, which is still in force, runs as follows :—

Any amendment or amendments to this Constitution may be proposed to the Senate and Assembly ; and if the same be agreed to by a majority of the members elected to each of the two Houses, such amendment or amendments shall be entered on their journals with the " Yeas " and " Nays " taken thereon, and referred to the Legislature to be chosen at the next general election, and shall be published for three months previous to the time of making such choice ; and if, in the Legislature so next chosen as aforesaid, such proposed amendment or amendments shall be agreed to by a majority of all the members elected to each House, then it shall be the duty of the Legislature to submit such proposed amendment or amendments to the people in such manner and at such time as the Legislature shall prescribe ; and if the people shall approve and ratify such amendment or amendments by a majority of the electors qualified to vote for members of the Legislature voting thereon, such amendment or amendments shall become part of the Constitution.

Section 2 of the Article provides an alternative mode of amendment.

At the general election to be held (in each twentieth year), and also at such time as the Legislature may by law provide, the question " Shall there be a Convention to revise the Constitution and amend the same ? " shall be decided by the electors qualified to vote for members of the Legislature, and in case a majority of the electors so qualified voting at such election shall decide in favour of a Convention for such purpose, the Legislature at the next Session shall provide by law for the election of delegates to such Convention.

These provisions of the Constitution of New York, regulating the procedure to be followed in constitutional amendments, and therefore in measures extending or altering the electoral franchise, are substantially repeated in the Constitutions of nearly all the American States. Where there are variations, they are generally in the direction of greater stringency. The Constitution of Ohio, for example, requires that there shall be at the least a three-fifths majority in each branch of the Legislature proposing an amendment, and a two-thirds majority is necessary if it is sought to summon a Convention. When an amendment is proposed in Massachusetts, a two-thirds majority is demanded in the Lower House ; and the same majority must be obtained in both Houses before the Constitution of Louisiana can be amended. The Constitution of New Jersey gives greater precision to the provision of the New York Constitution for the ultimate ratification of the proposed amendment by the constituencies, by inserting, after the words " the people shall ratify and approve," the words " at a special election to be held for that purpose only." The same Constitution declares that " no amendment shall be submitted to the people more than once in five years ; " and, like the Constitutions of several other States, it gives no power to summon a revising Convention.

No doubt therefore is possible as to the mode in which these American State Constitutions settle the formidable questions which the discussion of 1884 has shown to be unsettled in this country. First of all, it is to be noted that the electoral body recognised by all the Constitutions, without exception, as having an exclusive jurisdiction over amendments of the Constitution, is the existing electoral body, and not any electoral body of the future. Next, the most ample notice is given to it that an amendment of the Constitution will be brought before the next Legislature which it is called upon to choose ; both branches of the outgoing Legislature must record a resolution with the numbers of the division upon it, and this resolution must be published three months before a general election. It is quite clear, therefore, that the representatives chosen at this election will have what may be called a " Mandate." The amendment must then be agreed to by an absolute majority of the members of both Houses of the new Legislature ; or, as is required in some States, by a two-thirds or three-fifths majority in both Houses, or one of them. But there is a final security in addition. The Mandate must be ratified. The amendment must be submitted to the people in any way which the Legislature may provide ; and, as is shown by the

Constitution of New Jersey, the ratification is usually placed in the hands of a special legislature specially elected for the purpose of giving or refusing it.

Such are the securities against surprise or haste in conducting the most important part of legislation, which American political sagacity has devised. They may very well suggest to the English politician some serious reflections. What was most remarkable in the discussion of twelve months since was, far less the violent and inflammatory language in which it was carried on, than the extreme vagueness of the considerations upon which it has turned. The House of Lords, for instance, was threatened with extinction or mutilation for a certain offence. Yet when the offence is examined, it appears to have consisted in the violation of some rule or understanding, never expressed in writing, at variance with the strict law, and not perhaps construed in precisely the same way by any two thinking men in the country. Political history shows that men have at all times quarrelled more fiercely about phrases and formulas, than even about material interests ; and it would seem that the discussion of British Constitutional legislation is distinguished from the discussion of all other legislation by having no fixed points to turn upon, and therefore by its irrational violence. Is it therefore idle to hope that at some calmer moment—now that the creation of two or three million more voters has

been accomplished—we may borrow a few of the
American securities against surprise and irreflection
in constitutional legislation, and express them with
something like the American precision? Is it always
to be possible in this country that a great amendment
of the Constitution should, first of all, be attempted to
be carried by tumultuary meetings of the population,
enfranchised'and unenfranchised—next, that it should
be conducted through Parliament by a process which
practically excluded Parliament from all share in
shaping its provisions—and, lastly, that it should
hardly become law before it was hurriedly altered for
the purpose of giving votes to a particular class of
paupers ? Some have supposed that the only remedy
would be one which involved the conversion of the
unwritten Constitution of Great Britain into a written
Constitution. But a great part of our Constitution is
already written. Many of the powers of the Crown
—many of the powers of the House of Lords, including the whole of its judicial powers—much of the
constitution of the House of Commons and its entire
relation to the electoral body—have long since been
defined by Act of Parliament. There does not seem
to be any insuperable objection, first of all, to making
a distinction between ordinary legislation and legislation which in any other country would be called
Constitutional ; and next, to requiring for the last a
special legislative procedure, intended to secure

caution and deliberation, and as near an approach
to impartiality as a system of party government will
admit of. The alternative is to leave unsettled all the
questions which the controversy of 1884 brought to
light, and to give free play to a number of tendencies already actively at work. It is quite plain
whither they are conducting us. We are drifting
towards a type of government associated with terrible
events—a single Assembly, armed with full powers
over the Constitution, which it may exercise at
pleasure. It will be a theoretically all-powerful Convention, governed by a practically all-powerful secret
Committee of Public Safety, but kept from complete
submission to its authority by Obstruction, for which
its rulers are always seeking to find a remedy in some
kind of moral guillotine.

ESSAY III.

THE AGE OF PROGRESS.

THERE is no doubt that some of the most inventive, most polite, and best instructed portions of the human race are at present going through a stage of thought which, if it stood by itself, would suggest that there is nothing of which human nature is so tolerant, or so deeply enamoured, as the transformation of laws and institutions. A series of political and social changes, which a century ago no man would have thought capable of being effected save by the sharp convulsion of Revolution, is now contemplated by the bulk of many civilised communities as sure to be carried out, a certain number of persons regarding the prospect with exuberant hope, a somewhat larger number with equanimity, many more with indifference or resignation. At the end of the last century, a Revolution in France shook the whole civilised world ; and the consequence of the terrible events and bitter disappointments which it brought with it was to arrest all improvement in Great Britain for

thirty years, merely because it was innovation. But
in 1830 a second explosion occurred in France, followed by the reconstruction of the British electorate
in 1832, and with the British Reformed Parliament
began that period of continuous legislation through
which, not this country alone, but all Western Europe
appears to be passing. It is not often recognised how
excessively rare in the world was sustained legislative
activity till rather more than fifty years ago, and thus
sufficient attention has not been given to some characteristics of this particular mode of exercising sovereign
power, which we call Legislation. It has obviously
many advantages over Revolution as an instrument
of change ; while it has quite as trenchant an edge,
it is milder, juster, more equable, and sometimes
better considered. But in one respect, as at present
understood, it may prove to be more dangerous than
revolution. Political insanity takes strange forms,
and there may be some persons in some countries who
look forward to " The Revolution " as implying a series
of revolutions. But, on the whole, a Revolution is
regarded as doing all its work at once. Legislation,
however, is contemplated as never-ending. One stage
of it is doubtless more or less distinctly conceived. It
will not be arrested till the legislative power itself,
and all kinds of authority at any time exercised by
States, have been vested in the People, the Many, the
great majority of the human beings making up each

community. The prospect beyond that is dim, and perhaps will prove to be as fertile in disappointment as is always the morrow of a Revolution. But doubtless the popular expectation is that, after the establishment of a Democracy, there will be as much reforming legislation as ever.

This zeal for political movement, gradually identifying itself with a taste for Democracy, has not as yet fully had its way in all the societies of Western Europe. But it has greatly affected the institutions of some of them ; even when it is checked or arrested, it is shared by considerable minorities of their population ; and when (as in Russia) these minorities are very small, the excessive concentration of the passion for change has a manifest tendency to make it dangerously explosive. The analogies to this state of feeling in the Past must be sought rather in the history of Religion than in the history of Politics. There is some resemblance between the period of political reform in the nineteenth century and the period of religious reformation in the sixteenth. Now, as then, the multitude of followers must be distinguished from the smaller group of leaders. Now, as then, there are a certain number of zealots who desire that truth shall prevail. Some of them conceive the movement which they stimulate as an escape from what is distinctly bad ; others as an advance from what is barely tolerable to what is

K

greatly better ; and a few as an ascent to an ideal state, sometimes conceived by them as a state of Nature, and sometimes as a condition of millennial blessedness. But, behind these, now as then, there is a crowd which has imbibed a delight in change for its own sake, who would reform the Suffrage, or the House of Lords, or the Land Laws, or the Union with Ireland, in precisely the same spirit in which the mob behind the reformers of religion broke the nose of a saint in stone, or made a bonfire of copes and surplices, or shouted for the government of the Church by presbyteries. The passion for religious reform is, however, far more intelligible than the passion for political change, as we now see it in operation. In an intensely believing society, the obligation to think aright was enforced by tremendous penalties ; and the sense of this obligation was the propelling force of the Reformation, as at an earlier date it had been the propelling force of the rise and spread of Christianity. But what propelling force is there behind the present political movement, of such inherent energy that it not only animates the minority, who undoubtedly believe in their theories of democracy, or reform, or regeneration, but even makes itself felt by the multitude which reasons blindly or does not reason at all? " If you have wrong ideas about Justification, you shall perish everlastingly," is a very intelligible proposition ; but it is not exactly

a proposition of the same order as that into which
most English democratic philosophy translates itself:
"If you vote straight with the Blues, your great-
grandchild will be on a level with the average citizen
of the United States." The truth seems to be, that
a great number of persons are satisfied to think that
democracy is inevitable and the democratic movement
irresistible ; which means that the phenomenon exists,
that they see no way of arresting it, and that they
feel no inclination to throw themselves in its way.
There are others who appear to think that when a
man submits to the inevitable it is "greatly to his
credit" ; as it was to Mr. Gilbert's nautical hero
to remain an Englishman because he was born an
Englishman. So they baptise the movement with
various complimentary names, of which the com-
monest is Progress, a word of which I have never
seen any definition, and which seems to have all sorts
of meanings, many of them extraordinary ; for some
politicians in our day appear to employ it for mere
aimless movement, while others actually use it for
movement backwards, towards a state of primitive
nature.

It is an inquiry of considerable interest, whether
the passion for change which has possession of a certain number of persons in this age, and the acquiescence in it which characterises a much larger number,
are due to any exceptional causes affecting the sphere

of politics, or whether they are universal and permanent phenomena of human nature. There are some striking facts which appear to point to the first conclusion as the more correct. The most remarkable is the relatively small portion of the human race which will so much as tolerate a proposal or attempt to change its usages, laws, and institutions. Vast populations, some of them with a civilisation considerable but peculiar, detest that which in the language of the West would be called reform. The entire Mahommedan world detests it. The multitudes of coloured men who swarm in the great Continent of Africa detest it, and it is detested by that large part of mankind which we are accustomed to leave on one side as barbarous or savage. The millions upon millions of men who fill the Chinese Empire loathe it and (what is more) despise it. There are few things more remarkable and, in their way, more instructive, than the stubborn incredulity and disdain which a man belonging to the cultivated part of Chinese society opposes to the vaunts of Western civilisation which he frequently hears ; and his confidence in his own ideas is alike proof against his experience of Western military superiority and against that spectacle of the scientific inventions and discoveries of the West which overcame the exclusiveness of the undoubtedly feebler Japanese. There is in India a minority, educated at the feet of English

politicians and in books saturated with English
political ideas, which has learned to repeat their
language ; but it is doubtful whether even these, if
they had a voice in the matter, would allow a finger
to be laid on the very subjects with which European
legislation is beginning to concern itself, social and
religious usage. There is not, however, the shadow
of a doubt that the enormous mass of the Indian
population hates and dreads change, as is natural in
the parts of a body-social solidified by caste. The
chief difficulty of Indian government is even less the
difficulty of reconciling this strong and abiding sentiment with the fainter feeling of the Anglicised
minority, than the practical impossibility of getting
it understood by the English people. It is quite
evident that the greatest fact in Anglo-Indian history,
the Mutiny of the mercenary Sepoy Army, is as much
a mystery to the average man of the West as are
certain colours to the colour-blind ; and even historians are compelled to supply wholly or partially
fictitious explanations of the events of 1857 to a
public which cannot be brought to believe that a vast
popular uprising was produced by a prejudice about
a greased cartridge. The intense conservatism
of much the largest part of mankind is, however,
attested by quite as much evidence as is the pride of
certain nations in railways, electric telegraphs, or
democratic governments.

In spite of overwhelming evidence (I wrote in 1861), it is most difficult for a citizen of Western Europe to bring thoroughly home to himself the truth that the civilisation which surrounds him is a rare exception in the history of the world. The tone of thought common among us, all our hopes, fears, and speculations, would be materially affected, if we had vividly before us the relation of the progressive races to the totality of human life. It is indisputable that much the greatest part of mankind has never shown a particle of desire that its civil institutions should be improved, since the moment when external completeness was first given to them by their embodiment in some permanent record. One set of usages has occasionally been violently overthrown and superseded by another; here and there a primitive code, pretending to a supernatural origin, has been greatly extended and distorted into the most surprising forms; but, except in a small section of the world, there has been nothing like the gradual amelioration of a legal system. There has been material civilisation, but instead of the civilisation expanding the law, the law has limited the civilisation.[1]

To the fact that the enthusiasm for change is comparatively rare must be added the fact that it is extremely modern. It is known but to a small part of mankind, and to that part but for a short period during a history of incalculable length. It is not older than the free employment of legislation by

---

[1] *Ancient Law*, chap. ii. pp. 22, 23. These opinions were adopted by Mr. Grote. See his *Plato*, vol. ii. chap. v. p. 253 (note)

popular governments. There are few historical errors more serious than the assumption that popular governments have always been legislating governments. Some of them, no doubt, legislated on a scale which would now be considered extremely moderate; but, on the whole, their vigour has shown itself in struggles to restore or maintain some ancient constitution, sometimes lying far back in a partly real and partly imaginary Past, sometimes referred to a wholly unhistorical state of nature, sometimes associated with the great name of an original legislator. We, Englishmen, have had for several centuries a government in which there was a strong popular element, and for two centuries we have had a nearly unqualified popular government.[2] Yet what our forefathers contended for was not a typical constitution in the Future, but a typical constitution in the Past. Our periods of what would now be called legislative reforming activity have been connected with moments, not of violent political but of violent religious emotion—with the outbreak of feeling at the Reformation, with the dominion of Cromwell and the Independents (the true precursors of the modern Irreconcileables), and with the revival of dread and dislike of the Roman Catholic Church during the reign of James II. During the period at which English popular government was attracting to itself the admiration of the

[2] See above, p. 6.

educated classes throughout the civilised world, the Parliament of our Hanoverian Kings was busy with controlling executive action, with the discussion of foreign policy, with vehement debates on foreign wars ; but it hardly legislated at all. The truth is that the enthusiasm for legislative change took its rise, not in a popularly governed but in an autocratically governed country, not in England but in France. The English political institutions, so envied and panegyrised on the Continent, could not be copied without sweeping legislative innovations, but the grounds and principles on which these innovations were demanded were, as we shall see, wholly unlike anything known to any class of English politicians. Nevertheless, in their final effects, these French ideas have deeply leavened English political thought, mixing with another stream of opinion which is of recent but still of English origin.

An absolute intolerance even of that description of change which in modern language we call political thus characterises much the largest part of the human race, and has characterised the whole of it during the largest part of its history. Are there then any reasons for thinking that the love for change which in our day is commonly supposed to be overpowering, and the capacity for it which is vulgarly assumed to be infinite, are, after all, limited to a very narrow sphere of human action, that which we call politics,

and perhaps not even to the whole of this sphere ?
Let us look at those parts of human nature which
have no points of contact with politics, because the
authority of the sovereign state is not brought to
bear upon them at all, or at most remotely and indirectly. Let us attend for a moment to human
Habits, those modes of conduct and behaviour which
we follow either quite unconsciously or with no better
reason to assign for them than that we have always
followed them.   Do we readily change our habits ?
Man is a creature of habit, says an adage which
doubtless sums up a vast experience.   It is true that
the tenacity with which men adhere to habit is not
precisely the same in all parts of the globe.   It is
strictest in the East.   It is relaxed in the West, and
of all races the English and their descendants, the
Americans, are least reluctant to submit to a considerable change of habit for what seems to them an
adequate end.   Yet the exception is one of the sort
which proves the rule.   The Englishman, who trans-
ports himself to Australia or to India, surrounds
himself, under the greatest difficulties, with as close
an imitation of English life as he can contrive, and
submits all the while to a distasteful exile in the
hope of some day returning to the life which he lived
in his youth or childhood, though under somewhat
more favourable conditions.   The truth is that men
do alter their habits, but within narrow limits, and

almost always with more or less of reluctance and pain. And it is fortunate for them that they are so constituted, for most of their habits have been learned by the race to which they belong through long experience, and probably after much suffering. A man cannot safely eat or drink, or go downstairs, or cross a street, unless he be guided and protected by habits which are the long result of time. One set in particular of these habits, and perhaps the most surprising, that which enables us to deal safely with the destructive element of fire, was probably not acquired by mankind without infinite pain and injury. And all this, for all we know, may be true of the public usages which men follow in common with their fellows.

Let us turn from Habits to Manners, that is, to those customs of behaviour which we not only practise ourselves, but expect other men to follow. Do these suggest that men are naturally tolerant of departure from a usage or an accustomed line of conduct? Rarely as the subject is examined, it is a very curious one. What is the exact source of the revulsion of feeling which is indubitably caused by a solecism in manners or speech, and of the harshness of the judgment passed on it? Why should the unusual employment of a fork or a finger-glass, or the mispronunciation of a vowel or an aspirate, have the effect of instantly quenching an appreciable

amount of human sympathy? Some things about
the sentiment are certain. It is not modern, but very
ancient, and probably as old as human nature. The
incalculably ancient distinctions between one race and
another, between Greek and Barbarian, with all the
mutual detestation they carried with them, appear to
have been founded originally on nothing more than
dislike of differences in speech. Again, the sentiment
is not confined to the idle and possibly superfine
regions of society. It goes down to the humblest
social spheres, where, though the code of manners is
different, it is even more rigidly enforced. Whatever
else these facts may suggest, they assuredly do not
suggest the changeableness of human nature.

There are, however, other facts, even more remarkable and instructive, which point to the same
conclusion. One half of the human race—at this
moment and in our part of the world, the majority of
it—have hitherto been kept aloof from politics; nor,
till quite recently, was there any evidence that any
portion of this body of human beings cared more to
embark in politics than to engage in war. There is
therefore in all human societies a great and influential
class, everywhere possessed of intellectual power, and
here of intellectual cultivation, which is essentially
non-political. Are, then, Women characterised by a
passion for change? Surely there is no fact witnessed
to by a greater amount of experience than that, in all

communities, they are the strictest conservators of usage and the sternest censors of departure from accepted rules of morals, manners, and fashions. *Souvent femme varie*, says indeed the French song attributed to Francis I. ; but subtler observers of female nature than a French king of extraordinary dissoluteness have come to a very different conclusion, and, even in the relations of the sexes, have gone near to claiming constancy as a special and distinctive female virtue. This seems to have been an article of faith with Thackeray and Trollope, but the art which Thackeray and Trollope followed is itself furnishing striking illustrations of the conservatism of Women. During the last fifteen years, it has fallen very largely into their hands. What, then, is the view of life and society which is taken on the whole by this literature of Fiction, produced in enormous and ever-growing abundance, and read by multitudes ? I may at least say that, if no other part of the writings of this generation survived, the very last impression which this branch of literature would produce would be that we had lived in an age of feverish Progress. For in the world of novels, it is the ancient and time-hallowed that seems, as a rule, to call forth admiration or enthusiasm ; the conventional distinctions of society have a much higher importance given to them than belongs to them in real life ; wealth is on the whole regarded as ridi-

culous, unless associated with birth ; and zeal for
reform is in much danger of being identified with
injustice, absurdity, or crime. These books, ever
more written by Women, and read by increasing
multitudes of Women, leave no doubt as to the
fundamental character of female taste and opinion.
It must be admitted, on the other hand, that one
special set of customs, which we know collectively as
Fashion, have been left to the peculiar guardianship
of Women, and there is no doubt a common impression that Fashion is always changing. But is it true
that fashions vary very widely and very rapidly ?
Doubtless they do change. In some of the great
cities of Europe something like real genius is called
into activity, and countless experiments are tried, in
order that something may be devised which is new,
and yet shall not shock the strong attachment to the
old. Much of this ingenuity fails, some part of it
sometimes succeeds ; yet the change is very seldom
great, and it is just as often a reversion to the old as
an adoption of something new. " We speak," I said
in a former work, " of the caprices of Fashion ; yet,
on examining them historically, we find them extra-
ordinarily limited, so much so that we are sometimes
tempted to regard Fashion as passing through cycles
of form ever repeating themselves." [3] The eccen-

[3] I quote the whole of the passage in which this sentence
occurs in Note A appended to this chapter.

tricities of female dress mentioned in the Old Testament may still be recognised; the Greek lady
represented by the so-called Tanagra figures[4] is
surprisingly like a lady of our time ; and, on looking
through a volume of mediæval costumes, we see
portions of dress which, slightly disguised, have been
over and over again revived by the dressmaking
inventiveness of Paris. Here, again, we may observe
that it is extremely fortunate for a large part of the
human race that female fashions do not alter extensively and rapidly. For sudden and frequent changes
in them—changes which would more or less affect
half of mankind in the wealthiest regions of the
world—would entail industrial revolutions of the
most formidable kind. One may ask oneself what is
the most terrible calamity which can be conceived as
befalling great populations. The answer might perhaps be—a sanguinary war, a desolating famine, a
deadly epidemic disease. Yet none of these disasters
would cause as much and as prolonged human suffering as a revolution in fashion under which women
should dress, as men practically do, in one material
of one colour. There are many flourishing and
opulent cities in Europe and America which would
be condemned by it to bankruptcy or starvation, and

[4] The chief differences are that the Greek lady is without
stays, and occasionally wears a parasol as a fixed part of her head-
dress

it would be worse than a famine or a pestilence in China, India, and Japan.

This view of the very slight changeableness of human nature when left to itself, is much strengthened by the recent inquiries which have extended the history of the human race in new directions. The investigations inconveniently called prehistoric are really aimed at enlarging the domain of history, by collecting materials for it beyond the point at which it began to be embodied in writing. They proceed by the examination of the modes of life and social usages of men in a savage, barbarous, or semi-civilised condition, and they start from the assumption that the civilised races were once in that state, or in some such state. Unquestionably, these studies are not in a wholly satisfactory stage. As often happens where the labourers are comparatively few and the evidence as yet scanty, they abound in rash conclusions and peremptory assertions. But they have undoubtedly increased our knowledge of social states which are no longer ours, and of civilisations which are unlike ours. And on the whole, they suggest that the differences which, after ages of change, separate the civilised man from the savage or barbarian, are not so great as the vulgar opinion would have them. Man has changed much in Western Europe, but it is singular how much of the savage there still is in him, independently of the identity of

the physical constitution which has always belonged
to him.   There are a number of occupations which
civilised men follow with the utmost eagerness, and a
number of tastes in which they indulge with the
keenest pleasure, without being able to account for
them intellectually, or to reconcile them with accepted
morality.   These pursuits and tastes are, as a rule,
common to the civilised man and the savage.   Like
the savage, the Englishman, Frenchman, or American
makes war ; like the savage, he hunts ; like the
savage, he dances ; like the savage, he indulges in
endless deliberation ; like the savage, he sets an
extravagant value on rhetoric ; like the savage, he is
a man of party, with a newspaper for a totem, instead
of a mark on his forehead or arm ; and, like a savage,
he is apt to make of his totem his God.   He submits
to having these tastes and pursuits denounced in
books, speeches, or sermons ; but he probably derives
acuter pleasure from them than from anything else he
does.

If, then, there is any reason for supposing that
human nature, taken as a whole, is not wedded to
change, and that, in most of its parts, it changes
only by slow steps, or within narrow limits—if the
maxim of Seneca be true of it, *non fit statim ex diverso
in diversum transitus*—it is worth our while to inves-
tigate the probable causes of the exceptional enthusiasm for change in politics which seems to grow

up from time to time, giving to many minds the
sense of having in their presence an inflexible, inex-
orable, predetermined process. I may first observe
that, in the popular mind, there is a manifest association of political innovation with scientific advance.
It is not uncommon to hear a politician supporting
an argument for a radical reform by asserting that
this is an Age of Progress, and appealing for proof of
the assertion to the railway, the gigantic steamship,
the electric light, or the electric telegraph. Now it
is quite true that, if Progress be understood with its
only intelligible meaning, that is, as the continued
production of new ideas, scientific invention and
scientific discovery are the great and perennial sources
of these ideas. Every fresh conquest of Nature by
man, giving him the command of her forces, and every
new and successful interpretation of her secrets, gene-
rates a number of new ideas, which finally displace
the old ones, and occupy their room. But, in the
Western world, the mere formation of new ideas does
not often or necessarily create a taste for innovating
legislation. In the East, no doubt, it is otherwise.
Where a community associates the bulk of its social
usages with a religious sanction, and again associates
its religion with an old and false interpretation of
Nature, the most elementary knowledge of geography
or physics may overthrow a mass of fixed ideas concerning the constitution of society. An Indian youth

L

learns that a Brahman is semi-divine, and that it is
a deadly sin to taste the flesh of a cow, but he also
learns that Ceylon, which is close to India, is an
island peopled with demons ; and the easy exposure
of such delusions may change his entire view of
human life, and indeed is the probable explanation
of the great gulf which in India divides the educated
class from the uneducated.　A similar revolution of
ideas is very rare in the West, and indeed experience
shows that innovating legislation is connected not so
much with Science as with the scientific air which
certain subjects, not capable of exact scientific treatment, from time to time assume.　To this class of
subjects belonged Bentham's scheme of Law-Reform,
and, above all, Political Economy as treated by
Ricardo.　Both have been extremely fertile sources
of legislation during the last fifty years.　But both
have now fallen almost entirely out of fashion ; and
their present disfavour may serve as a warning
against too hastily assuming that the existing friendly
alliance between advanced politicians and advancing
science will always continue.　When invention has
been successfully applied to the arts of life, the disturbance of habits and displacement of industries,
which the application occasions, has always been at
first profoundly unpopular.　Men have submitted to
street-lighting and railway-travelling, which they
once clamoured against ; but Englishmen never sub-

mitted to the Poor Law—the first great effort of economical legislation—and it has got to be seen whether they will submit to Free Trade. The prejudices of the multitude against scientific inventions are dismissed by the historian [5] with a sarcasm ; but, when the multitude is all-powerful, this prejudice may afford material for history.

The principal cause of an apparent enthusiasm for innovating legislation is not as often assigned as it should be. Legislation is one of the activities of popular government ; and the keenest interest in these activities is felt by all the popularly governed communities. It is one great advantage of popular government over government of the older type, that it is so intensely interesting. For twenty years, we had close to our shores a striking example of this point of inferiority in absolute monarchies during the continuance of the Second Bonapartist Empire in France. It never overcame the disadvantage it suffered through the dulness of its home politics. The scandal, the personalities, the gossip, and the trifling which occupied its newspapers proved no substitute for the political discussions which had filled them while the Republic and the Constitutional Monarchy

[5] Macaulay, *History*, I. c. iii. p. 283. "There were fools in that age (1685) who opposed the introduction of what was called the new light, as strenuously as fools in our age have opposed the introduction of vaccination and railroads."

lasted. The men who ruled it were acutely conscious of the danger involved in this decline of excitement and amusement suitable to cultivated and masculine minds ; and their efforts to meet it led directly to their overthrow, by tempting them to provide the French public with distractions of a higher order, through adventurous diplomacy and war. There are, again, good observers who trace the political inse-curity of Russia, the aggressiveness of her govern-ment abroad, and the wild attempts on it at home, to the general dulness of Russian life during peace. Englishmen would find it almost impossible to con-ceive what would compensate them for the with-drawal of the enthralling drama which is enacted before them every morning and evening. A cease-less flow of public discussion, a throng of public events, a crowd of public men, make up the spectacle. Nevertheless, in our country at all events, over-indulgence in what has no doubt become a passion with elevated minds is growing to be dangerous. For the plot of the performance which attracts such multitudes turns, now-a-days, almost always on the fortunes of some legislative measure. The English Parliament, as has been said, legislated very little until fifty years since, when it fell under the influence of Bentham and his disciples. Ever since the first Reform Act, however, the volume of legislation has been increasing, and this has been very much owing

to the unlooked-for operation of a venerable constitutional form, the Royal Speech at the commencement
of each Session.   Once it was the King who spoke,
now it is the Cabinet as the organ of the party who
supports it ; and it is rapidly becoming the practice
for parties to outbid one another in the length of the
tale of legislation to which they pledge themselves in
successive Royal Speeches.

There is undoubted danger in looking upon
politics as a deeply interesting game, a never-ending
cricket-match between Blue and Yellow.   The practice is yet more dangerous when the ever-accumulating stakes are legislative measures upon which the
whole future of this country is risked ; and the
danger is peculiarly great under a constitutional
system which does not provide for measures reforming the Constitution any different or more solemn procedure than that which is followed in ordinary
legislation.   Neither experience nor probability
affords any ground for thinking that there may be
an infinity of legislative innovation, at once safe and
beneficent.   On the contrary, it would be a safer
conjecture that the possibilities of reform are strictly
limited.   The possibilities of heat, it is said, reach
2,000 degrees of the Centigrade thermometer ; the
possibilities of cold extend to about 300 degrees
below its zero ; but all organic life in the world is
only possible through the accident that temperature

in it ranges between a maximum of 120 degrees and
a minimum of a few degrees below zero of the Centigrade.   For all we know, a similarly narrow limitation may hold of legislative changes in the structure
of human society.   We can no more argue that,
because some past reforms have succeeded, all reforms
will succeed, than we can argue that, because the
human body can bear a certain amount of heat, it can
bear an indefinite amount.

There are, however, many accidents of their
history, and particularly of their recent history,
which blind Englishmen to the necessity of caution
while they indulge in the pastime of politics, particularly when the two sides into which they divide
themselves compete in legislative innovation.   We
are singularly little sensible, as a nation, of the
extraordinary good luck which has befallen us
since the beginning of the century.   Foreign observers (until perhaps the other day) were always
dwelling on it, but Englishmen, as a rule, do not
notice it, or (it may be) secretly believe that they
deserve it.   The fact is that, since the century began,
we have been victorious and prosperous beyond all
example.   We have never lost a battle in Europe or
a square mile of territory ; we have never taken a
ruinous step in foreign politics ; we have never made
an irreparable mistake in legislation.   If we compare
our history with recent French history, there is

nothing in it like the disaster at Sedan or the loss of
Alsace-Lorraine ; nothing like the gratuitous quarrel
with Germany about the vacant Crown of Spain ;
nothing like the law of May 1850, which, by altering
the suffrage, gave the great enemy of the Republic the
opportunity for which he had been waiting.   Yet, if
we multiply occasions for such calamities, it is possible and even probable that they will occur ; and it
is useless to deny that, with the craving for political
excitement which is growing on us every day, the
chances of a great false step are growing also.

I do not think it likely to be denied, that the
activity of popular government is more and more
tending to exhibit itself in legislation, or that the
materials for legislation are being constantly supplied
in ever-increasing abundance through the competition
of parties, or, lastly, that the keen interest which the
community takes in looking on, as a body of specta-
tors, at the various activities of popular government,
is the chief reason of the general impression that ours
is an Age of Progress, to be indefinitely continued.
There are, however, other causes of this impression or
belief, which are much less obvious and much less
easily demonstrated to the ordinary English politician.
At the head of them, are a group of words, phrases,
maxims, and general propositions, which have their
root in political theories, not indeed far removed from
us by distance of time, but as much forgotten by the

mass of mankind as if they had belonged to the remotest antiquity. How is one to convince the advanced English politician who announces with an air of pride that he is Radical, and indeed a Radical and something more, that he is calling himself by a name which he would never have had the courage to adopt, so deep was its disrepute, if Jeremy Bentham had not given it respectability by associating it with a particular theory of legislation and politics ? How is one to persuade him, when he speaks of the Sovereign People, that he employs a combination of words which would never have occurred to his mind if in 1762 a French philosopher had not written a speculative essay on the origin of society, the forma-tion of States, and the nature of government ? Neither of these theories, the theory of Rousseau which starts from the assumed Natural Rights of Man, or the theory of Bentham which is based on the hypothetical Greatest Happiness principle, is now-a-days explicitly held by many people. The natural rights of man have indeed made their appearance in recent political discourse, producing much the same effect as if a professed lecturer on astronomy were to declare his belief in the Ptolemaic spheres and to call upon his audience to admire their music ; but, of the two theories mentioned above, that of Rousseau which recognises these rights is much the most thoroughly forgotten. For the attempt to apply it

led to terrible calamities, while the theory of Bentham
has at present led to nothing worse than a certain
amount of disappointment. How is it then that
these wholly or partially exploded speculations still
exercise a most real and practical influence on political thought ? The fact is that political theories are
endowed with the faculty possessed by the hero of
the Border-ballad. When their legs are smitten off
they fight upon their stumps. They produce a host
of words, and of ideas associated with those words,
which remain active and combatant after the parent
speculation is mutilated or dead. Their posthumous
influence often extends a good way beyond the
domain of politics. It does not seem to me a fantastic assertion that the ideas of one of the great
novelists of the last generation may be traced to
Bentham, and those of another to Rousseau. Dickens,
who spent his early manhood among the politicians
of 1832 trained in Bentham's school, hardly ever
wrote a novel without attacking an abuse. The
procedure of the Court of Chancery and of the
Ecclesiastical Courts, the delays of the Public Offices,
the costliness of divorce, the state of the dwellings of
the poor, and the condition of the cheap schools in
the North of England, furnished him with what he
seemed to consider, in all sincerity, the true moral of
a series of fictions. The opinions of Thackeray have
a strong resemblance to those to which Rousseau

gave popularity. It is a very just remark of Mill,
that the attraction which Nature and the State of
Nature had for Rousseau may be partly accounted for
as a reaction against the excessive admiration of civilisation and progress which took possession of educated men during the earlier part of the eighteenth
century. Theoretically, at any rate, Thackeray hated
the artificialities of civilisation, and it must be owned
that some of his favourite personages have about
them something of Rousseau's natural man as he
would have shown himself if he had mixed in real
life—something, that is, of the violent blackguard.

The influence which the political theory originating in France and the political theory originating in
England still exercise over politics seems to me as
certain as anything in the history of thought can be.
It is necessary to examine these theories, because
there is no other way of showing the true value of
the instruments, the derivative words and derivative
ideas, through which they act. I will take first the
famous constitutional theory of Rousseau, which,
long unfamiliar or discredited in this country, is the
fountain of many notions which have suddenly
become popular and powerful among us. There is
much difficulty in the attempt to place it in a clear
light, for reasons well known to all who have given
attention to the philosophy of the remarkable man
who produced it. This philosophy is the most strik-

ing example extant of a confusion which may be
detected in all corners of non-scientific modern
thought, the confusion between what is and what
ought to be, between what did as a fact occur
and what under certain conditions would have
occurred. The "Contrat Social," which sets forth the
political theory on which I am engaged, appears at
first sight to give an historical account of the emer-
gence of mankind from a State of Nature. But
whether it is meant that mankind did emerge in this
way, whether the writer believes that only a happily
circumstanced part of the human race had this experience, or whether he thinks that Nature, a beneficent legislatress, intended all men to have it, but
that her objects were defeated, it is quite impossible
to say with any confidence. The language of Rousseau sometimes suggests that he meant his picture
of early social transformations to be regarded as imaginary ;[6] but nevertheless the account given of them

<hr />

[6] "Comment ce changement s'est-il fait ? Je l'ignore."—
Contrat Social, chap. i.   I have myself no doubt that very much
of the influence of Rousseau over the men of his own generation,
and of the next, arose from the belief widely spread among them
that his account of natural and of early political society was
literally true.   There is a remarkable passage in the *Pensées* of
Pascal (III. 8) which describes the powerful revolutionary effects
which may be produced by contrasting an existing institution with
some supposed "fundamental and primitive law" of the State.
The reflection was obviously suggested by the sedition of the
Fronde.   The Parliament of Paris firmly believed in the "funda-

is so precise, detailed, and logically built up, that it is quite inconceivable its author should not have intended it to express realities. This celebrated theory is briefly as follows. Rousseau, who in his earlier writings had strongly insisted on the disadvantages which man had sustained through the loss of his natural rights, begins the " Contrat Social " with the position that Man was originally in the State of Nature. So long as he remained in it, he was before all things free. But, in course of time, a point is reached at which the obstacles to his continuance in the natural condition become insuperable. Mankind then enter into the Social Compact under which the State, society, or community is formed. Their consent to make this compact must be unanimous ; but the effect of its completion is the absolute alienation or surrender, by every individual human being, of his person and all his rights to the aggregate community.[7] The community then becomes the sovereign, the true and original Sovereign People, and it is an autocratic sovereign. It ought to maintain liberty and equality among its subjects, but only because the subjection of

mental and primitive laws" of France ; and, a century later, the disciples of Rousseau had exactly the same faith in the State of Nature and the Social Compact.

[7] " Le pacte social se réduit aux termes suivants : chacun de nous mit en commun sa personne et toute sa puissance sous la suprême direction de la volonté générale ; et nous recevons encore chaque membre comme partie individuelle du tout."—*Contrat Social*, c. i. 6.

one individual to another is a loss of force to the State, and because there cannot be liberty without equality.[8] The collective despot cannot divide, or alienate, or delegate his power. The Government is his servant, and is merely the organ of correspondence between the sovereign and the people. No representation of the people is allowed. Rousseau abhorred the representative system ; but periodical assemblies of the entire community are to be held, and two questions are to be submitted to them—whether it is the pleasure of the sovereign to maintain the present form of government—and whether the sovereign pleases to leave the administration of its affairs to the persons who now conduct it.[9] The autocracy of the aggregate community and the indivisibility, perpetuity, and incommunicable character of its power, are insisted upon in every part of the "Contrat Social" and in every form of words.

As is almost always the case with sweeping theories, portions of Rousseau's ideas may be discovered in the speculations of older writers. A part may be found, a century earlier, in the writings of Hobbes ; another part in those of the nearly contemporary school of French Economists. But the theory, as he put it together, owes to him its extraordinary

[8] *Contrat Social*, ii. 11.
[9] *Contrat Social*, iii. 18.   The decision is in this case to be by majority ; Rousseau requires unanimity for the consent to enter into the Social Compact, but not otherwise.

influence ; and it is the undoubted parent of a host
of phrases and associated notions which, after having
long had currency in France and on the Continent,
are beginning to have serious effect in this country, as
the democratic element in its Constitution increases.
From this origin sprang the People (with a capital
P), the Sovereign People, the People the sole source
of all legitimate power. From this came the sub-
ordination of Governments, not merely to electorates
but to a vaguely defined multitude outside them, or
to the still vaguer mastership of floating opinion.
Hence began the limitation of legitimacy in governments to governments which approximate to democracy. A vastly more formidable conception be-
queathed to us by Rousseau is that of the omnipotent
democratic State rooted in natural right ; the State
which has at its absolute disposal everything which
individual men value, their property, their persons,
and their independence ; the State which is bound
to respect neither precedent nor prescription ; the
State which may make laws for its subjects ordaining
what they shall drink or eat, and in what way they
shall spend their earnings ; the State which can con-
fiscate all the land of the community, and which,
if the effect on human motives is what it may
be expected to be, may force us to labour on it when
the older incentives to toil have disappeared. Nevertheless this political speculation, of which the remote

and indirect consequences press us on all sides, is of
all speculations the most baseless.   The natural condition from which it starts is a simple figment of the
imagination.   So far as any research into the nature
of primitive human society has any bearing on so mere
a dream, all inquiry has dissipated it.   The process by
which Rousseau supposes communities of men to have
been formed, or by which at all events he wishes us to
assume that they were formed, is again a chimera.
No general assertion as to the way in which human
societies grew up is safe, but perhaps the safest of all
is that none of them were formed in the way imagined
by Rousseau.   The true relation of some parts of the
theory to fact is very instructive.   Some particles of
Rousseau's thought may be discovered in the mental
atmosphere of his time.   " Natural law " and " natural rights " are phrases properly belonging to a
theory not of politics, but of jurisprudence, which,
originating with the Roman jurisconsults, had a
great attraction for the lawyers of France.   The
despotic sovereign of the " Contrat Social," the all-
powerful community, is an inverted copy of the King
of France invested with an authority claimed for him
by his courtiers and by the more courtly of his lawyers, but denied to him by all the highest minds in
the country, and specially by the great luminaries of
the French Parliaments.   The omnipotent democracy
is the King-Proprietor, the lord of all men's fortunes

and persons ; but it is the French King turned upside down. The mass of natural rights absorbed by
the sovereign community through the Social Compact
is, again, nothing more than the old divine right of
kings in a new dress. As for Rousseau's dislike of
representative systems and his requirement that the
entire community should meet periodically to exercise
its sovereignty, his language in the " Contrat Social "
suggests that he was led to these opinions by the example of the ancient tribal democracies. But at a later
date he declared that he had the Constitution of Geneva
before his mind ;[1] and he cannot but have known that
the exact method of government which he proposed
still lived in the oldest cantons of Switzerland.

This denial to the collective community of all
power of acting in its sovereign capacity through
representatives is so formidable, as apparently to forbid any practical application of Rousseau's theory.
Rousseau, indeed, expressly says[2] that his principles
apply to small communities only, hinting at the same
time that they may be adapted to States having a
large territory by a system of confederation ; and in
this hint we may suspect that we have the germ of
the opinion, which has become an article of faith in
modern Continental Radicalism, that freedom is best
secured by breaking up great commonwealths into

[1] *Lettres écrites de la Montagne*, part i. letter 6, p. 328.
[2] *Contrat Social*, iii. 15.

small self-governing communes. But the time was
not ripe for such a doctrine at the end of the last
century ; and real vitality was for the first time
given to the speculation of Rousseau by that pamphlet of Siéyès, "Qu'est-ce que le Tiers État ? " which
did so much to determine the early stages of the
French Revolution. As even the famous first page[3]
of this pamphlet is often misquoted, what follows it
is not perhaps always carefully read, and it may have
escaped notice that much of it[4] simply reproduces
the theory of Rousseau. But then Siéyès reproduces
this theory with a difference. The most important
claim which he advanced, and which he succeeded
in making good, was that the Three Orders should
sit together and form a National Assembly. The
argument by which he reaches this conclusion is substantially that of the " Contrat Social." With Siéyès,
as with Rousseau, man begins in the natural condition ; he enters society by a social compact ; and by
virtue of this compact an all-powerful community is
formed. But then Siéyès had not the objection of
Rousseau to representation, which indeed was one of

[3] The first page runs : " 1. Qu'est-ce que le Tiers État ?—Tout.
2. Qu'a-t-il été jusqu'à présent dans l'ordre politique ?—Rien.
3. Que demande-t-il ?—À être quelque chose." It is misquoted
by Alison, *History of Europe during the French Revolution*, vol. i.
c. iii. p. 453.

[4] The argument fills the long chapter v. The edition before
me is the third, published in 1789.

his favourite subjects of speculation during life. He allows the community to make a large preliminary delegation of its powers by representation. Thus is formed the class of representative bodies to which the future National Assembly of France was to belong. Siéyès calls them *extraordinary*, and describes them as exercising their will like men in a state of nature, as standing in place of the nation, as incapable of being tied down to any particular decision or line of legislation. *Ordinary* representative bodies are, on the other hand, legislatures deriving their powers from a Constitution which the extraordinary Assembly has formed and strictly confined to the exercise of these powers. The extraordinary assembly is thus the sovereign community of Rousseau ; the ordinary assembly is his government. To the first class belong those despotic bodies which, under the name of National Assembly or Convention, have four times governed France, never successfully and sometimes disastrously. To the second belong the Legislative Assemblies and Chambers of Deputies so often overthrown by revolution.

The other theory, from which a number of political phrases and political ideas now circulating among us have descended, is of English origin, and had Jeremy Bentham for its author. Its contribution to this currency is at this moment smaller than that which may be traced to a French source in the " Contrat Social," but it was at one time much larger. It must be carefully borne in mind that during the earlier and greater part of his long life Bentham was not a reformer of Constitutions, but a reformer of Law. He was the first Englishman to see clearly how the legislative powers of the State, very sparingly employed for this object before, could be used to rearrange and reconstruct civil jurisprudence and adapt it to its professed ends. He became a Radical Reformer —an expression to which, as I said before, he gave a new respectability—through sheer despair.[5] The British Constitution in his day might no doubt have been improved in many of its parts, but, in his impatience of delay in legislative reforms, he attributed to inherent defects in the Constitution obstructions which were mainly owing to the effects produced on the entire national mind by detestation of principles, strongly condemned by himself, which had brought on France the Reign of Terror and on the entire Continent the military despotism of Napoleon Bonaparte. Superficially, the ideal political system for which he argued in a series of pamphlets has not a little resemblance to that of Rousseau and Siéyès. There was to be a single-chambered democracy, one all-powerful representative assembly, with powers unrestricted theoretically, but with its action facili-

[5] See the Introduction to his plan of Parliamentary Reform. *Works*, iii. 436.

tated and guided by a strange and complex apparatus of subordinate institutions.[6] The real difference between his plans and those of the French theorist lay in their philosophical justification. The system of Rousseau was based on the pretended Natural Rights of men, and it owes to this basis a hold on weaker and less instructed minds, which is rather increasing than diminishing. But Bentham utterly repudiated those Natural Rights, and denounced the conception of them as absurd and anarchical. During the first or law-reforming period of his life, which lasted till he was more than sixty years old, he had firmly grasped the " greatest happiness of the greatest number " (a form of words found in Beccaria) as the proper standard of legislative reform ; but, observing the close association of law with morals, he had made the bolder attempt to reform moral ideas on the same principle, and by a sort of legislation to force men to think and feel, as well as to act, in conformity with his standard. As the great war proceeded, the time became more and more unfavourable for Bentham's experiment, and finally he himself declared that the cause of reform was lost on the plains of Waterloo. It was then that he began his attack on the British Constitution, and published his proposals for reconstructing it from base to apex. As the classes which it placed in power refused to recognise or promote

[6] *Constitutional Code. Works,* ix. 1.

the greatest happiness of the greatest number, he proposed to displace them and to hand over all political authority to the greatest number itself. It must necessarily follow his standard, he argued ; every man and every number of men seeks its own happiness, and the greatest number armed with legislative power must legislate for its own happiness. This reasoning had great effect on some of the most powerful minds of Bentham's day. His disciples— Grote, the two Mills, Molesworth, the two Austins, and Roebuck—did really do much to transform the British Constitution. Some of them, however, lived long enough to be disenchanted by the results ; [7] and, I have attempted to show in a former Essay, many of these results would have met with the deepest disapproval from Bentham himself. The truth is, there was a serious gap in his reasoning. Little can be

[7] I quote the following passage from the Preface to John Austin's *Plea for the Constitution.* " In the course of the following Essay I have advanced opinions which are now unpopular, and which may possibly expose me to some obloquy, though I well remember the time (for I was then a Radical) when the so-called Liberal opinions which are now predominant exposed the few who professed them to political and social proscription. I have said that the bulk of the working-classes are not yet qualified for political power. . . . I have said this because I think so. I am no worshipper of the great and rich, and have no fancy for their style of living. I am by origin, and by my strongest sympathies, a man of the people ; and I have never desired, for a single moment, to ascend from the modest station which I have always occupied."

said against "the greatest happiness of the greatest number" as a standard of legislation, and indeed it is the only standard which the legislative power, when once called into action, can possibly follow. It is inconceivable that any legislator should deliberately propose or pass a measure intended to diminish the happiness of the majority of the citizens. But when this multitudinous majority is called to the Government for the purpose of promoting its own happiness, it now becomes evident that, independently of the enormous difficulty of obtaining any conclusion from a multitude of men, there is no security that this multitude will know what its own happiness is, or how it can be promoted. On this point it must be owned that Rousseau shows himself wiser than Bentham. He claimed for the entire community that it should be sovereign and that it should exercise its sovereignty in the plenitude of power, because these were its Natural Rights ; but, though he claimed for it that it should be all-powerful, he did not claim that it was all-wise, for he knew that it was not. The People, he said, always meant well ; but it does not always judge well.

Comment une multitude aveugle, qui souvent ne sait ce qu'elle veut, parce qu'elle sait rarement ce qui lui est bon, exécuterait-elle d'elle-même une entreprise aussi grande, aussi difficile, qu'un système de législation ? De lui-même le peuple veut toujours le bien, mais de lui-même il ne le voit pas toujours.   La volonté générale est toujours droite, mais le jugement qui la guide n'est pas toujours éclairé. [8]

Rousseau was led by these misgivings almost to doubt the practical possibility of wise legislation by his ideal democracy.   He seems to have thought that the legislator who could properly guide the people in the exercise of their sovereign powers would only appear at long intervals, and must virtually be semi-divine.   In connection with these ideas, he made a prediction which has contributed nearly as much to his fame as any of his social and political speculations. Sharing the general interest and sympathy which the gallant struggle of the Corsicans for independence had excited in his day, he persuaded himself that the ideal legislator would most probably arise in Corsica. " J'ai quelque pressentiment," he writes, "qu'un jour, cette petite ile étonnera l'Europe."   The prophecy has been repeatedly taken to mean that Rousseau foresaw the birth in Corsica, seven years later, of a military genius after whom the Code Civil of France would be named.

One further remark, not perhaps at first sight obvious, ought to be made of these political theories of Rousseau and Bentham which contribute so largely to the mental stock of the classes now rising to power in Europe.   These theories were, in their origin,

[8] *Contrat Social*, ii. 6.   The latter part of this chapter is replete with good sense.

theories not of constitutional reform, but of law-reform. It is unnecessary to give new proof of this assertion as respects Bentham. But it is also true of Rousseau. The conceptions of Nature, of Natural Law, and of Natural Right, which prompted and shaped his political speculations, are first found in the language of the Roman lawyers. It is more than doubtful whether these illustrious men ever believed in the State of Nature as a reality, but they seem to have thought that, under all the perverse technicalities of ancient law, there lay a simple and symmetrical system of rules which were in some sense those of Nature. Their natural law was, for all practical purposes, simple or simplified law. This view, with all its philosophical defects, led to a great simplification of law both in the Roman State and in modern Europe, and indeed was the chief source of law-reform until the system of Bentham, which also aimed at the simplification of law, made its appearance. But the undoubted descent both of the French and the English political theory from theories of law-reform points to a serious weakness in them. That because you can successfully reform jurisprudence on certain principles, you can successfully reform Constitutions on the same principles, is not a safe inference. In the first place, the simplification of civil law, its disentanglement from idle forms, technicalities, obscurities, and illogicalities, can scarcely be other than a

beneficial process. It may indeed lead to disappointment. Bentham thought that, if law were reformed
on his principles, litigation would be easy, cheap, and
expeditious ; yet, now that nearly all his proposals
have been adopted, the removal of legal difficulties
seems to have brought into still greater nakedness
the difficulties of questions of fact. But, though the
simplification of law may lead to disappointment, it
can scarcely lead to danger. It is, however, idle to
conceal from oneself that the simplification of political
institutions leads straight to absolutism, the absolutism not of an expert judge, but of a single man or
of a multitude striving to act as if it were a single
man. The illogicalities swept away in the process may
really be buttresses which helped to support the vast
burden of government, or checks which mitigated the
consequences of the autocrat's undeniable fallibility.
Again, a mistake in law-reform is of small importance. It mainly affects a class of whose grievances,
I may observe, Bentham had far too exalted a
notion, the small part of the community which actually "goes to law." If committed, it can be corrected
with comparative ease. But a mistake in constitutional innovation directly affects the entire community
and every part of it. It may be fraught with calamity
or ruin, public or private. And correction is virtually
impossible. It is practically taken for granted among
us, that all constitutional changes are final and must

be submitted to, whatever their consequences. Doubt-less this assumption arises from a general belief that, in these matters, we are propelled by an irresistible force on a definite path towards an unavoidable end —towards Democracy, as towards Death.

If there be force in the considerations which I have urged, the ideas current among us as to the Age of Progress through which we are supposed to be passing will stand in need of a great deal of modi-fication. In one important particular, they will have to be exactly reversed. The natural condition of mankind (if that word "natural" is used) is not the progressive condition. It is a condition not of changeableness but of unchangeableness. The immobility of society is the rule ; its mobility is the exception. The toleration of change and the belief in its advantages are still confined to the smallest portion of the human race, and even with that portion they are extremely modern. They are not much more than a century old on the Continent of Europe ; and not much more than half a century old in Great Britain. When they are found, the sort of change which they contemplate is of a highly special kind, being exclusively political change. The process is familiar enough to Englishmen. A number of per-sons, often a small minority, obtain the ear of the governing part of the community, and persuade it to force the entire community to conform itself to their ideas. Doubtless there is a general submission to this process, and an impression even among those who dislike it that it will go very far. But when the causes of this state of feeling are examined, they appear to arise in a very small degree from intelligent conviction, but to a very great extent from the remote effects of words and notions derived from broken-down political theories. If this be the truth, or even an approximation to the truth, it suggests some very simple and obvious inferences. If modern society be not essentially and normally change-able, the attempt to conduct it safely through the unusual and exceptional process of change is not easy but extremely difficult. What is easy to a man is that which has come to him through a long-in-herited experience, like walking or using his fingers; what is difficult to him is that in which such expe-rience gives him little guidance or none at all, like riding or skating. It is extremely probable that the Darwinian rule, "small changes benefit the organism," holds good of communities of men, but a sudden sweeping political reform constantly places the com-munity in the position of an individual who should mount a horse solely on the strength of his studies in a work on horsemanship.

These conclusions, which I venture to think are conclusions of common sense, go a long way to ex-plain a series of facts which at first sight are not quite intelligible. What is the reason of the advantage which historical Constitutions, Constitutions gradually developed through the accumulation of experience, appear as a fact to enjoy over à priori Constitutions, Constitutions founded on speculative assumptions remote from experience? That the advantage exists, will hardly be denied by any educated Englishman. With Conservatives this is of course an axiom, but there are few really eminent men on the opposite side who do not from time to time betray the same opinion, especially in presence of a catastrophe suffered by some Constitution of the last-mentioned type. Not many persons in the last century could have divined from the previous opinions of Edmund Burke the real substructure of his political creed, or did in fact suspect it till it was uncovered by the early and comparatively slight miscarriage of French revolutionary institutions. A great disillusion has always seemed to me to separate the " Thoughts on the Present Discontents in 1770 " and the " Speech on American Taxation in 1774 " from the magnificent panegyric on the British Constitution in 1790.

Our political system is placed in a just correspondence and symmetry with the order of the world and with the mode of existence decreed to a permanent body composed of transitory parts; wherein, by the disposition of a stupendous wisdom, moulding together the great mysterious incorporation of the human race, the whole, at one time, is never old, or middle-aged, or young, but in a condition of unchangeable constancy moves on through the varied tenour of perpetual decay, fall, renovation, and progression. Thus, in preserving that method of nature in the conduct of the State, in what we improve we are never wholly new; in what we retain, we are never wholly obsolete.[9]

Macaulay, again, happened to have to close his account of the Revolution of 1688 just when a new French experiment in *à priori* Constitution-building had spread confusion through the Continent of Europe, and his picture of the events which gave birth to the party that had a monopoly of his admiration would almost rob them of their historical name of " Revolution Whigs," which he nevertheless claimed for them.

As our Revolution was a vindication of ancient rights, so it was conducted with strict attention to ancient formalities. In almost every word and act may be discerned a profound reverence for the Past. The Estates of the Realm deliberated in the old halls and according to the old rules. . . . The speeches present an almost ludicrous contrast to the revolutionary oratory of every other country. Both the English parties agreed in treating with solemn respect the ancient constitutional traditions of the State. The only question was, in what sense these traditions were to be understood. The assertors of liberty said nothing about the natural equality of men and the inalienable sovereignty of the people, about

[9] Burke, *Reflections on the Revolution in France*, vol. v. of *Works*, p. 70.

Harmodius or Timoleon, Brutus the elder or Brutus the younger. When they were told that, by the English law, the Crown, at the moment of a demise, must descend to the next heir, they answered that, by the English law, a living man could have no heir. When they were told that there was no precedent for declaring the throne vacant, they produced from among the records in the Tower a roll of parchment, near three hundred years old, on which, in quaint characters and barbarous Latin, it was recorded that the Estates of the Realm had declared vacant the throne of a perfidious and tyrannical Plantagenet. When at length the dispute had been accommodated, the new sovereigns were proclaimed with the old pageantry. All the fantastic pomp of heraldry was there, Clarencieux and Norroy, Portcullis and Rouge Dragon, the trumpets, the banners, the grotesque coats embroidered with lions and lilies. The title of King of France, assumed by the conqueror of Cressy, was not omitted in the royal style. To us, who have lived in the year 1848, it may seem almost an abuse of terms to call a proceeding, conducted with so much deliberation, with so much sobriety, and with such minute attention to prescriptive etiquette, by the terrible name of Revolution.[1]

In the light of historical facts neither the rhetoric of Burke nor the rhetoric of Macaulay is unjust. I will not undertake to hold the balance of success or failure among the 350 Constitutions which a modern writer[2] declares to have come into existence since the beginning of this century ; but if we take our stand-

[1] Macaulay, *History of England*, chap. x. *Works*, ii. 395, 396.

[2] Lieber, *Civil Liberty and Self-government.* Introduction.

ing ground at the end of the century preceding, when *à priori* Constitutions first appeared, we find it certain that among all historical Constitutions there have been no failures so great and terrible as those of Constitutions of the other class. There have been oppressive Constitutions of the historical type ; there have been Constitutions which mischievously obstructed the path of improvement ; but with these there has been nothing like the disastrous course and end of the three Constitutions which announce their character by beginning with a Declaration of the Rights of Man, the French semi-monarchical Constitution of 1791, the French Republican Constitution of 1793, and the French Republican-Directorial Constitution of 1795. Nor has any historical Constitution had the ludicrous fate of the Constitution of December 1799, which came from the hands of Siéyès a marvel of balanced powers, and became by a single transposition the charter of a pure despotism. All this, however, is extremely intelligible, if human nature has always a very limited capacity, as in general it has very slight taste, for adjusting itself to new conditions. The utmost it can do is to select parts of its experience and apply them tentatively to these conditions ; and this process is always awkward and often dangerous. A community with a new *à priori* political constitution is at best in the disagreeable position of a British traveller whom a hospitable

Chinese entertainer has constrained to eat a dinner
with chopsticks.   Let the new institutions be extra-
ordinarily wide of experience, and inconvenience becomes imminent peril.   The body-politic is in that
case like the body-natural transported to a new
climate, unaccustomed food, and strange surround-
ings.   Sometimes it perishes altogether.   Sometimes
the most unexpected parts of its organisation develop
themselves at the expense of others ; and when the
ingenious legislator had counted on producing a
nation of self-denying and somewhat sentimental
patriots, he finds that he has created a people of
Jacobins or a people of slaves.

It is in a high degree likely that the British
Parliament and the British electorate will soon have
to consider which of these two principles, assumption
or experience, they will apply to a great and ancient
institution, of all our institutions the one which on
the whole has departed least from its original form.
I put aside the question which of them it is that has
been applied to the constituent body of the House of
Commons.   That is over, and its consequences, in
Homeric phrase, "lie upon the knees of the gods."
But, surprising as was the way in which the question
of Franchise and Redistribution ended, and in which
the question of reconstructing the House of Lords,
which had been mixed up with it, fell suddenly into
the background, no observant man can doubt that

the last question will before long press again for attention. The very variety of opinion which, as I pointed out in the last Essay, prevails among politicians of every party colour as to the mode in which the legal power of the House of Lords should be exercised, is an earnest of a controversy soon to be revived ; and indeed the mere demand for continuous important legislation will soon force into notice so great an addition to the supply as the reform of the Upper House. The quarrel which raged for a while on platforms and in the newspapers threw up a great number of suggestions for change, out of which very few were worthy of consideration. They varied from a proposal to dispense altogether with a Second Chamber to proposals for a Chamber of Peers nominated for life ; proposals for empowering the Crown to select a limited number of Peers out of the present body for service in each Parliament ; proposals for giving to the entire present House of Lords the right to elect this limited number ; proposals for a Second Chamber of experienced executive officers, and proposals for a Senate to which the Local Government Circles (as yet unformed) should furnish constituencies. But, amid these loose guesses at a reasonable solution of a great question, there was much language employed which seemed to me to betray serious misconception of the nature of a Second or Upper House, and these opinions merit some consideration.

N

Let me take first the most trenchant of the proposals recently before the country, the scheme for
governing through a Parliament consisting of a single
Chamber. This plan was advocated by Mr. J. S.
Mill in one of his later writings, but it is just to him
to bear in mind that in the single Chamber he proposed there was to be a minutely accurate representation of minorities. This condition was dropped in
the late controversy, and it was thought enough to
quote the well-known epigram of Siéyès on the subject of Second Chambers. "If," it runs, "a Second
Chamber dissents from the First, it is mischievous ;
if it agrees, it is superfluous." It has perhaps escaped
notice that this saying is a conscious or unconscious
parody of that reply of the Caliph Omar about the
books of the Alexandrian Library which caused them
to be burnt. "If the books," said the Commander of
the Faithful to his lieutenant, "differ from the book
of the Prophet, they are impious ; if they agree, they
are useless." The reasoning is precisely the same in
both cases, and starts from the same assumption. It
takes for granted that at a particular utterance is divine.
If the Koran is the inspired and exclusive word of
God, Omar was right ; if Vox Populi, Vox Dei, expresses a truth, Siéyès was right. If the decisions
of the community, conveyed through one particular
organ, are not only imperative but all-wise, a Second
Chamber is a superfluity or an impertinence. There

is no question that the generality of First Chambers,
or popularly elected Houses, do make the assumption
on which this argument rests. They do not now-a-
days rest their claim to authority on the English
theory of the advantages of a balance of the historical
elements in a given society. They do not appeal to
the wise deduction from experience, as old as Aristotle, which no student of constitutional history will
deny, that the best Constitutions are those in which
there is a large popular element. It is a singular
proof of the widespread influence of the speculations
of Rousseau that, although very few First Chambers
really represent the entire community (indeed, there
is no agreement as to what the entire community is,
and nobody is quite sure how it can be represented),
nevertheless in Europe they almost invariably claim
to reflect it, and, as a consequence, they assume an
air of divinity which, if it rightfully belonged to
them, would be fatal to all argument for a Second
Chamber.

There appears to me to be no escaping from the
fact that all such institutions as a Senate, a House of
Peers, or a Second Chamber, are founded on a denial
or a doubt of the proposition that the voice of the
people is the voice of God. They express the revolt
of a great mass of human common sense against it.
They are the fruit of the agnosticism of the political
understanding. Their authors and advocates do

not assert that the decisions of a popularly elected
Chamber are always or generally wrong. These
decisions are very often right. But it is impossible
to be sure that they are right. And the more the
difficulties of multitudinous government are probed,
and the more carefully the influences acting upon it
are examined, the stronger grows the doubt of the
infallibility of popularly elected legislatures. What,
then, is expected from a well-constituted Second
Chamber is not a rival infallibility, but an additional
security. It is hardly too much to say that, in this
view, almost any Second Chamber is better than
none. No such Chamber can be so completely un-
satisfactory that its concurrence does not add some
weight to a presumption that the First Chamber is in
the right; but doubtless Upper Houses may be so
constituted, and their discussions so conducted, that
their concurrence would render this presumption
virtually conclusive. The conception of an Upper
House as a mere revising body, trusted with the
privilege of dotting i's and crossing t's in measures
sent up by the other Chamber, seems to me as irrational as it is poor. What is wanted from an Upper
House is the security of its concurrence, after full
examination of the measure concurred in.

It requires some attention to facts to see how
widely spread is the misgiving as to the absolute
wisdom of popularly elected Chambers. I will not

stop to examine the American phenomena of this class, but will merely observe in passing, that the one thoroughly successful institution which has been established since the tide of modern democracy began to run, is a Second Chamber, the American Senate. On the Continent of Europe there are no States without Second Chambers, except three—Greece, Servia, and Bulgaria—all resembling one another in having long been portions of the Turkish Empire, and in being now very greatly under the influence of the Russian Government. Russia has not, Turkey never had, any true aristocracy, any " root of gentlemen," to repeat Bacon's expression ; and we shall see presently that the framers of Constitutions, in their search for materials of a Second Chamber other than the ordinary forms of popular election, have constantly had to build, at all events partially, on the foundation of an aristocracy. But, with the exception of the three communities just mentioned, all the European States have Second Chambers, varying from that of Norway, where, after a single general election, a certain number of the deputies returned are told off to make an Upper House, to the ultra-aristocratic House of Magnates established from the earliest time [3] under the ancient Hungarian Constitu-

---

[3] Since this essay appeared in its first form, the House of Magnates has undergone a reform which still leaves it a highly aristocratic body.

tion. Hereditary Peers, generally mixed with Life
Peers and elective Peers, are still common in the
Second Chambers of the Continent ; they are found
in Cis-Leithan Austria, in Prussia, in Bavaria, in
many of the smaller German States, in Spain, and in
Portugal. There is much reason to believe that the
British House of Lords would have been exclusively,
or at all events much more extensively, copied in the
Constitutions of the Continent, but for one remarkable difficulty. This is not in the least any dislike
or distrust of the hereditary principle, but the extreme numerousness of the nobility in most Continental societies, and the consequent difficulty of
selecting a portion of them to be exclusively privileged. Siéyès, in his famous pamphlet, observes
that in 1789 the higher French aristocracy was eager[4]
to have a House of Lords engrafted on the new
French Constitution ; and this ambition, as Burke
noticed, was the secret of the fervour—the suicidal
fervour, as it afterwards turned out—with which a
certain number of the noblest French families threw
in their lot with the Revolutionary movement.
Siéyès, however, pointed out the fatal obstacle to
these hopes. It was the number and the theoretical
equality of the nobles. His calculation was that, in

---

[4] Siéyès, *Qu'est-ce que le Tiers Etat ?* chap. iv. "Tout ce
qui tient aux quatre cents familles les plus distinguées soupire
après l'établissement d'une Chambre Haute, semblable à celle
d'Angleterre."

all France, there were no less than 110,000 noble-
men ; there were 10,000 in Brittany alone. The
proportions which this difficulty sometimes still
assumes on the Continent may be inferred from one
curious instance. The combined Parliament of the
two small States called respectively Mecklenburg-
Schwerin and Mecklenburg-Strelitz is a mediæval
Diet, very slightly changed. It now consists of 731
members, of whom 684 are persons of knightly rank,
holding land by knightly tenure. As a rule, however, this numerousness of the nobility causes the
privilege of sitting in the Upper House to be confined
to comparatively few Peers of very high and universally acknowledged rank, and hereditary Peers
are seldom found without an intermixture of Life
Peers. Life Peers also occur by themselves, but the
Crown is generally directed by the Constitution to
select them from certain classes of distinguished men.
The best example of an Upper House formed by this
method is the Italian Senate.

In the French Republic and in most of the Monarchical European States, elective Senators are found,
either by themselves or together with Life Senators
or Hereditary Peers. The mode of choosing them
deserves careful attention. Sometimes the Senatorial
electorate is different from that which chooses the
Lower House ; where, for instance, there is a property qualification, it is often higher in the case of

Senatorial electors than in the case of electors for a
Chamber of Deputies. More often, however, as in
the case of France, Sweden, Denmark, the Netherlands, and Belgium, the elective Senators are chosen
by an electorate which in principle is the same with
that which returns the other Chamber. But then
the electors are differently grouped. Provinces,
cities, communes, elect the Senators; while the
Deputies are assumed to be chosen by the nation
at large. Nothing brings out so clearly as does this
class of contrivances a fundamental doubt afflicting
the whole Democratic theory. It is taken for granted
that a popular electorate will be animated by a different spirit according as it is grouped; but why
should there be any connection between the grouping
of the People and the Voice of the People? The
truth is, that as soon as we begin to reflect seriously
on modes of practically applying the democratic principle, we find that some vital preliminary questions
have never been settled. Granting that the People is
entitled of right to govern, how is it to give its decisions and orders? Rousseau answers that all the
people must meet periodically in assembly. Siéyès
replies that it may speak through representatives, but
he spent a life and displayed marvels of ingenuity
in devising systems of representation; and the difficulties which he never succeeded in solving still
perplex the absolute theorist. Vox Populi may be

Vox Dei, but very little attention shows that there never has been any agreement as to what Vox means or as to what Populus means. Is the voice of the People the voice which speaks through *scrutin d'arrondissement* or through *scrutin de liste*, by Plébiscite or by tumultuary assembly? Is it a sound in which the note struck by minorities is entirely silent? Is the People which speaks, the People according to household suffrage, or the People according to universal suffrage, the People with all the women excluded from it, or the People, men, women, and children together, assembling casually in voluntary meeting? None of these questions have been settled ; some have hardly been thought about. In reality, the devotee of Democracy is much in the same position as the Greeks with their oracles. All agreed that the voice of an oracle was the voice of a god ; but everybody allowed that when he spoke he was not as intelligible as might be desired, and nobody was quite sure whether it was safer to go to Delphi or to Dodona.

It is needless to say that none of these difficulties embarrass the saner political theorist who holds that, in secular matters, it is better to walk by sight than by faith. As regards popularly elected Chambers, he will be satisfied that, to Englishmen as to Greeks, experience has shown the best Constitutions to be those in which the popular element is large; and he

will readily admit that, as the structure of each
society of men slowly alters, it is well to alter
and amend the organisation by which this element
makes itself felt. But, as regards the far more
difficult undertaking of reconstructing an Upper
House, he will hope that it will fall into the hands of
men who have thoroughly brought home to themselves the truth, that only two Second Chambers
have as yet had any duration to speak of—the
American Senate, with all its success a creation of
yesterday, and the ancient English House of Lords.
It is very difficult to obtain from the younger institution any lessons which can be of use in the reconstruction of the older. The Senate of the United
States is, in strictness, no more a democratic institution than the House of Lords. As I shall point
out in the following Essay, it is founded on inequality of representation, not on equality. But then,
on the other hand, thirteen of the States which
severally depute the senators to Washington are of
older origin than the Federal Union ; they still retain
some portion of sovereignty ; and thus no artificial
Local Government circles which may be created in this
country will have more than a superficial resemblance
to them. It is only, I am persuaded, by careful
examination of infirmities which experience has shown
to exist in the House of Lords, and by careful consideration of doubts which have actually arisen as to

the principles proper for it to follow in exercising its
legal powers, that hints of any kind can be gathered
respecting its possible improvement. The most com-
petent reformers of the House of Lords will probably
be those who understand it from belonging to it ;
and doubtless there are times when the maxim of
Portalis applies, " Il faut innover quand la plus
funeste de toutes les innovations serait de ne point
innover." Meantime, there does not seem to me to
be anything in the thought and tendencies of our day
which lends support to the vague propositions—
powerful, I admit, through their very vagueness—
which suggest that the improvement of the House of
Lords is a desperate undertaking. One hears it said
that the House of Lords consists of great landowners,
and that the history of landed property in great
masses is nearly ended ; that the privileges of the
Peers are hereditary, and that an hereditary right to
share in government is absurd ; and that the age of
aristocracies and of aristocratic ascendency is gone
for ever. These are very broad generalities, against
which may be set off other generalities, perhaps
equally broad, but much better supported by experience and observation. It certainly does appear
that, for the moment, landed property is seriously
threatened. Yet it demands but little penetration of
mind to see that most of the current objections to it
are objections to all private property, and there may

again be a time when it is recognised that the possession of a great estate, as is natural in a form
of ownership probably descended from a form of
sovereignty,[5] implies more administrative power and
kindlier relations with other classes having subordinate interests than almost any other kind of superiority founded on wealth. The assertion of the
inherent absurdity of an hereditary legislature will
seem itself absurd to those who can follow the course
of scientific thought in our day. Under all systems
of government, under Monarchy, Aristocracy, and
Democracy alike, it is a mere chance whether the
individual called to the direction of public affairs will
be qualified for the undertaking; but the chance of
his competence, so far from being less under Aristocracy than under the other two systems, is distinctly
greater. If the qualities proper for the conduct of
government can be secured in a limited class or body
of men, there is a strong probability that they will
be transmitted to the corresponding class in the next
generation, although no assertion be possible as to
individuals. Whether—and this is the last objection
—the age of aristocracies be over, I cannot take upon
myself to say. I have sometimes thought it one of
the chief drawbacks on modern democracy that, while
it gives birth to despotism with the greatest facility,

---

[5] I have discussed this point in an earlier work, *Early History
of Institutions*, pp. 115 *et seq.* and pp. 130 *et seq.*

it does not seem to be capable of producing aristocracy, though from that form of political and social
ascendency all improvement has hitherto sprung.
But some of the keenest observers of democratic
society in our day do not share this opinion. Noticing
that the modern movement towards democracy is
coupled with a movement towards scientific perfection,
they appear to be persuaded that the world will some
day fall under intellectual aristocracies. Society is
to become the Church of a sort of political Calvinism,
in which the Elect are to be the men with exceptional brains. This seems to be the view suggested
by French democratic society to M. Ernest Renan.[6]
Whether such an aristocracy, if it wielded all the
power which the command of all scientific results
placed in its hands, would be exactly beneficent, may
possibly be doubted. The faults to which the older
privileged orders are liable are plain enough and at

[6] Renan, *Dialogues Philosophiques.* Third Dialogue. A
younger writer, M. Paul Bourget, expresses himself as follows in
a remarkable book called *Essais de Psychologie contemporaine.*
" Il est possible, en effet, qu'une divergence éclate entre ces deux
grandes forces des sociétés modernes : la démocratie et la science.
Il est certain que la première tend de plus en plus à niveler,
tandis que la seconde tend de plus en plus à créer des différences.
' Savoir, c'est pouvoir,' disait le philosophe de l'induction, savoir
dix fois plus qu'un autre homme, c'est pouvoir dix fois ce qu'il peut,
et comme la chimère d'une instruction également répartie sur
tous les individus est, sans aucun doute, irréalisable, par suite de
l'inégalité des intelligences, l'antinomie se manifestera de plus en
plus entre les tendances de la démocratie et les résultats sociaux
de la science " (pp. 106, 107).

times very serious. They are in some characters
idleness, luxuriousness, insolence, and frivolity ; in
others, and more particularly in our day, they are
timidity, distrust of the permanence of anything
ancient and great, and (what is worse) a belief that
no reputation can be made by a member of an ancient
and great institution except by helping to pull it
down. But, assuming the utmost indulgence in
these faults, I may be permitted to doubt whether
mankind would derive unmixed advantage from
putting in their place an ascetic aristocracy of men
of science, with intellects perfected by unremitting
exercise, absolutely confident in themselves and absolutely sure of their conclusions. The question, however, will not long or deeply trouble those who, like
me, have the strongest suspicion that, if there really
arise a conflict between Democracy and Science,
Democracy, which is already taking precautions
against the enemy, will certainly win.

NOTE A.[7]

" Mr. Tylor has justly observed that the true
" lesson of the new science of Comparative Mythology

[7] This Note is taken from my *Early History of Institutions*,
pp. 225–230.

" is the barrenness in primitive times of the faculty
" which we most associate with mental fertility, the
" Imagination.   Comparative Jurisprudence, as might
" be expected from the natural stability of law and
" custom, yet more strongly suggests the same infer-
" ence, and points to the fewness of ideas and the
" slowness of additions to the mental stock as among
" the most general characteristics of mankind in its
" infancy."

" The fact that the generation of new ideas does not
" proceed in all states of society as rapidly as in that
" to which we belong, is only not familiar to us through
" our inveterate habit of confining our observation of
" human nature to a small portion of its phenomena.
" When we undertake to examine it, we are very apt
" to look exclusively at a part of Western Europe and
" perhaps of the American Continent.   We constantly
" leave aside India, China, and the whole Mahometan
" East.   This limitation of our field of vision is per-
" fectly justifiable when we are occupied with the
" investigation of the laws of Progress.   Progress is, in
" fact, the same thing as the continued production of
" new ideas, and we can only discover the law of this
" production by examining sequences of ideas where
" they are frequent and of considerable length.   But
" the primitive condition of the progressive societies is
" best ascertained from the observable condition of
" those which are non-progressive; and thus we leave

"a serious gap in our knowledge when we put aside
" the mental state of the millions upon millions of men
" who fill what we vaguely call the East as a pheno-
" menon of little interest and of no instructiveness.
" The fact is not unknown to most of us that, among
" these multitudes, Literature, Religion, and Art—or
" what corresponds to them—move always within a
" distinctly drawn circle of unchanging notions ; but
" the fact that this condition of thought is rather the
" infancy of the human mind prolonged than a dif-
" ferent maturity from that most familiar to us, is
" very seldom brought home to us with a clearness
" rendering it fruitful of instruction.

" I do not, indeed, deny that the difference between
" the East and the West, in respect of the different
" speed at which new ideas are produced, is only a
" difference of degree. There were new ideas produced
" in India even during the disastrous period just before
" the English entered it, and in the earlier ages this
" production must have been rapid.   There must have
" been a series of ages during which the progress of
" China was very steadily maintained, and doubtless
" our assumption of the absolute immobility of the
" Chinese and other societies is in part the expression
" of our ignorance. Conversely, I question whether
" new ideas come into being in the West as rapidly
" as modern literature and conversation sometimes
" suggest. It cannot, indeed, be doubted that causes,

" unknown to the ancient world, lead among us to the
" multiplication of ideas.   Among them are the never-
" ceasing discovery of new facts of nature, inventions
" changing the circumstances and material conditions
" of life, and new rules of social conduct ; the chief of
" this last class, and certainly the most powerful in the
" domain of law proper, I take to be the famous maxim
" that all institutions should be adapted to produce the
" greatest happiness of the greatest number.   Never-
" theless, there are not a few signs that even conscious
" efforts to increase the number of ideas have a very
" limited success.   Look at Poetry and Fiction.   From
" time to time one mind endowed with the assemblage
" of qualities called genius makes a great and sudden
" addition to the combinations of thought, word, and
" sound which it is the province of those arts to pro-
" duce ; yet as suddenly, after one or a few such efforts,
" the productive activity of both branches of invention
" ceases, and they settle down into imitativeness for
" perhaps a century at a time.   An humbler example
" may be sought in rules of social habit.   We speak
" of the caprices of Fashion ; yet, on examining them
" historically, we find them singularly limited, so much
" so, that we are sometimes tempted to regard Fashion
" as passing through cycles of form ever repeating
" themselves.   There are, in fact, more natural limita-
" tions on the fertility of intellect than we always
" admit to ourselves, and these, reflected in bodies

" of men, translate themselves into that weariness of
" novelty which seems at intervals to overtake whole
" Western societies, including minds of every degree
" of information and cultivation.

  " My present object is to point out some of the
" results of mental sterility at a time when society is in
" the stage which we have been considering. Then,
" the relations between man and man were summed up
" in kinship. The fundamental assumption was that
" all men, not united with you by blood, were your
" enemies or your slaves. Gradually the assumption
" became untrue in fact, and men, who were not blood
" relatives, became related to one another on terms of
" peace and mutual tolerance or mutual advantage.
" Yet no new ideas came into being exactly harmonis-
" ing with the new relation, nor was any new phraseo-
" logy invented to express it. The new member of
" each group was spoken of as akin to it, was treated as
" akin to it, was thought of as akin to it. So little
" were ideas changed that, as we shall see, the very
" affections and emotions which the natural bond
" evoked were called forth in extraordinary strength
" by the artificial tie. The clear apprehension of these
" facts throws light on several historical problems, and
" among them on some of Irish history. Yet they
" ought not greatly to surprise us, since, in a modified
" form, they make part of our everyday experience.
" Almost everybody can observe that, when new cir-

" cumstances arise, we use our old ideas to bring them
"home to us; it is only afterwards, and sometimes
"long afterwards, that our ideas are found to have
"changed. An English Court of Justice is in great
"part an engine for working out this process. New
" combinations of circumstance are constantly arising,
" but in the first instance they are exclusively inter-
"preted according to old legal ideas. A little later
"lawyers admit that the old ideas are not quite what
" they were before the new circumstances arose.

" The slow generation of ideas in ancient times
" may first be adduced as necessary to the explanation
" of that great family of Fictions which meet us on
"the threshold of history and historical jurispru-
" dence."

ESSAY IV.

THE CONSTITUTION OF THE UNITED STATES.

THE Constitution of the United States of America is much the most important political instrument of modern times. The country, whose destinies it controls and directs, has this special characteristic, that all the territories into which its already teeming population overflows are so placed, that political institutions of the same type can be established in every part of them. The British Empire contains a much larger population, but its portions lie far apart from one another, divided by long stretches of sea, and it is impossible to apply the popular government of the British Islands to all of them, and to none of them can it be applied without considerable modifications. Russia has something like the compactness of the United States, and her population is at present more numerous, although her numbers seem likely to be overtaken in no long time by those included in the American Federation. All the Russian Empire is nominally governed through the sole authority of the

Emperor, but there are already great differences between the bureaucratic despotism of Western Russia
and the military autocracy which presides over the
East ; and, whenever the crisis comes through which
Russian institutions seem doomed to pass, the difference between the eastern and western systems of
Russian Government cannot fail to be accentuated.
But the United States of America, from the Atlantic
to the Pacific, from the Canadian lakes to the Mexican
border, appear destined to remain for an indefinite
time under the same political institutions ; and there
is no evidence that these will not continue to belong
to the popular type. Of these institutions, the most
important part is defined by the Federal Constitution.
The relative importance, indeed, of the Government
of the United States and of the State Governments
did not always appear to be as clearly settled as it
appears at the present moment. There was a time
at which the authority of the several States might be
thought to be gaining at the expense of the authority
of the United States ; but the War of Secession reversed this tendency, and the Federation is slowly but
decidedly gaining at the cost of the States. Thus,
the life and fortunes of the most multitudinous and
homogeneous population in the world will, on the
whole and in the main, be shaped by the Constitution
of the United States.

The political liberty of the United States exercises

more or less influence upon all forms of free government in the older world. But to us of the present generation it has the greatest interest for another reason. The success of the United States has sustained the credit of Republics—a word which was once used with a good deal of vagueness to signify a government of any sort without an hereditary king at its head, but which has lately come to have the additional meaning of a government resting on a widely extended suffrage. It is not at all easy to bring home to the men of the present day how low the credit of Republics had sunk before the establishment of the United States. I called attention in my first Essay to the language of contempt in which the writers of the last century speak of the Republics then surviving. The authors of the famous American collection of papers called the "Federalist," of which I shall have much to say presently, are deeply troubled by the ill-success and ill-repute of the only form of government which was possible for them. The very establishment of their independence had left them a cluster of Republics in the old sense of the word, and, as hereditary kingship was out of the question, their Federal Constitution was necessarily Republican. They tried to take their own Republic out of the class as commonly understood. What they chiefly dreaded was disorder, and they were much impressed by the turbulence, the "fugitive and turbulent existence," of the ancient Republics. But these, they said,[1] were not Republics in the true sense of the name. They were "democracies," commonwealths of the primitive type, governed by the vote of the popular assembly, which consisted of the whole mass of male citizens met together in one place. The true Republic must always be understood as a commonwealth saved from disorder by representative institutions.

But soon after the emancipated Americans began their great experiment, its credit had to be sustained against a much more terrible exemplification of the weaknesses of republican institutions, for the French Republic was established. The black shadow of its crimes still hangs over the century, though it is fading imperceptibly into the distance. But what has not been sufficiently noticed, is its thorough political miscarriage. It tried every expedient by which weak governments, directed by unscrupulous men, attempt to save themselves from open discomfiture. It put to death all who were likely to oppose it, and it con-ducted its executions on a scale which, for the quantity of blood spilt within narrow limits of time, had been unknown since the Tartar invasions. It tried foreign war, and it obtained success in the field beyond its wildest hopes. It tried military usurpation, and it sent the most distinguished and virtuous of the new constitutional school of French politicians, which was

[1] *Federalist*, No. 10 (Madison).

beginning to control it, to perish in tropical swamps.
Yet it sank lower and lower into contempt, and died
without a struggle. There are not many of the
charges brought against Napoleon Bonaparte which
are altogether unjust, but he must at any rate be
acquitted of having destroyed a Republic, if by a
Republic is to be understood a free government.
What he destroyed was a military tyranny, for this
had been the character of the French Government
since the September of 1797; and he substituted for
this military tyranny another still severer and infinitely more respected.

As a matter of fact, there is no doubt that the
credit of American Republican institutions, and of
such institutions generally, did greatly decline through
the miserable issue of the French experiment. The
hopes of political freedom, which the Continental communities were loth to surrender, turned in another
direction, and attached themselves exclusively to
Constitutional Monarchy. American publicists note
the first fifteen years of the present century as the
period during which their country was least respected
abroad and their Government treated with most con-
tumely by European diplomacy.[2] And just when
the American Federation was overcoming the low

---

[2] See the language employed by Canning, as lately as 1821,
in conversation with John Quincy Adams, then American Minister
in London (Morse's *Life of J. Q. Adams*, p. 141).

opinion of all Republics which had become common, a set of events happened close to its doors which might have overwhelmed it in general shame. The Spanish Colonies in North, Central, and South America revolted, and set up Republics in which the crimes and disorders of the French Republic were repeated in caricature. The Spanish American Republicans were to the French what Hébert and Anacharsis Clootz had been to Danton and Robespierre. This absurd travesty of Republicanism lasted more than fifty years, and even now the curtain has not quite fallen upon it. Independently, therefore, of the history of the United States, it would have seemed quite certain what the conclusion of political philosophy must have been upon the various forms of Government as observed under the glass of experience. If we clear our mental view by adopting the Aristotelian analysis, and classify all governments as governments of the One, governments of the Few, and governments of the Many, we shall see that mankind had had much experience of government by the One, and a good deal of government by the Few, and also some very valuable experience of attempts at combining these two forms of Government, but that of government by the Many it had very slight experience, and that whatever it had was on the whole decidedly unfavourable. The antecedent doubt, whether government by the Many was really possible

—whether in any intelligible sense, and upon any theory of volition, a multitude of men could be said to have a common will—would have seemed to be strengthened by the fact that, whenever government by the Many had been tried, it had ultimately produced monstrous and morbid forms of government by the One, or of government by the Few. This conclusion would, in truth, have been inevitable, but for the history of the United States, so far as they have had a history. The Federal Constitution has survived the mockery of itself in France and in Spanish America. Its success has been so great and striking, that men have almost forgotten that, if the whole of the known experiments of mankind in government be looked at together, there has been no form of government so unsuccessful as the Republican.

The antecedents of a body of institutions like this, and its mode of growth, manifestly deserve attentive study ; and fortunately the materials for the inquiry are full and good. The papers called the " Federalist," which were published in 1787 and 1788 by Hamilton, Madison, and Jay, but which were chiefly from the pen of Hamilton, were originally written to explain the new Constitution of the United States, then awaiting ratification, and to dispel misconstructions of it which had got abroad. They are thus, undoubtedly, an *ex post facto* defence of the new institutions, but they show us with much clearness

either the route by which the strongest minds among
the American statesmen of that period had travelled
to the conclusions embodied in the Constitution, or
the arguments by which they had become reconciled to
them. The " Federalist" has generally excited something like enthusiasm in those who have studied it,
and among these there have been some not at all
given to excessive eulogy. Talleyrand strongly
recommended it ; and Guizot said of it that, in the
application of the elementary principles of government
to practical administration, it was the greatest work
known to him. An early number of the " Edinburgh
Review" (No. 24) described it as a " work little known
in Europe, but which exhibits a profundity of research and an acuteness of understanding which
would have done honour to the most illustrious
statesmen of modern times." The American com-
mendations of the "Federalist " are naturally even less
qualified. " I know not," wrote Chancellor Kent, " of
any work on the principles of free government that is
to be compared in instruction and in intrinsic value
to this small and unpretending volume of the ' Federalist ' ; not even if we resort to Aristotle, Cicero,
Machiavel, Montesquieu, Milton, Locke, or Burke.
It is equally admirable in the depth of its wisdom,
the comprehensiveness of its views, the sagacity of
its reflections, and the freshness, patriotism, candour,
simplicity, and eloquence, with which its truths are

uttered and recommended." Those who have atten-
tively read these papers will not think such praise
pitched, on the whole, too high. Perhaps the part
of it least thoroughly deserved is that given to their
supposed profundity of research. There are few
traces in the " Federalist " of familiarity with previous
speculations on politics, except those of Montesquieu
in the " Esprit des Lois," the popular book of that
day. The writers attach the greatest importance to
all Montesquieu's opinions. They are much discom-
posed by his assertion, that Republican government
is necessarily associated with a small territory, and,
they are again comforted by his admission, that this
difficulty might be overcome by a confederate Republic. Madison indeed had the acuteness to see
that Montesquieu's doctrine is as often polemical as
philosophical, and that it is constantly founded on a
tacit contrast between the institutions of his own
country, which he disliked, with those of England,
which he admired. But still his analysis, as we shall
hereafter point out, had much influence upon the
founders and defenders of the American Constitution.
On the whole, Guizot's criticism of the " Federalist "
is the most judicious. It is an invaluable work on
the application of the elementary principles of government to practical administration. Nothing can be
more sagacious than its anticipation of the way in
which the new institutions would actually work, or

more conclusive than its exposure of the fallacies which underlay the popular objections to some of them.

It is not to be supposed that Hamilton, Jay, and Madison were careless of historical experience. They had made a careful study of many forms of government, ancient and modern. Their observations on the ancient Republics,[3] which were shortly afterwards to prove so terrible a snare to French political theorists, are extremely just. The cluster of commonwealths woven together in the " United Netherlands "[4] is fully examined, and the weaknesses of this anomalous confederacy are shrewdly noted. The remarkable structure of the Romano-German Empire[5] is depicted, and there is reason to suspect that these institutions, now almost forgotten, influenced the framers of the American Constitution, both by attraction and by repulsion. But far the most important experience to which they appealed was that of their own country, at a very recent date. The earliest link had been supplied to the revolted colonies by the first or

[3] *Federalist*, No. 14 (Madison).
[4] *Ibid*. No. 20 (Hamilton and Madison).
[5] *Ibid*. No. 19 (Hamilton and Madison).   Nos. 19 and 20 are attributed to Hamilton and Madison in Mr. J. C. Hamilton's edition of the *Federalist*, but Hamilton's share in them is not acknowledged in the list left by Madison.   See Bancroft, *History of the Formation of the Constitution of the United States*, ii. p. 336.

American " Continental" Congress, which issued the Declaration of Independence. There had subsequently been the " Articles of Confederation," ratified in 1781. These earlier experiments, their demonstrable miscarriage in many particulars, and the disappointments to which they gave rise, are a storehouse of instances and a plentiful source of warning and reflection to the writers who have undertaken to show that their vices are removed in the Constitution of 1787–89.

Nevertheless, there is one fund of political experience upon which the " Federalist" seldom draws, and that is the political experience of Great Britain. The scantiness[6] of these references is at first sight inexplicable. The writers must have understood Great Britain better than any other country, except their own. They had been British subjects during most of their lives. They had scarcely yet ceased to breathe the atmosphere of the British Parliament and to draw strength from its characteristic disturbances. Next to their own stubborn valour, the chief secret of the colonists' success was the incapacity of the English generals, trained in the stiff Prussian system soon to perish at Jena, to adapt themselves to new conditions of warfare, an incapacity which newer generals, full of admiration for a newer German system, were again to

[6] References to Great Britain occur in *Federalist*, No. 5 (Jay); and (for the purpose of disproving a supposed analogy) in *Federalist*, No. 69 (Hamilton).

manifest at Majuba Hill against a meaner foe. But
the colonists had also reaped signal advantage from
the encouragements of the British Parliamentary
Opposition. If the King of France gave " aid," the
English Opposition gave perpetual " comfort " to the
enemies of the King of England. It was a fruit of
the English party system which was to reappear,
amid much greater public dangers, in the Peninsular
War ; and the revelation of domestic facts, the assertion of domestic weakness, were to assist the arms of
a military tyrant, as they had assisted the colonists
fighting for independence. Various observations[7]
in the " Federalist" on the truculence of party spirit
may be suspected of having been prompted by the
recollection of what an Opposition can do. But there
could be no open reference to this in its pages ; and,
on the whole, it cannot but be suspected that the
fewness of the appeals to British historical examples
had its cause in their unpopularity. The object of
Madison, Hamilton, and Jay was to persuade their
countrymen ; and the appeal to British experience
would only have provoked prejudice and repulsion.
I hope, however, to show that the Constitution of the
United States is coloured throughout by political
ideas of British origin, and that it is in reality a
version of the British Constitution, as it must have

---

[7] *Federalist*, No. 70 (Hamilton).

presented itself to an observer in the second half of the last century.

It has to be carefully borne in mind that the construction of the American Constitution was extremely unlike that process of founding a new Constitution which in our day may be witnessed at intervals of a few years on the European Continent, and that it bore even less resemblance to the foundation of a new Republic, as the word is now understood. Whatever be the occasion of one of these new European Constitutions, be it ill success in war, or escape from foreign dominion, or the overthrow of a government by the army or the mob, the new institutions are always shaped in a spirit of bitter dissatisfaction with the old, which, at the very best, are put upon their trial. But the enfranchised American colonists were more than satisfied with the bulk of their institutions, which were those of the several colonies to which they belonged. And, although they had fought a successful war to get rid of the King of Great Britain and of the British Parliament, they had no quarrel with kings or parliaments as such. Their contention was that the British King and the British Parliament had forfeited by usurpation whatever rights they had, and that they had been justly punished by dispossession. Born free Englishmen, they were not likely to deny the value of parliaments, and, even as to kings, it is probable that many of them had at one time shared the youthful opinion of Alexander Hamilton, who, while totally denying the claim of parliamentary supremacy over the British colonies, except so far as they had conceded it, had argued that the "connecting, pervading principle," necessary to unite a number of individual communities under one common head, could only be found in the person and prerogative of the King, who was " King of America by virtue of a compact between the colonists and the Kings of Great Britain." [8] When once, however, the war had been fought out, and the connection with the Parliament and the King alike had been broken, the business in hand was to supply their place.   This new constitutional link had now to be forged from local materials.   Among these, there were none for making an hereditary King, hardly any for manufacturing an hereditary Second Chamber ; but yet the means of enabling the now separated portion of the British Empire to discharge the functions of a fully organised State, as completely as they had been performed by the kingdom from which it was severed, must somehow be found on the west of the Atlantic.   The Constitution of the United States was the fruit of signal sagacity and prescience applied to these necessities.   But, again, there was almost no analogy between the new undertaking and the establishment

* See Preface to J. C. Hamilton's edition of the *Federalist*, p. 10.

P

of a modern Continental Republic. The commonwealth founded in America was only called a Republic
because it had no hereditary king, and it had no
hereditary king because there were no means of having
one. At that time every community without an
hereditary monarchy was considered to be republican.
There was a King of Poland elected for life, but his
kingdom was styled the Polish Republic. In the
style of the elective Romano-German Empire there
were still traces of the old Roman Republican Constitution. The Venetian Republic was a stern oligarchy ; and, in fact, the elective Doges of Venice
and Genoa were as much kings of the old type as
those ancient Kings of Rome who originally gave its
name to Royal authority. Many of the Swiss Cantons were Republics of the most primitive kind,
where the whole population met once a year in
assembly to legislate and elect public officers ; but
one section in some cantons severely governed the
others, and some cantons held their dependent territories in the hardest subjection. Now-a-days, however,
the establishment of a Republic means the substitu-
tion, in all the functions of government, of the Many
for the One or the Few—of the totality of the community for a determinate portion of it—an experiment
of tremendous and perhaps insuperable difficulty,
which the colonists never thought of undertaking.
The suffrage, as I shall have to show, was extremely

limited in many of the States, and it is unnecessary
to state that about half of them were slaveholding
communities.

I now propose to take in turn the great Federal
institutions set up by the Americans—the President
of the United States, the Supreme Court, the Senate,
and the House of Representatives—and, in sum-
marily considering them, to point out their relation
to pre-existing European, and especially British, institutions.   What I may say will perhaps serve in some
degree as a corrective of the vague ideas betrayed,
not only in the loose phraseology of the English
platform, but by the historical commonplaces of the
Americans themselves.

On the face of the Constitution of the United
States, the resemblance of the President of the United
States to the European King, and especially to the
King of Great Britain, is too obvious for mistake.
The President has, in various degrees, a number of
powers which those who know something of Kingship in its general history recognise at once as
peculiarly associated with it and with no other institution.   The whole Executive power is vested in
him.[9]   He is Commander-in-Chief of the Army and
Navy.[1]   He makes treaties with the advice and consent of the Senate, and with the same advice and
consent he appoints Ambassadors, Ministers, Judges,

---

[9] C. of U.S. Art. II.   [1] Ibid. 1, 2.

and all high functionaries. He has a qualified veto on legislation. He convenes Congress, when no special time of meeting has been fixed. It is conceded in the "Federalist" that the similarity of the new President's office to the functions of the British King was one of the points on which the opponents of the Constitution fastened. Hamilton replies [2] to their arguments, sometimes with great cogency, sometimes, it must be owned, a little captiously. He urges that the only alternative to a President was a plural Executive, or Council, and he insists on the risk of a paralysis of Executive authority produced by party opposition in such a body. But he mainly relies on the points in which the President differs from the King—on the terminability of the office, on the participation of the Senate in the exercise of several of his powers, on the limited nature of his veto on Bills passed by Congress. It is, however, tolerably clear that the mental operation through which the framers of the American Constitution passed was this : they took the King of Great Britain, went through his powers, and restrained them whenever they appeared to be excessive or unsuited to the circumstances of the United States. It is remarkable that the figure they had before them was not a generalised English king nor an abstract Constitutional monarch ; it was no anticipation of Queen Victoria, but George III.

[2] *Federalist*, No. 69 (Hamilton).

himself whom they took for their model. Fifty years
earlier, or a hundred years later, the English king
would have struck them in quite a different light.
There had been a tacit compact between the first
two Georges and the Whig aristocracy, that the
King should govern Hanover and the Whig Ministry
Great Britain ; and such differences as arose between
the King and his subjects were attributable to the
fact that European wars began in the Hanoverian
department. But George III. cared nothing for
Hanover and much for governing England. He at
once took a new departure in policy by making peace,
and setting himself to conduct the government of
England in his own way. Now, the original of the
President of the United States is manifestly a treaty-
making king, and a king actively influencing the
Executive Government. Mr. Bagehot insisted that
the great neglected fact in the English political system
was the government of England by a Committee
of the Legislature, calling themselves the Cabinet.
This is exactly the method of government to which
George III. refused to submit, and the framers of the
American Constitution take George III.'s view of
the kingly office for granted. They give the whole
Executive Government to the President, and they do
not permit his Ministers to have seat or speech in
either branch of the Legislature. They limit his
power and theirs, not, however, by any contrivance

known to modern English constitutionalism, but by making the office of President terminable at intervals of four years.

If Hamilton had lived a hundred years later, his comparison of the President with the King would have turned on very different points. He must have conceded that the Republican functionary was much the more powerful of the two. He must have noted that the royal veto on legislation, not thought in 1789 to be quite lost, was irrevocably gone. He must have observed that the powers which the President shared with the Senate had been altogether taken away from the King. The King could make neither war nor treaty ; he could appoint neither Ambassador nor Judge ; he could not even name his own Ministers. He could do no executive act. All these powers had gone over to Mr. Bagehot's Committee of Parliament. But, a century ago, the only real and essential difference between the Presidential and the Royal office was that the first was not hereditary. The succession of President to President cannot therefore have been copied from Great Britain. But there is no reason to suppose that the method of election was suddenly evolved from the brain of American statesmen. Two features of the original plan have very much fallen out of sight. The President, though appointed for four years only, was to be indefinitely re-eligible ; [3] the practical limitation of the term of office to a maximum period of eight years was finally settled only the other day. And again, the elaborate machinery of election [4] provided in the Constitution was intended to be a reality. Each State was to appoint Electors, and the choice of a President was to be the mature fruit of an independent exercise of judgment by the electoral college. Knowing what followed, knowing how thoroughly the interposition of electors became a futile fiction, and what was the effect on the character of elections to the Presidency, one cannot but read with some melancholy the prediction of Hamilton, that " this process of election affords a moral certainty that the office of President will seldom fall to the lot of any man who is not in an eminent degree endowed with the requisite qualifications." Understanding, then, that there was to be a real election, by a selected body, of a President who might conceivably serve for life, we must recollect that elective Kings had not died out of Europe. Not long before the War of Independence, at the commencement of the troubles about the American Stamp Act, a King of the Romans—who, as Joseph II., turned out to be much more of a Radical Reformer than ever was George Washington—had been elected by the Electoral College of the Empire, and the unfortunate Govern-

[3] *Federalist*, No. 69 (Hamilton).   [4] *Ibid.* No. 68 (Hamilton).

ment called the Polish Republic had chosen its last King, the luckless Stanislaus Poniatowski. It seems probable that the framers of the Constitution of the United States deliberately rejected the last example, but were to a considerable extent guided by the first. The American Republican Electors are the German Imperial Electors, except that they are chosen by the several States. The writers in the "Federalist" had made an attentive study of the Romano-German Empire, which is analysed in much detail by Hamilton and Madison.[5] They condemn it as a government which can only issue commands to governments themselves sovereign, but not for the mode of electing its executive head. There is some interest in observing that the Electoral Colleges of the United States and of the Empire failed in exactly the same way. The electors fell under the absolute control of the factions dominant in the country. The German electors came to belong[6] to the French or Austrian party, just as the American electors took sides with the Federalists, or with the old Republicans, or with the Whigs, the new Republicans, or the Democrats.

[5] *Federalist*, No. 19 (Hamilton and Madison). But see note at p. 205.

[6] The account of the intrigues, French and Austrian, which preceded the election of a king of the Romans forms one of the most amusing portions of the Duc de Broglie's recent work, *Frédéric II. et Marie Thérèse.*

The Supreme Court of the United States, which
is the American Federal institution next claiming
our attention, is not only a most interesting but a
virtually unique creation of the founders of the Constitution. The functions which the Judges of this
Court have to discharge under provisions of the
Constitution arise primarily from its very nature.[7]
The Executive and Legislative authorities of the
United States have no powers, except such as are
expressly conferred on them by the Constitution itself; and, on the other hand, the several States are
forbidden by the Constitution to do certain acts
and to pass certain laws. What then is to be done
if these limitations of power are transgressed by
any State, or by the United States? The duty of
annulling such usurpations is confided by the Third
Article of the Constitution to the Supreme Court,
and to such inferior Courts as Congress may from
time to time ordain and establish. But this remarkable power is capable only of indirect exercise; it is
called into activity by " cases," by actual controversies,[8] to which individuals, or States, or the
United States, are parties. The point of unconsti-

---

[7] See on this subject the valuable remarks of Mr. A. V. Dicey
in a paper on " Federal Government," in the first number of the
Law Quarterly Review (Jan. 1885). Before the Revolution, the
British Privy Council had adjudicated on certain questions
arising between Colony and Colony.

[8] *Const. of U.S.* Art. III. s. 2.

tutionality is raised by the arguments in such controversies ; and the decision of the Court follows the view which it takes of the Constitution. A declaration of unconstitutionality, not provoked by a definite dispute, is unknown to the Supreme Court.

The success of this experiment has blinded men to its novelty. There is no exact precedent for it, either in the ancient or in the modern world. The builders of Constitutions have of course foreseen the violation of constitutional rules, but they have generally sought for an exclusive remedy, not in the civil, but in the criminal law, through the impeachment of the offender. And, in popular governments, fear or jealousy of an authority not directly delegated by the people has too often caused the difficulty to be left for settlement to chance or to the arbitrament of arms. "Je ne pense pas," wrote De Tocqueville, in his "Démocratie en Amérique," "que jusqu'à présent aucune nation du monde ait constitué le pouvoir judiciaire de la même manière que les Américains."

Yet, novel as was the Federal Judicature established by the American Constitution as a whole, it nevertheless had its roots in the Past, and most of their beginnings must be sought in England. It may be confidently laid down, that neither the institution of a Supreme Court, nor the entire structure of the Constitution of the United States, were the least likely to occur to anybody's mind before the publication of the "Esprit des Lois." We have

already observed that the "Federalist" regards the
opinions of Montesquieu as of paramount authority,
and no opinion had more weight with its writers
than that which affirmed the essential separation of
the Executive, Legislative, and Judicial powers.
The distinction is so familiar to us, that we find it
hard to believe that even the different nature of the
Executive and Legislative powers was not recognised
till the fourteenth[9] century ; but it was not till the
eighteenth that the "Esprit des Lois" made the
analysis of the various powers of the State part of
the accepted political doctrine of the civilised world.
Yet, as Madison saw, Montesquieu was really writing
of England and contrasting it with France.

The British[1] Constitution was to Montesquieu what
Homer has been to the didactic writers on Epic poetry.   As
the latter have considered the works of the immortal bard
the perfect model from which the principles and rules of the
epic art were to be drawn, and by which all similar works
were to be judged, so the great political critic appears to
have viewed the Constitution of England as the standard, or,
to use his own expression, as the mirror, of political liberty ;
and to have delivered, in the form of elementary truths, the
several characteristic principles of that particular system.

The fact was that, in the middle of the eighteenth
century, it was quite impossible to say where the

---

[9] It occurs in the *Defensor Pacis* of the great Ghibelline
jurist, Marsilio da Padova (1327), with many other curious anti-
cipations of modern political ideas.

[1] *Federalist*, No. 47.

respective provinces of the French King and of the French Parliaments in legislation, and still more of the same authorities in judicature,[2] began and ended. To this indistinctness of boundary Montesquieu opposed the considerable but yet incomplete separation of the Executive, Legislative, and Judicial powers in England ; and he founded on the contrast his famous generalisation.

Montesquieu adds to his analysis the special proposition, " There is no liberty, if the Judicial power be not separated from the Legislative and the Executive ; " and here we have, no doubt, the principal source of the provisions of the American Constitution respecting the Federal Judicature. It is impossible to read the chapter (chap. vi. liv. xi.) of the " Esprit des Lois," in which the words occur, without perceiving that they must have been suggested to the writer by what was, on the whole, the English practice. There were, however, other practices of their English kinsmen which must have led the framers of the American Constitution to the same conclusion. They must have been keenly alive to the inconvenience of discussing questions of constitutional law in legislative assemblies. The debates in both Houses of Parliament, from the accession of George III. to the recognition of American Independence, are asto-

[2] A good account of this confusion is given by M. Louis de Loménie in the twelfth chapter of his *Beaumarchais et Son Temps*.

nishingly unlike those of the present day in one particular. They turn to a surprising extent on law,
and specially on Constitutional law. Everybody in
Parliament is supposed to be acquainted with law,
and, above all, the Ministers. The servants of the
Crown may not plead the authority of its Law officers
for their acts ; nay, even the Attorney- and Solicitor-
General may not publicly admit that they have been
consulted beforehand, but have to pretend that they
are arguing the legal question before the House on
the spur of the moment. There is an apparent survival of these strange fictions in the doctrine which
still prevails, that the opinions of the Law Officers
of the Crown are strictly confidential. During the
whole period of the bitter controversies provoked by
the grievances of Wilkes and the discontent of the
colonies, it is hard to say whether Parliament or the
Courts of Justice are the proper judges of the points
of law constantly raised. Sometimes a Judge of great
eminence speaks with authority, as did Lord Camden
on general warrants, and Lord Mansfield on Wilkes's
outlawry ; but Parliament is just as often the field to
which the perpetual strife is transferred. The confusion reaches its height when Lord Chatham in the
House of Lords declares the House of Commons to
be open to a civil action for not giving Wilkes a seat,
when Lord Mansfield covers this opinion with ridicule,
and when Lord Camden to some extent supports

Lord Chatham.   These are the true causes of the un-
satisfactory condition of English Constitutional law,
and of its many grave and dangerous uncertainties.

The impression made on American minds by a
system under which legal questions were debated with
the utmost acrimony, but hardly ever solved, must
have been deepened by their familiarity with the very
question at issue between the mother-country and the
colonies.   On this question Englishmen, content as is
their wont with the rough rule of success or failure
as the test of right or wrong in national undertakings,
have generally accepted the view which was, on the
whole, that of the Whig Opposition.   And it must
be allowed that the statesmen of the most unpopular
country in Europe ought to have known that it could
not attempt to subdue a great and distant dependency,
without bringing its most powerful European enemies
on its back.   As for American opinion, the merits
of the issue have been buried deep in the nauseous
grandiloquence of the American panegyrical historians.
Yet, in reality, the question was in the highest degree technical, in the highest degree difficult, in the
highest degree fitted for adjudication by an impartial
Court, if such a tribunal could have been imagined.
What was the exact significance of the ancient constitutional formula which connected taxation with
representation ?   When broadly stated by the colonists,
it must have struck many Englishmen of that day

as a mischievous paradox, since it seemed to deny the right of Parliament to tax, not only Massachusetts, but Manchester and Birmingham, which were not represented in any intelligible sense in the House of Commons. On the other hand, the American contention is largely accounted for by the fact, that the local assemblies in which the colonists were represented " were not formally instituted, but grew up by themselves, because it was in the nature of Englishmen to assemble." [3] They were a natural product of soil once become British. The truth is that, from the popular point of view, either the affirmation or the denial of the moot point led straight to an absurdity ; and when the dispute was over, its history must have suggested to thoughtful men, who had once recovered their calmness, the high expediency of judicial mediation in questions between State and State acknowledging the same sovereignty.

Let me finally note that the Constitution of the United States imposes (Art. III. s. 2) on the Judges of the Supreme Court a method of adjudication which is essentially English. No general proposition is laid down by the English tribunal, unless it arises on the facts of the actual dispute submitted to it for adjudication. The success of the Supreme Court of the

[3] See Seeley, *The Expansion of England.* Professor Seeley, at p. 67 of this excellent book, quotes from Hutchinson the statement: "This year (1619) a House of Burgesses *broke out* in Virginia."

United States largely results from its following this mode of deciding questions of constitutionality and unconstitutionality. The process is slower, but it is freer from suspicion of pressure, and much less provocative of jealousy, than the submission of broad and emergent political propositions to a judicial body ; and this submission is what an European foreigner thinks of when he contemplates a Court of Justice deciding on alleged violations of a constitutional rule or principle.

The Congress or Legislature of the United States, sharply separated from the Executive in conformity with Montesquieu's principle, consists, I need scarcely say, of the Senate and the House of Representatives. And here I follow Mr. Freeman in noting this two-chambered legislature as a plain mark of the descent of the American Federal Constitution, as it was at an earlier date of the descent of American Colonial Constitutions, from a British original. If we could conceive a political architect of the eighteenth century endeavouring to build a new Constitution in ignorance of the existence of the British Parliament, or with the deliberate determination to neglect it, he might be supposed to construct his Legislature with one Chamber, or three, or four ; he would have been in the highest degree unlikely to construct it with two. The " Federalist," no doubt, seems [4] to regard the

Federalist, No. 63 (Hamilton).

Senates of the ancient world as in some sense Second Chambers of a Legislature, but these peculiar bodies, originally consisting of the old men of the community, would have been found on closer inspection to answer very slightly to this conception.[5] The first real anticipation of a Second Chamber, armed with a veto on the proposals of a separate authority, and representing a different interest, occurs in that much-misunderstood institution, the Roman Tribunate. In the modern feudal world, the community naturally distributed itself into classes or Estates, and there are abundant traces of legislatures in which these classes were represented according to various principles. But the Estates of the Realm were grouped in all sorts of ways. In France, the States-General were composed of three orders, the Clergy, the Nobility, and the rest of the Nation as the Tiers État. There were three orders also in Spain. In Sweden there were four, the Clergy, the Nobility, the Burghers, and the Peasants. The exceptional two Houses of the British Constitution arose from special causes. The separate Parliamentary representation of the Clergy came early to an end in England, except so far the great dignitaries of the Church were summoned to the House of Lords ; and the Knights of the Shire, who represented the great mass of landed

[5] See Maine, *Early Law and Custom*, pp. 24, 25.

Q

proprietors, were disjoined from the nobility, and sat with the representatives of the towns in the House of Commons.

The Senate of the United States, constituted under section 3 of the First Article of the Federal Constitution, is at this moment one of the most powerful political bodies in the world. In point of dignity and authority, it has in no wise disappointed the sanguine expectations of its founders. As I have already said, it is not possible to compare the predictions of the " Federalist " with the actual history of the Presidency of the United States, without being forced to acknowledge that in this particular the hopes of Hamilton and his coadjutors have failed of fulfilment. But the Senate has, on the whole, justified the hopes of it which they expressed.

Through the medium of the State legislatures, which are select bodies of men, and who are to appoint the members of the National Senate, there is reason to expect that this branch will generally be composed with peculiar care and judgment; that these circumstances promise greater knowledge and more comprehensive information in the national annals; and that, on account of the extent of country from which will be drawn those to whose direction they will be committed, they will be less apt to be tainted by the spirit of faction, and more out of the reach of those occasional ill-humours, or temporary prejudices and propensities, which in smaller societies frequently contaminate the public deliberations, beget injustice and oppression towards a part of the community, and engender schemes which, though they gratify a momentary inclination or desire, terminate in general distress, dissatisfaction, and disgust.[6]

We may not reasonably doubt that the Senate is indebted for its power—a power which has rather increased than diminished since the Federal Constitution came into force—and for its hold on the public respect, to the principles upon which it was deliberately founded, to the mature age of the Senators, to their comparatively long tenure of office, which is for six years at least, and above all to the method of their election by the Legislatures of the several States.

It is very remarkable that the mode of choosing the Senate finally adopted did not commend itself to some of the strongest minds employed on the construction of the Federal Constitution. Its First Article provides (in s. 3) that "the Senate of the United States shall be composed of two Senators from each State, chosen by the Legislatures thereof, for six years." Hence it follows that the Senate is a political body, of which the basis is not equality, but inequality. Each State elects no more and no fewer than two Senators. Rhode Island, Delaware, and Maryland have the same representation in the Senate, as the great and populous States of New York and Pennsylvania. The Constitutional composition of

---

[6] *Federalist*, No. 27 (Hamilton).

the Senate is therefore a negation of equality. Now, the writer whose prediction I quoted above is Alexander Hamilton, and Hamilton himself had proposed a very different mode of constituting a Senate. His plan had been that the Senate should consist of "persons to be chosen by Electors, elected for that purpose by the citizens and inhabitants of the several States who shall have in their own right, or in right of their wives, an estate in land for not less than life, or a term of years whereof, at the time of giving their votes, there shall be at least fourteen years unexpired." The scheme further provided that each Senator should be elected from a District, and that the number of Senators should be apportioned between the different States according to a rule roughly representing population. The blended political and economical history of Europe has now shown us that Hamilton's plan would not, in all probability, have proved durable. It is founded on inequality of property, and specially on inequality of landed property. We are now, however, in a position to lay down, as the result of experience and observation, that, although popular government has steadily extended itself in the Western world, and although liberty is the parent of inequalities in fortune, these inequalities are viewed by democratic societies with a peculiar jealousy, and that no form of property is so much menaced in such societies as property in land. When the Federal

Constitution was framed, there were property qualifications for voting in the greater number of the
American States, and it will be seen that these limitations of the suffrage were allowed to have influence
in - the House of Representatives. But they have
given way almost everywhere to a suffrage very little
short of universal, and the foundation of Hamilton's
Senate would probably have undergone a similar
change. Nevertheless, though inequalities of fortune
are resented by modern democracy, historical inequalities do not appear to be resented in the same degree
—possibly to some extent because the consideration
which Science has finally secured for the heredity of
the individual has insensibly extended to the heredity
of commonwealths. Now the Senate of the United
States reflects the great fact of their history, the
original political equality of the several States. Since
the War of Secession and its event in the triumph of
the North, this fact has become purely historical ; but
it illustrates all the more an apparent inference from
modern European experiments in constitution-building—from the actual history in Europe of Constitutional Kings, Presidents of a Republic, and Second
Legislative Chambers—that nothing but an historical
principle can be successfully opposed to the principle
of making all public powers and all parliamentary
assemblies the mere reflection of the average opinion
of the multitude. On all questions connected with

the Federal Senate, Hamilton unconsciously took the less Conservative side. Not only would he have distinguished the electoral body choosing the Senate from the electoral body choosing the House of Representatives by a property qualification solely, but he would have annulled from the first the self-government of the States by giving the appointment of the Governor or President of each separate State to Federal authority.[7]

The House of Representatives, which shares with the Senate the legislative powers of the United States, is unquestionably a reproduction of the House of Commons. No Constitution but the British could have suggested section 7 of Article I. of the Federal Constitution, which lays down a British principle, and settles a dispute which had arisen upon it in a particular way. "All Bills raising Revenue shall originate in the House of Representatives ; but the Senate may propose or concur with amendments as in other Bills." There is a common impression in this country, that the American House of Representatives was somehow intended to be a more democratic assembly than our House of Commons. But this is a vulgar error. The Constitutional provision on the subject is contained in section 2 of the First Article, which is to the effect that the House is to be

---

[7] Alexander Hamilton's scheme of a Constitution is printed at page 31 of Mr. J. C. Hamilton's edition of the *Federalist*.

composed of members chosen every second year by
the people of the several States, and that the electors
in each State are to " have the qualifications requisite
for Electors of the most numerous branch of the
State Legislature." The "Federalist" expressly
tells us that the differences in the qualification were
at that time "very material." " In every State," it
adds,[8] "a certain proportion of the inhabitants are
deprived of this right by the Constitution of the State."
Nor had the provision for biennial elections the significance which would have been attached to it at a
later date. Our present ideas have been shaped by
the Septennial Act, but it is quite evident that in
Hamilton's day the Septennial Act was still regarded
as a gross usurpation, and that the proper English
system was thought to be one of triennial Parliaments.
Election every two years seems to have been taken as
a fair mean between the systems of the States which
made up the Federation. There were septennial
elections in Virginia, which had been one of the most
forward of the States in pressing on the Revolution ;
but in Connecticut and Rhode Island there were
actually half-yearly elections, and annual elections in
South Carolina.

The House of Representatives is a much more
exclusively legislative body than either the Senate of

---

[8] *Federalist*, No. 51 (Hamilton).

the United States or than the present British House
of Commons.   Many of the Executive powers vested
in the President cannot be exercised save with the
consent of the Senate.   And, as the Congress has
not yet repealed the legislation by which it sought to
trammel the recalcitrant President, Andrew Johnson,
after the War of Secession, the Executive authority
of the Senate is now probably wider than it was
ever intended to be by the framers of the Constitution.   The House of Representatives has no similar
rights over the province of the Executive ; and this
restriction of power is itself a feature connecting it
with the British House of Commons, as known to
the American statesmen of the Revolution.   The far-
reaching and perpetual interference with the Executive
Government, which is now exercised by the House of
Commons through the interrogation of the Ministers,
was then at most in its first feeble beginnings ; and
moreover the right of the House to designate the
public servants, who are nominally the Ministers of
the Crown, had for a considerable time been successfully disputed by the King.   George I. and George II.
had, on the whole, carried out the understanding that
their Ministers should be taken from a particular
class ; but George III. had conducted the struggle
with the Colonists through servants of his own choosing, and, when the Americans were framing their
Constitution, he had established his right for the rest

of his reign.   It is to be observed that the Constitution of the United States settles the quarrel in the
sense contended for by the King of England.   The
heads of the Executive Departments subordinated to
the President do not sit in the Senate or in the
House.   They are excluded from both by section 6
of Article I., which provides that "no person holding
any office under the United States shall be a member
of either House during his continuance in office."

We are here brought to one of the most interesting subjects which can engage the attention of the
Englishman of our day, the points of difference between the Government of the United States, as it
works under the provisions of the Federal Constitution, and the Government of Great Britain as it has
developed itself independently of any express controlling instrument.   In order to bring out a certain
number of these differences clearly, I will first describe the manner in which the American House of
Representatives carries on its legislation, and its
method of regulating that occasional contact between
the Executive authorities and the Legislature, which
is inseparable from free government.   I will then
contrast the system with that which is followed by
the British House of Commons at this moment.   The
difference will be found to be striking, and, to an
Englishman, perhaps disquieting.

The House of Representatives distributes itself,

under its Tenth Rule, into no less than forty Standing Committees, independently of Joint-Committees
of Senators and Representatives. The subjects over
which these Committees have jurisdiction comprise
the whole business of Government, from Financial,
Foreign, and Military Affairs, to the Codification of
the Law and the Expenditure on Public Buildings.
The Eleventh Rule provides that " all proposed legislation shall be referred to the Committees named in
the Tenth Rule." As there are no officials in the
House, all Bills are necessarily introduced by private
members, who draft them as they please. I believe
that, practically, every such Bill is allowed to go to
the appropriate Committee, but that the proportion
of them which are "reported" by the Committees
and come back to the House is extremely small.
Lawyers abound in the House, and the Committee,
in fact, re-draws the Bill. Every measure, therefore,
has its true beginning in the bosom of a strictly
legislative body. How this contrasts with the early
stages of British legislation will be seen presently.
The differences in the mode of contact between the
House and the Executive Departments differ still
more widely in the two countries. This contact is
governed in the United States by the Twenty-fourth
Rule of the House. First of all, if information be
required from the Secretary of State or other
Ministers, a resolution of the House must be ob-

tained. Once a week, under the Rule, and on that occasion only, "resolutions of inquiry directed to the heads of the Executive Departments shall be in order for reference to appropriate Committees, which resolutions shall be reported to the House within one week thereafter." Sometimes, I believe, the Minister attends the Committee ; but, if he pleases, he may answer the resolution by a formal communication addressed to the Speaker of the House. This carefully guarded procedure answers to the undefined and irregular practice of putting and answering questions in our own House of Commons.

The procedure of the American House of Representatives, both in respect of the origination of bills and of the interrogation of Ministers, is that of a political body which considers that its proper functions are not executive, but legislative. The British House of Commons, on the other hand, which the greatest part of the world regards as a legislative assembly (though it never quite answered to that description), has, since 1789, taken under its supervision and control the entire Executive government of Great Britain, and much of the government of her colonies and dependencies. There are no theoretical limits to its claim for official information, not merely concerning general lines of policy, but concerning the minute details of administration. It gives effect to its claim by questions put publicly to Ministers on the Treasury Bench, and, independently of all other results of this practice, the mere time consumed by the multitude of questions and replies is beginning to encroach very seriously on the time available for legislation. A singularly small number of these questions appear to have their origin in the interest which a member of the House of Commons may legitimately feel in foreign and domestic policy. Some, no doubt, spring from innocent curiosity; some from pardonable vanity; but not a few are deliberately intended to work public mischief. It is a minor objection, that the number of questions which are flagrantly argumentative is manifestly increasing.

All legislative proposals which have any serious chance of becoming law, proceed in the United States from Committees of the Senate or of the House of Representatives. Where are we to place the birth of an English legislative measure? He who will give his mind to this question will find it one of the obscurest which ever perplexed the political observer. Some Bills undoubtedly have their origin in the Executive Departments, where the vices of existing laws or systems have been disclosed in the process of actual administration. Others may be said to be conceived in the House of Commons, having for their embryo either the Report of a Committee of the House or of a resolution passed by it which, according to a modern practice, suggested no doubt by the difficulties of legislation, has taken the place of the private member's Bill. But if we may trust the experience of 1883, by far the most important measures, measures fraught with the gravest consequence to the whole future of the nation, have a much more remarkable beginning. One of the great English political parties, and naturally the party supporting the Government in power, holds a Conference of gentlemen, to whom I hope I may without offence apply the American name " wire-pullers," and this Conference dictates to the Government, not only the legislation which it is to submit to the House of Commons, but the order in which it is to be submitted. Here we are introduced to the great modern paradox of the British Constitution. While the House of Commons has assumed the supervision of the whole Executive Government, it has turned over to the Executive Government the most important part of the business of legislation. For it is in the Cabinet that the effective work of legislation begins. The Ministers, hardly recruited from the now very serious fatigues of a Session which lasts all but to the commencement of September, assemble in Cabinet in November, and in the course of a series of meetings, extending over rather more than a fortnight, determine what legislative proposals are to be submitted to Parliament. These proposals, sketched, we may believe, in not more than outline, are then placed in the hands of the Government draftsman ; and, so much is there in all legislation which consists in the manipulation of detail and in the adaptation of vaguely conceived novelties to pre-existing law, that we should not probably go far wrong if we attributed four-fifths of every legislative enactment to the accomplished lawyer who puts into shape the Government Bills.   From the measures which come from his hand, the tale of Bills to be announced in the Queen's Speech is made up, and at this point English legislation enters upon another stage.

The American political parties of course support and oppose particular legislative measures.   They are elated at the success of a particular Bill, and disappointed by its failure.   But no particular consequences beyond disappointment follow the rejection of a Bill.   The Government of the country goes on as before.   In England it is otherwise.   Every Bill introduced into Parliament by the Ministry (and we have seen that all the really important Bills are thus introduced) must be carried through the House of Commons without substantial alteration, or the Ministers will resign, and consequences of the gravest kind may follow in the remotest parts of an empire extending to the ends of the earth.   Thus a Government Bill has to be forced through the House of Commons with the whole strength of party organisation, and in a shape very closely resembling that which the Executive

Government gave to it. It should then in strictness pass through a searching discussion in the House of Lords ; but this stage of English legislation is becoming merely nominal, and the judgment on it of the Crown has long since become a form. It is therefore the Executive Government which should be credited with the authorship of English legislation. We have thus an extraordinary result. The nation whose constitutional practice suggested to Montesquieu his memorable maxim concerning the Executive, Legislative, and Judicial powers, has in the course of a century falsified it. The formal Executive is the true source of legislation ; the formal Legislature is incessantly concerned with Executive Government.

After its first birth, nothing can be more equable and nothing can be more plain to observation than the course of an American legislative measure. A Bill, both in the House of Representatives and the Senate, goes through an identical number of stages of about equal length. When it has passed both Houses, it must still commend itself to the President of the United States, who has a veto on it which, though qualified, is constantly used, and is very difficult to overcome. An English Bill begins in petty rivulets or stagnant pools. Then it runs underground for most of its course, withdrawn from the eye by the secrecy of the Cabinet. Emerging into the House of Commons, it can no more escape from its embankments than the water of a canal ; but once dismissed from that House, it overcomes all remaining obstacles with the rush of a cataract, and mixes with the trackless ocean of British institutions.

The very grave dangers entailed on our country by this eccentric method of legislation arise from its being followed, not only in the enactment of ordinary laws, but in the amendment of what, if it be still permitted to us to employ the word, is called the British Constitution. "En Angleterre," writes De Tocqueville, "la Constitution peut changer sans cesse ; *ou plutôt elle n'existe pas.*" There are doubtless strong Conservative forces still surviving in England ; they survive because, though our political institutions have been transformed, the social conditions out of which they originally grew are not extinct. But of all the infirmities of our Constitution in its decay, there is none more serious than the absence of any special precautions to be observed in passing laws which touch the very foundations of our political system. The nature of this weakness, and the character of the manifold and elaborate securities which are contrasted with it in America, may be well illustrated by considering two famous measures—the Reform of the London Corporation, which is still unaccomplished, and the County Franchise Bill, now become law. The reconstruction of the London Municipality, though a very difficult undertaking, would belong in America to the

ordinary State Legislatures. The Legislature of New
York State has, in fact, several times attempted to re-
model the municipality of New York City, which has
repeatedly shown itself to be corrupt, unmanageable,
and inefficient ; and these attempts call for no special
remark, except that they have hitherto met with only
the most moderate success. But a measure distantly
resembling the English County Franchise Bill would
be, both from the point of view of the several States
and from the point of view of the United States, a
Constitutional amendment. In the least considerable,
the least advanced, and the most remote American
State, its enactment would have to be coupled with
the carefully devised precautionary formalities which
I described in the latter part of the Second Essay. If
an American County Franchise Bill were proposed to
be enforced by Federal authority, the designed difficulty of carrying it would be vastly greater. As a
rule, the Federal Constitution does not interfere with
the franchise ; it leaves the right of voting to be regulated by the several States, gradually and locally,
according to the varying circumstances of each, and
the political views prevailing in it. But the rule has
now been departed from in the new Article, securing
the suffrage to the negroes ; and there is no question
that, if a measure were contemplated in America,
bearing to the entirety of American institutions the
same relation which the County Franchise Bill bore

R

to the entirety of ours—nay, even if a simple change
in the franchise had to be introduced into all the
States, or into the bulk of them, simultaneously—the
object could only be effected by an amendment of the
Constitution of the United States. It would therefore
have to be dealt with under the Fifth Article of the
Constitution. This article, which is the keystone of
the whole Federal fabric, runs as follows :—

> The Congress, whenever two-thirds of both Houses shall
> deem it necessary, shall propose Amendments to this Con-
> stitution; or, on the application of the Legislatures of two-
> thirds of the several States, shall call a Convention for
> proposing Amendments which, in either case, shall be valid
> to all intents and purposes as part of this Constitution, when
> ratified by the Legislatures of three-fourths of the several
> States or by Conventions in three-fourths thereof, as one or
> the other mode of ratification may be proposed by the
> Congress.

The mode, therefore, of proceeding with a measure
requiring an amendment of the Constitution would be
this. First of all, the Senate of the United States and
the House of Representatives must resolve, by a two-
thirds majority of each Chamber, that the proposed
amendment is desirable. The amendment has then
to be ratified by the Legislatures of three-fourths of
the several States. Now, there are at the present moment thirty-eight States in the American Union. The
number of Legislatures which must join in the ratifi-

cation is therefore twenty-nine. I believe, however, that there is no State in which the Legislature does not consist of two Houses, and we arrive, therefore, at the surprising result that, before a constitutional measure of the gravity of the English County Franchise Bill could become law in the United States, it must have at the very least in its favour the concurring vote of no less than fifty-eight separate legislative chambers, independently of the Federal Legislature, in which a double two-thirds majority must be obtained. The alternative course permitted by the Constitution, of calling separate special Conventions of the United States and of the several States, would prove probably in practice even lengthier and more complicated.

The great strength of these securities against hasty innovation has been shown beyond the possibility of mistake by the actual history of the Federal Constitution. On March 4, 1789, the day fixed for commencing the operation of the new Federal Government, the Constitution had been ratified by all the States then established, except three. One of the first acts of the new Congress was to propose to the States, on September 25, 1789, a certain number of amendments on comparatively unimportant points, which had no doubt been suggested by the discussions on the draft-Constitution, and the several States ratified these amendments in the course of the following year. An amendment of more importance, relating to the power of the Supreme Court, was declared to have been ratified on September 5, 1794 ; and another, remedying a singular inconvenience which had disclosed itself in the original rule regulating the election of the President and of the Vice-President, had its ratification completed in September 1804. After these early amendments, which were comparatively easy of adoption through the small number of the original States, there was no change in the Federal Constitution for sixty years. The Thirteenth, Fourteenth, and Fifteenth Amendments, which became part of the Constitution in the period between the beginning of 1865 and the beginning of 1870, were the fruits of the conquest of the South by the North. They abolish slavery, provide against its revival, forbid the abridgment of the right to vote on the ground of race or colour, impose penalties on the vanquished adherents of the seceding States, and incidentally give a constitutional guarantee to the Public Debt of the Federation. But they could not have been either proposed or ratified, if the South had not lain under the heel of the North. The military forces of the United States controlled the Executive Governments of the Southern States, and virtually no class of the population, except the negroes, was represented in the Southern Legislatures. The War of Secession, which was itself a war of Revolution, was in fact succeeded by a Revolutionary period of several

years,[9] during which not only the institutions of the
Southern States, but the greater part of the Federal
institutions were more or less violently distorted to
objects not contemplated by the framers of the Constitution. But the form of the Federal institutions was
always preserved, and they gradually recovered their
reality, until at the present moment the working of the
Constitution of the United States does not, save for the
disappearance of negro slavery, differ from the mode of
its operation before the civil convulsion of 1861–65.

The powers and disabilities attached to the
United States and to the several States by the Federal
Constitution, and placed under the protection of the
deliberately contrived securities we have described,
have determined the whole course of American history. That history began, as all its records abun-
dantly show, in a condition of society produced by
war and revolution, which might have condemned
the great Northern Republic to a fate not unlike that
of her disorderly sisters in South America. But the
provisions of the Constitution have acted on her like
those dams and dykes which strike the eye of the
traveller along the Rhine, controlling the course of a
mighty river which begins amid mountain torrents,
and turning it into one of the most equable water-

---

[9] A striking account of the perversion of the Constitution
during this revolutionary interval, now brought to a close, may
be found in the work of Mr. Louis J. Jennings, *Republican
Government in the United States*.

ways in the world. The English Constitution, on the other hand, like the great river of England, may perhaps seem to the observer to be now-a-days always more or less in flood, owing to the crumbling of the banks and the water poured into it from millions of drain-pipes. The observation is, however, worth making, that the provisions of the Constitution of the United States which have most influenced the destinies of the American people are not always those which the superficial student of it would first notice. Attention is easily attracted by Article IV. section 4, which makes the United States guarantee to every State in the Union a Republican form of government, and, on the other hand, protection against domestic violence; and again, by sections 9 and 10 of Article I., which prohibit the United States and the several States from granting titles of Nobility. No man can mistake the importance of the portions of the First Article which forbid the several States to enter into any treaty, alliance, or confederation, to make anything but gold or silver coin a tender in payment of debts, and (without the consent of Congress) to keep troops or ships of war in time of peace. But a hasty reader might under-estimate the practical effects of the provisions in Article I. which empower the United States "to promote the progress of science and the useful arts, by securing for limited times to authors and inventors the exclusive right to their respective writings and discoveries;" and, again, of the parts of the same Article which prohibit the United States and the several States from laying any tax or duty on articles exported from any State; and, lastly, of the remarkable provision which forbids a State to pass any law impairing the obligation of contracts. The power to grant patents by Federal authority has, however, made the American people the first in the world for the number and ingenuity of the inventions by which it has promoted the "useful arts"; while, on the other hand, the neglect to exercise this power for the advantage of foreign writers has condemned the whole American community to a literary servitude unparalleled in the history of thought. The prohibition against levying duties on commodities passing from State to State is again the secret both of American Free-trade and of American Protection. It secures to the producer the command of a free market over an enormous territory of vast natural wealth, and thus it secondarily reconciles the American people to a tariff on foreign importations as oppressive as ever a nation has submitted to. I have seen the rule which denies to the several States the power to make any laws impairing the obligation of contracts criticised as if it were a mere politico-economical flourish; but in point of fact there is no more important provision in the whole Constitution. Its principle was much extended by a decision of the Supreme Court,[10] which ought now to interest a large number of Englishmen, since it is the basis of the credit of many of the great American Railway Incorporations. But it is this prohibition which has in reality secured full play to the economical forces by which the achievement of cultivating the soil of the North American Continent has been performed ; it is the bulwark of American individualism against democratic impatience and Socialistic fantasy. We may usefully bear in mind that, until this prohibition, as interpreted by the Federal Courts, is got rid of, certain communistic schemes of American origin, which are said to have become attractive to the English labouring classes because they are supposed to proceed from the bosom of a democratic community, have about as much prospect of obtaining practical realisation in the United States as the vision of a Cloud-Cuckoo-borough to be built by the birds between earth and sky.

It was not to be expected that all the hopes of the founders of the American Constitution would be fulfilled. They do not seem to have been prepared for the rapid development of party, chiefly under the influence of Thomas Jefferson, nor for the thorough organisation with which the American parties before long provided themselves. They may have expected

[10] In *Dartmouth College* v. *Woodward*, a case argued by Daniel Webster in 1818.

the House of Representatives, which is directly elected by the people, to fall under the dominion of faction, but the failure of their mechanism for the choice of a President was a serious disappointment. I need hardly say that the body intended to be a true Electoral College has come to consist of mere deputies of the two great contending parties, and that a Presidential Elector has no more active part in choosing a President than has a balloting paper. The miscarriage has told upon the qualities of American Presidents. An Electoral College may commit a blunder, but a candidate for the Presidency, nominated for election by the whole people, will, as a rule, be a man selected because he is not open to obvious criticism, and will therefore in all probability be a mediocrity. But, although the President of the United States has not been all which Washington and Hamilton, Madison and Jay, intended him to be, nothing has occurred in America to be compared with the distortion which the Presidency has suffered at the hands of its copyists on the European Continent. It is probable that no foreigner but an Englishman can fully understand the Constitution of the United States, though even an Englishman is apt to assume it to have been much more of a new political departure than it really was, and to forget to compare it with the English institutions of a century since. But, while it has made the deepest possible impression on

Continental European opinion, it has been hardly ever comprehended. Its imitators have sometimes made the historical mistake of confounding the later work-ing of some of its parts with that originally intended by its founders. And sometimes they have fallen into the practical error of attempting to combine its characteristics with some of the modern character-istics of the British Constitution. The President of the Second French Republic was directly elected by the French people in conformity with the modern practice of the Americans, and the result was that, confident in the personal authority witnessed to by the number of his supporters, he overthrew the Re-public and established a military despotism. The President of the Third French Republic is elected in a different and a safer way ; but the Ministers whom he appoints have seats in the French Legisla-ture, mix in its debates, and are responsible to the Lower House, just as are the members of an English Cabinet. The effect is, that there is no living func-tionary who occupies a more pitiable position than a French President. The old Kings of France reigned and governed. The Constitutional King, according to M. Thiers, reigns, but does not govern. The Pre-sident of the United States governs, but he does not reign. It has been reserved for the President of the French Republic neither to reign nor yet to govern.

The Senate has proved a most successful institution except in one particular. Congress includes many honourable as well as very many able men, but it would be affectation to claim for the American Federal Legislature as a whole that its hands are quite clean. It is unnecessary to appeal on this point to satire or fiction; the truth is, that too many Englishmen have been of late years concerned with Congressional business for there to be any want of evidence that much money is spent in forwarding it which is not legitimately expended. One provision of the Constitution has here defeated another. One portion of the 6th section of the First Article provides securities against corruption on the part of Senators and Representatives, but the portion immediately preceding provides that " Senators and Representatives shall have a compensation for their services, to be ascertained by law and paid out of the Treasury of the United States." This system of payment for legislative services, which prevails throughout the whole of the Union, has produced a class of professional politicians, whose probity in some cases has proved unequal to the strain put upon it by the power of dealing with the public money and the public possessions of what will soon be the wealthiest community in the world. It is a point of marked inferiority to the British political system, even in its decline.

It may be thought that a great American institu-

tion failed on one occasion conspicuously and disastrously.   The Supreme Court of the United States
did not succeed in preventing by its mediation the
War of Secession.   But the inference is not just.
The framers of the Constitution of the United States,
like succeeding generations of American statesmen,
deliberately thrust the subject of Slavery as far as
they could out of their own sight.   It barely dis-
closes itself in the method of counting population
for the purpose of fixing the electoral basis of the
House of Representatives, and in the subsequently
famous provision of the Fourth Article, that persons
"bound to service or labour in one State" shall be
delivered up if they escape into another.   But, on
the whole, the makers of the Constitution pass by on
the other side.   They have not the courage of their
opinions, whatever they were.   They neither guarantee Slavery on the one hand, nor attempt to regulate
it on the other, or to provide for its gradual extinction.   When then, about seventy years afterwards,
the Supreme Court was asked to decide whether the
owner of slaves taking them into one of the territories of the Union, not yet organised as a State,
retained his right of ownership, it had not in reality
sufficient materials for a decision.   The grounds of
its judgment in the *Dred Scott* case may have been
perhaps satisfactory to lawyers, but in themselves
they satisfied nobody else.   It is extremely signifi-

cant that, in the one instance in which the authors of the Constitution declined of set purpose to apply their political wisdom to a subject which they knew to be all-important, the result was the bloodiest and costliest war of modern times.

Let me repeat the points which I trust I have done something towards establishing. The Constitution of the United States is a modified version of the British Constitution ; but the British Constitution which served as its original was that which was in existence between 1760 and 1787. The modifications introduced were those, and those only, which were suggested by the new circumstances of the American Colonies, now become independent. These circumstances excluded an hereditary king, and virtually excluded an hereditary nobility. When the American Constitution was framed, there was no such sacredness to be expected for it as before 1789 was supposed to attach to all parts of the British Constitution. There was every prospect of political mobility, if not of political disorder. The signal success of the Constitution of the United States in stemming these tendencies is, no doubt, owing in part to the great portion of the British institutions which were preserved in it ; but it is also attributable to the sagacity with which the American statesmen filled up the interstices left by the inapplicability of certain of the then existing British institutions to the emancipated colonies. This sagacity stands out in every part of the "Federalist," and it may be tracked in every page of subsequent American history. It may weil fill the Englishmen who now live *in fæce Romuli* with wonder and envy.

INDEX.

S

260

INDEX.

POPULATION

14, 20, 52 ; adopted in France, 14 ; in Spain, 15 ; in Germany, 17 ; experience of, in Europe, 18 ; armies of, 22 ; overturned by armies and mobs, 23 ; danger to, from Irreconcileables, 25 ; power of wire-pullers, 30 ; danger of subdivision of power, 30 ; inherent infirmities of, 41, 43, 87 ; stability and weakness of, 52 ; in Roman State, 80 ; originally identical with popular justice, 89 ; not necessarily legislative, 135 ; attractions of, 147 ; Rousseau's theories, 156 ; prospects of, in United States, 197 ; its extension in the West, 228 ; parent of inequality of fortune, 228

Population, theory of, 37 ; unpopularity of, in France and America, 37 ; in United States, Russia, &c., 196

President, the, of United States, 211 ; duration of office, 214 ; mode of election, 215, 244, 249 ; executive powers, 232 ; likely to be a mediocrity, 249

Privilege, opposed to democracy, 66 ; privileged classes, 4 ; their prejudices, 69 ; of House of Lords, 187

Progress, an undefined term, 131 ; ideas of, 145, 169 ; a "continued production of new ideas," 191

Property regarded as theft, 75 ; outcry against, 187

RACE and language, theories of, 27 Radicalism in Europe, 21, 160 ; associated with universal suffrage, 35 ; of Bentham and his pupils, 56, 82, 84, 152 ; subserviency to mobs, 77

"Referendum," the, of Swiss Government, 41, 67, 96

Reform, chiefly carried out by monarchies, 65, 214 ; not by democracies, 67 ; history of, 128 ; detested by large masses of mankind, 132 ; associated with religious emotion, 135 ; consequences of, in England, 148 ; dangers attending, 149, 171 ; "cause of, lost at Waterloo," 164 ; of laws (see Bentham); G. Washington as a reformer, 215

Reformation, propelling force of, 130

ROMAN

Religion, lack of, in France, 1 ; in England, 11 ; tenacity of, in ancient states, 66 ; affinity to party, 100 ; history of, 129

Renan, E., 42 n ; on French democratic society, 189

Representation, Government by, 92, 93 ; Rousseau's views, 155, 159 ; Sièyès' views, 161, 184 ; ordinary and extraordinary representative bodies, 161, 198 ; equality of, 186 ; and taxation, 222

Representatives, House of, in America, 211, 230, 249

Republican party, the, in America, 216

Republics, of Europe, 9, 199, 250 ; of America, 12, 18, 198, 201 ; of Rome and Athens, 80 ; universal suffrage in, 33 ; modern, formation of, 59 ; democratic, not reforming, 67 ; false ideas of, 68, 202 ; credit of, sustained by United States, 198 ; definition of, 199 ; most unsuccessful form of Government, 202

Revolution, characteristics of, 127 ; in Fashion, its probable effects, 142 ; in ideas more prevalent in the East than the West, 146

— French, blindness of privileged classes, 1 ; causes of, 2 ; influence on Popular Government, 12, 127, 200 ; detestation of, in England, 13, 103 ; its results, 66 ; suspicions of democracy, 71 ; discredited by its own crimes, 71, 200 ; oratory and literature of, 74 ; hindrance to progress, 82 ; influence on England, 103, 128 ; influenced by Sièyès' pamphlet, 160 ; compared with the English of 1688 by Macaulay, 172

— of 1830, 72, 128
— of 1848, 40

Ricardo, theories of political economy, 146

Riego, General, military insurrection of, 15

Rights, Natural, Rousseau's theory, 152, 163, 166

Roebuck, Mr., referred to, 165

Roman Catholic Church, a school of equality, 20

Roman Empire, cause of destruction of wealth in, 48 ; an example, 65

PRINTED BY

SPOTTISWOODE AND CO., NEW-STREET SQUARE

LONDON

ALBEMARLE STREET, LONDON,
July, 1892.

MR. MURRAY'S
GENERAL LIST OF WORKS.

ALBERT MEMORIAL. A Descriptive and Illustrated Account of the National Monument at Kensington. Illustrated by numerous Engravings. By DOYNE C. BELL. With 24 Plates. Folio. 12*l.*12*s.*
———— HANDBOOK. 16mo. 1*s.*; Illustrated, 2*s.* 6*d.*

ABBOTT (REV. J.). Memoirs of a Church of England Missionary in the North American Colonies. Post 8vo. 2*s.*

ABERCROMBIE (JOHN). Enquiries concerning the Intellectual Powers and the Investigation of Truth. Fcap. 8vo. 3*s.* 6*d.*

ACLAND (REV. C.). Manners and Customs of India. Post 8vo. 2*s.*

ACWORTH (W. M.) The Railways of England. With 56 Illustrations. 8vo. 14*s.*
———— The Railways of Scotland Map. Crown 8vo. 5*s.*
———— The Railways and the Traders. The Railway Rates Question in Theory and Practice. Crown 8vo. 6*s.*, or *Popular Edit.*1*s.*

ÆSOP'S FABLES. A New Version. By REV. THOMAS JAMES. With 100 Woodcuts, by TENNIEL and WOLFE. Post 8vo. 2*s.* 6*d.*

AGRICULTURAL (ROYAL) JOURNAL.

AINGER (A. C.). Latin Grammar. [See ETON.]
———— An English-Latin Gradus, or Verse Dictionary. On a New Plan, with carefully Selected Epithets and Synonyms. Intended to Simplify the Composition of Latin Verses. Crown 8vo. (450 pp.) 9*s.*

ALICE (PRINCESS); GRAND DUCHESS OF HESSE. Letters to H.M. THE QUEEN. With a Memoir bv H.R.H. Princess Christian. Portrait. Crown 8vo. 7*s.* 6*d.*, or Original Edition, 12*s.*

AMBER-WITCH (THE). A most interesting Trial for Witchcraft. Translated by LADY DUFF GORDON. Post 8vo. 2*s.*

AMERICA (THE RAILWAYS OF). Their Construction, Development, Management, and Appliances By Various Writers. With an Introduction by T. M COOLEY. With 200 Illustrations. Large 8vo. 31*s.*6*d.*
———— [See BATES, NADAILLAC, RUMBOLD.]

APOCRYPHA: With a Commentary Explanatory and Critical. By Dr. Salmon, Prof. Fuller, Archdeacon Farrar, Archdeacon Gifford, Canon Rawlinson, Dr. Edersheim, Rev. J. H. Lupton, Rev. C. J. Ball. Edited by HENRY WACE, D.D. 2 vols. Medium 8vo. 50*s.*

ARCHITECTURE: A Profession or an Art. Thirteen short Essays on the qualifications and training of Architects. Edited by R. NORMAN SHAW, R.A., and T. G. JACKSON, A.R.A. 8vo.

ARGYLL (DUKE OF). Unity of Nature. 8vo. 12*s.*
———— Reign of Law. Crown 8vo. 5*s.*
———— Neglected Elements in Economic Science. 8vo.

ARISTOTLE. [See GROTE.]

ARTHUR'S (LITTLE) History of England. By LADY CALLCOTT. New Edition, continued to 1878. With Woodcuts. Fcap. 8vo. 1*s.* 6*d.*
———— History of France, from the Earliest Times to the Fall of the Second Empire. With Woodcuts. Fcp. 8vo 2*s.* 6*d.*

AUSTIN (JOHN). GENERAL JURISPRUDENCE; or, The Philosophy of Positive Law. Edited by ROBERT CAMPBELL. 2 Vols. 8vo. 32*s.*

B

AUSTIN (John'. Student's Edition, compiled from the above
work, by Robert Campbell. Post 8vo. 12s.

———————— Analysis of. By Gordon Campbell. Post 8vo. 6s.

AUSTRALIA. [See Lumholtz.]

BABER (E. C.). Travels in W. China. Maps. Royal 8vo. 5s.

BAINES (Thomas). Greenhouse and Stove Plants, Flower-
ing and Fine Leaved. Palms, Ferns, and Lycopodiums. With full
details of the Propagation and Cultivation. 8vo. 8s. 6d.

BALDWIN BROWN (Prof G.). The Fine Arts. With Illustrations. Crown 8vo. 3s. 6d. (University Extension Series.)

BARKLEY (H. C.). Five Years among the Bulgarians and Turks
between the Danube and the Black Sea. Post 8vo. 10s. 6d.

———————— Bulgaria Before the War. Post 8vo. 10s. 6d.

———————— My Boyhood. Woodcuts. Post 8vo. 6s.

———————— Studies in the Art of Rat-catching. Post 8vo.
3s. 6d.

———————— Ride through Asia Minor and Armenia. With
Sketches of the Character, Manners, and Customs of both the Mussul-
man and Christian Inhabitants. Crown 8vo. 10s. 6d.

BARROW (John). Life of Sir Francis Drake. Post 8vo. 2s.

BATES (H. W.). Records of a Naturalist on the Amazons during
Eleven Years' Adventure and Travel. Illustrations. Post 8vo. 7s. 6d.

BATTLE ABBEY ROLL. [See Cleveland.]

BEACONSFIELD'S (Lord) Letters, and "Correspondence with
his Sister," 1830—1852. Portrait. Crown 8vo. 2s.

BEATRICE, H.R.H. Princess. Adventures in the Life of Count
George Albert of Erbach. A True Story. Translated from the German.
Portraits and Woodcuts. Crown 8vo. 10s. 6d.

BECKETT (Sir Edmund), (Lord Grimthorpe). "Should the
Rev'sed New Testament be Authorised?" Post 8vo. 6s.

BELL (Doyne C.). Notices of the Historic Persons buried in
the Chapel of the Tower of London. Illustrations. Crown 8vo. 14s.

BENJAMIN'S Persia & the Persians. Illustrations. 8vo. 24s.

BENSON (Archbishop). The Cathedral; its necessary place in
the Life and Work of the Church. Post 8vo. 6s.

BERKELEY (Hastings). Wealth and Welfare : Crown 8vo. 6s.

———————— Japanese Letters ; Eastern Impressions of
Western Men and Manners, as contained in the Correspondence of
Tokiwara and Yashiri. Post 8vo 6s.

BERTHELOT ON EXPLOSIVES. [See Cundill.]

BERTRAM (Jas. G.). Harvest of the Sea : an Account of British
Food Fishes, Fisheries and Fisher Folk. Illustrations. Post 8vo. 9s.

BIBLE COMMENTARY. Explanatory and Critical. With
a Revision of the Translation. By Bishops and Clergy of the
Anglican Church. Edited by Canon F. C. Cook, M.A.

THE OLD TESTAMENT. 6 Vols. Medium 8vo. 6l. 15s.

Vol. I. 30s. } Genesis—Deuteronomy.	Vol. IV. 24s. } Job—Song of Solomon.
Vol. II. 20s. } Joshua—Kings.	Vol. V. 20s. Isaiah—Jeremiah.
Vol. III. 18s. } Kings ii.—Esther.	Vol. VI. 25s. } Ezekiel—Malachi.

THE NEW TESTAMENT. 4 Vols. Medium 8vo. 4l. 14s.

Vol. I. 18s. } St. Matthew—St. Luke.	Vol. III. 28s. } Romans—Philemon.
Vol. II. 20s. } St. John —Acts of the Apostles.	Vol. IV. 28s. } Hebrews — Revela-tion.

BIBLE COMMENTARY. The Apocrypha. By Various Writers.
Edited by Henry Wace, D.D. 2 vols. Medium 8vo. 50s.
———————— The Student's Edition. Abridged and Edited
by Rev. J. M. Fuller, M.A. 6 Vols Crown 8vo. 7s. 6d. each.
Old Testament. 4 Vols. New Testament. 2 Vols.
BIRD (Isabella). Hawaiian Archipelago; or Six Months among
the Palm Groves, Coral Reefs, and Volcanoes of the Sandwich Islands.
Illustrations. Crown 8vo. 7s. 6d.
———————— A Lady's Life in the Rocky Mountains. Illustrations.
Post 8vo. 7s. 6d.
———————— The Golden Chersonese and the Way Thither. Illustra-
tions. Post 8vo. 14s.
———————— Unbeaten Tracks in Japan : Including Visits to the
Aborigines of Yezo and the Shrines of Nikko and Isé. Illustra-
tions. Crown 8vo. 7s. 6d.
———————— Journeys in Persia and Kurdistan : with a Summer in the
Upper Karun Region, and a Visit to the Nestorian Rayahs. Maps and
36 Illustrations. 2 vols. Crown 8vo. 24s.
BISHOP (Mrs.). [See Bird (Isabella).]
BLACKIE (C.). Geographical Etymology; or, Dictionary of
Place Names. Third Edition. Crown 8vo. 7s.
BLUNT (Rev. J. J.). Undesigned Coincidences in the Writings of
the Old and New Testaments, an Argument of their Veracity. Post 8vo. 6s.
———————— History of the Christian Church in the First Three
Centuries. Post 8vo. 6s.
———————— The Parish Priest; His Duties, Acquirements, and
Obligations. Post 8vo. 6s.
BOOK OF COMMON PRAYER. Illustrated with Coloured
Borders. Initial Letters, and Woodcuts 8vo. 18s.
BORROW (George). The Bible in Spain ; or, the Journeys and
Imprisonments of an Englishman in an attempt to circulate the
Scriptures in the Peninsula. Portrait. Post 8vo. 2s. 6d.
———————— The Zincali. An Account of the Gipsies of Spain ;
Their Manners, Customs, Religion, and Language. 2s. 6d.
———————— Lavengro; Scholar—Gypsy—and Priest. 2s. 6d.
———————— Romany Rye. A Sequel to Lavengro. Post 8vo. 2s. 6d.
———————— Wild Wales : its People, Language, and Scenery.
Post 8vo. 2s. 6d.
———————— Romano Lavo-Lil. With Illustrations of the English
Gypsies; their Poetry and Habitations. Post 8vo. 5s.
BOSWELL'S Life of Samuel Johnson, LL.D. Including the
Tour to the Hebrides. Edited by Mr. Croker. Seventh Edition.
Portraits. 1 vol. Medium 8vo. 12s.
BOWEN (Lord Justice). Virgil in English Verse, Eclogues and
Æneid, Books I.—VI. Map and Frontispiece. 8vo. 12s
BRADLEY (Dean). Arthur Penrhyn Stanley ; Biographical
Lectures. Crown 8vo. 3s. 6d.
BREWER (Rev. J. S.). The Reign of Henry VIII.; from his
Accession till the Death of Wolsey. Illustrated from Original Docu-
ments. Edited by James Gairdner. With Portrait. 2 vols. 8vo. 30s.
———————— The Endowments and Establishment of the Church of
England. Edited by L. T. Dibdin, M.A. Post 8vo. 6s.
BRIDGES (Mrs. F. D.). A Lady's Travels in Japan, Thibet,
Yarkand, Kashmir, Java, the Straits of Malacca, Vancouver's Island, &c.
With Map and Illustrations from Sketches by the Author. Crown 8vo. 15s

BRITISH ASSOCIATION REPORTS. 8vo.

*** The Reports for the years 1831 to 1875 may be obtained at the Offices of the British Association.

Glasgow, 1876, 25s.	Southampton, 1882, 24s.	Bath, 1888, 24s.
Plymouth, 1877, 24s.	Southport, 1883, 24s.	Newcastle-upon-Tyne,
Dublin, 1878, 24s.	Canada, 1884, 24s.	1-89, 24s.
Sheffield, 1879, 24s.	Aberdeen, 1885, 24s.	Leeds, 1890, 74s.
Swansea, 1880, 24s.	Birmingham, 1886, 24s.	Cardiff, 1891, 24s.
York, 1881, 24s.	Manchester, 1887, 24s.	

BROADFOOT (Major W., R.E.) Services in Afghanistan, the Punjab, and on the N. W. Frontier of India. Compiled from his papers and those of Lords Ellenborough and Hardinge. Maps. 8vo. 15s.

BROCKLEHURST (T. U.). Mexico To-day: A Country with a Great Future. With a Glance at the Prehistoric Remains and Antiquities of the Montezumas. Plates and Woodcuts. Medium 8vo. 21s.

BRUCE (Hon. W. N.). Life of Sir Charles Napier. [See NAPIER.]

BRUGSCH (Professor). A History of Egypt under the Pharaohs. Derived entirely from Monuments. A New and thoroughly Revised Edition. Edited by M. BRODRICK. Maps. 1 Vol. 8vo. 18s.

BULGARIA. [See BARKLEY, HUHN, MINCHIN.]

BUNBURY (Sir E. H.). A History of Ancient Geography, among the Greeks and Romans, from the Earliest Ages till the Fall of the Roman Empire. Maps 2 Vols. 8vo, 21s.

BURBIDGE (F. W.). The Gardens of the Sun: or A Naturalist's Journal in Borneo and the Sulu Archipelago. Illustrations. Cr. 8vo. 14s.

BURCKHARDT'S Cicerone; or Art Guide to Painting in Italy. New Edition, revised by J. A. CROWE. Post 8vo. 6s.

BURGES (Sir JAMES BLAND, Bart.) Selections from his Letters and Papers, as Under-Secretary of State for Foreign Affairs. With Notices of his Life. Edited by JAMES HUTTON. 8vo. 15s.

BURGON (Dean). A Biography. Illustrated by Extracts from his Letters and Early Journals. By E. MEYRICK GOULBURN, D.D. Portraits. 2 Vols. 8vo. 24s.

———— The Revision Revised : (1.) The New Greek Text; (2.) The New English Version; (3.) Westcott and Hort's Textual Theory. Second Edition. 8vo. 14s.

———— Lives of Twelve Good Men. Martin J. Routh, H. J. Rose, Chas. Marriott, Edward Hawkins, Saml. Wilberforce, R. L. Cotton, Richard Gresswell, H. O. Coxe, H. L. Mansel, Wm. Jacobson, C. P. Eden, C. L. Higgins. New Edition. With Portraits. 1 Vol. 8vo. 16s.

BURN (Col.). Dictionary of Naval and Military Technical Terms, English and French—French and English. Crown 8vo. 15s.

BUTTMANN'S LEXILOGUS; a Critical Examination of the Meaning of numerous Greek Words, chiefly in Homer and Hesiod. By Rev. J. R. FISHLAKE. 8vo. 12s.

BUXTON (Charles). Memoirs of Sir Thomas Fowell Buxton, Bart. Portrait. 8vo. 16s. *Popular Edition.* Fcap. 8vo. 5s.

———— Notes of Thought. With a Biographical Notice. *Second Edition.* Post 8vo. 5s.

———— (Sydney C.). A Handbook to the Political Questions of the Day; with the Arguments on Either Side. Eighth Edition. 8vo. 10s. 6d.

———— Finance and Politics, an Historical Study. 1783–1885. 2 Vols. 26s.

———— Handbook to the Death Duties. Post 8vo. 3s. 6d.

BYRON'S (Lord) LIFE AND WORKS :—
LIFE, LETTERS, AND JOURNALS. By THOMAS MOORE. One
Volume, Portraits. Royal 8vo. 7s. 6d.
LIFE AND POETICAL WORKS. *Popular Edition.* Portraits.
2 Vols. Royal 8vo. 15s.
POETICAL WORKS. *Library Edition.* Portrait. 6 Vols. 8vo. 45s.
POETICAL WORKS. *Cabinet Edition.* Plates. 10 Vols. 12mo. 30s.
POETICAL WORKS. *Pocket Ed.* 8 Vols. 16mo. In a case. 21s.
POETICAL WORKS. *Popular Edition.* Plates. Royal 8vo. 7s. 6d.
POETICAL WORKS. *Pearl Edition.* Crown 8vo. 2s. 6d. Cloth.
3s. 6d.
CHILDE HAROLD. With 80 Engravings. Crown 8vo. 12s.
CHILDE HAROLD. 16mo. 2s. 6d.
CHILDE HAROLD. Vignettes. 16mo. 1s.
CHILDE HAROLD. Portrait. 16mo. 6d.
TALES AND POEMS. 16mo. 2s. 6d.
MISCELLANEOUS. 2 Vols. 16mo. 5s.
DRAMAS AND PLAYS. 2 Vols. 16mo. 5s.
DON JUAN AND BEPPO. 2 Vols. 16mo. 5s.

CAILLARD (E. M.). Electricity; The Science of the 19th
Century. A Sketch for General Readers. With Illustrations. Crown
8vo. 7s. 6d.
———— The Invisible Powers of Nature. Some
Elementary Lessons in Physical Science for Beginners. Post 8vo. 6s.

CALDECOTT (ALFRED). English Colonization and Empire.
Coloured Maps and Plans. Crown 8vo. 3s. 6d. (Univ. Extension Series.)

CAMPBELL (LORD). Autobiography, Journals and Correspon-
dence. By Mrs. Hardcastle. Portrait. 2 Vols. 8vo. 30s.
———— Lord Chancellors and Keepers of the Great
Seal of England. From the Earliest Times to the Death of Lord Eldon
in 1838. 10 Vols. Crown 8vo. 6s. each.
———— Chief Justices of England. From the Norman
Conquest to the Death of Lord Tenterden. 4 Vols. Crown 8vo. 6s. each.
———— (THOS.) Essay on English Poetry. With Short
Lives of the British Poets. Post 8vo. 3s. 6d.

CAREY (Life of). [See GEORGE SMITH.]

CARLISLE (BISHOP OF). Walks in the Regions of Science and
Faith—a Series of Essays. Crown 8vo. 7s. 6d.
———— The Foundations of the Creed. Being a Discussion
of the Grounds upon which the Articles of the Apostles' Creed may be
held by Earnest and Thoughtful Minds in the 19th Century. 8vo. 14s.

CARNARVON (LORD). Portugal, Gallicia, and the Basque
Provinces. Post 8vo. 3s. 6d.

CAVALCASELLE'S WORKS. [See CROWE.]

CESNOLA (GEN.). Cyprus; its Ancient Cities, Tombs, and Tem-
ples. With 400 Illustrations. Medium 8vo. 50s.

CHAMBERS (G. F.). A Practical and Conversational Pocket
Dictionary of the English, French, and German Languages. Designed
for Travellers and Students generally. Small 8vo. 6s.

CHILD-CHAPLIN (Dr.). Benedicite; or, Song of the Three Children;
being Illustrations of the Power, Beneficence, and Design manifested
by the Creator in his Works. Post 8vo. 6s.

CHISHOLM (Mrs.). Perils of the Polar Seas; True Stories of
Arctic Discovery and Adventure. Illustrations. Post 8vo. 6s.

CHURTON (Archdeacon). Poetical Remains. Post 8vo. 7s. 6d.

CLARKE (Major G. Sydenham), Royal Engineers. Fortification;
Its Past Achievemer ts, Recent Development, and Future Progress.
With Illustrations. Medium 8vo. 21s.

CLASSIC PREACHERS OF THE ENGLISH CHURCH.
Lectures delivered at St. James'. 2 Vols. Post 8vo. 7s. 6d. each.

CLEVELAND (Duchess of). The Battle Abbey Roll. With
some account of the Norman Lineages. 3 Vols. 8m. 4to. 48s.

CLIVE'S (Lord) Life. By Rev. G. R. Gleig. Post 8vo. 3s. 6d.

CLODE (C. M.). Military Forces of the Crown; their Administration and Government. 2 Vols. 8vo. 21s. each.

———— Administration of Justice under Military and Martial
Law, as applicable to the Army, Navy, and Auxiliary Forces. 8vo. 12s

COLEBROOKE (Sir Edward, Bart.). Life of the Hon. Mount-
stuart Elphinstone. With Portrait and Plans. 2 Vols. 8vo. 26s.

COLERIDGE (Samuel Taylor), and the English Romantic School.
By Prof. Brandl. With Portrait, Crown 8vo. 12s.

———————— Table-Talk. Portrait. 12mo. 3s. 6d.

COLES (John). Summer Travelling in Iceland. With a Chapter
on Askja. By E. D. Morgan. Map and Illustrations. 18s.

COLLINS (J. Churton). Bolingbroke: an Historical Study.
With au Essay on Voltaire in England. Crown 8vo. 7s. 6d.

COLONIAL LIBRARY. [See Home and Colonial Library.]

COOK (Canon F. C.). The Revised Version of the Three First
Gospels, considered in its Bearings upon the Record of Our Lord's
Words and Incidents in His Life. 8vo. 9s.

———————— The Origins of Language and Religion. 8vo. 15s.

COOKE (E. W.). Leaves from my Sketch-Book. With Descriptive Text 50 Plates. 2 Vols. Small folio. 31s. 6d. each.

———— (W. H.). History and Antiquities of the County of
Hereford. Vol. III. In continuation of Duncumb's History. 4to.
£2 12s. 6d.

———— Additions to Duncumb's History. Vol. II. 4to. 15s.

———— The Hundred of Grimsworth. Parts I. and II. 4to.
17s. 6d. each.

COOKERY (Modern Domestic). Adapted for Private Families.
By a Lady. Woodcuts Fcap. 8vo. 5s.

COOLEY (Thomas M.). [See America, Railways of.]

CORNEY GRAIN. By Himself. Post 8vo. 1s.

COURTHOPE (W. J.). The Liberal Movement in English
Literature. A Series of Essays. Post 8vo. 6s.

———————— Life and Works of Alexander Pope. With Portraits. 10 Vols. 8vo. 10s. 6d. each.

CRABBE (Rev. G.). Life & Works. Illustrations. Royal 8vo. 7s.

CRAIK (Henry). Life of Jonathan Swift. Portrait. 8vo. 18s.

CRIPPS (Wilfred). Old English Plate: Ecclesiastical, Decorative,
and Domestic, its Makers and Marks. New Edition. With Illustrations and 2010 facsimile Plate Marks. Medium 8vo. 21s.
. Tables of the Date Letters and Marks sold separately. 5s.

CROKER (Rt. Hon. J. W.). Correspondence and Journals, relating to the Political and Social Events of the first half of the present
Century. Edited by Louis J. Jennings, M.P. Portrait. 3 Vols.
8vo. 45s.

———————————————— Progressive Geography for Children.
18mo. 1s. 6d.

CROKER (Rt. Hon.J.W.). Boswell's Life of Johnson. [See Boswell.]
———— Historical Essay on the Guillotine. Fcap. 8vo. 1s.
CROWE and CAVALCASELLE. Lives of the Early Flemish
Painters. Woodcuts. Post 8vo, 7s. 6d.; or Large Paper 8vo, 15s.
———— Life and Times of Titian, with some Account of his
Family. Illustrations. 2 Vols. 8vo. 21s.
———— Raphael; His Life and Works. 2 Vols. 8vo. 33s.
CUMMING (R. Gordon). Five Years of a Hunter's Life in the
Far Interior of South Africa. Woodcuts. Post 8vo. 6s.
CUNDILL (Colonel J. P.), R.A., and HAKE (C. Napier). Re-
searches on the Power of Explosives. Translated and Condensed from
the French of M. Berthelot. With Illustrations. 8vo.
CUNNINGHAM (Prof.W.), D.D. The Use and Abuse of Money.
Crown 8vo. 2s. (University Extension Series.)
CURRIE (C. L.). An Argument for the Divinity of Jesus Christ.
Translated from the French of the Abbé Em. Bougaud. Post 8vo. 6s.
CURTIUS' (Professor) Student's Greek Grammar, for the Upper
Forms. Edited by Dr. Wm. Smith. Post 8vo. 6s.
————Elucidations of the above Grammar. Translated by
Evelyn Abbot. Post 8vo. 7s. 6d.
———— Smaller Greek Grammar for the Middle and Lower
Forms. Abridged from the larger work. 12mo. 3s. 6d.
———— Accidence of the Greek Language. Extracted from
the above work. 12mo. 2s. 6d.
———— Principles of Greek Etymology. Translated by A. S.
Wilkins and E. B. England. New Edition. 2 Vols. 8vo. 28s.
———— The Greek Verb, its Structure and Development.
Translated by A. S. Wilkins, and E. B. England. 8vo. 12s.
CURZON (Hon. Robert). Visits to the Monasteries of the Levant.
Illustrations. Post 8vo. 7s. 6d.
CUST (General). Warriors of the 17th Century—Civil Wars of
France and England. 2 Vols. 16s. Commanders of Fleets and Armies.
2 Vols. 18s.
———— Annals of the Wars—18th & 19th Century.
With Maps. 9 Vols. Post 8vo. 6s. each.
DAVY (Sir Humphry). Consolations in Travel; er, Last Days
of a Philosopher. Woodcuts. Fcap. 8vo. 3s. 6d.
———— Salmonia; or, Days of Fly Fishing. Woodcuts.
Fcap. 8vo. 3s. 6d.
DE COSSON (Major E. A.). The Cradle of the Blue Nile; a
Journey through Abyssinia and Soudan. Map and Illustrations.
2 Vols. Post 8vo. 21s.
———— Days and Nights of Service with Sir Gerald Graham's
Field Force at Suakim. Plan and Illustrations. Crown 8vo. 14s.
DENNIS (George). The Cities and Cemeteries of Etruria.
20 Plans and 200 Illustrations. 2 Vols. Medium 8vo. 21s.
———— (Robert). Industrial Ireland. Suggestions for a Prac-
tical Policy of "Ireland for the Irish." Crown 8vo. 6s.
DARWIN'S (Charles) Life and Letters, with an autobiographical
Chapter. Edited by his Son, Francis Darwin, F.R.S. Portraits.
3 Vols. 8vo. 36s.
———————— Biography, founded on the above work. By
Francis Darwin. 1 Vol. Crown 8vo.
———————— An Illustrated Edition of the Voyage of a
Naturalist Round the World in H.M.S. Beagle. With Views of Places
Visited and Described. By R. T. Pritchett. 100 Illustrations.
Medium 8vo. 21s.

DARWIN (Charles) *continued.*

JOURNAL OF A NATURALIST DURING A VOYAGE ROUND THE
WORLD. Popular Edition. With Portrait. 3s. 6d.

ORIGIN OF SPECIES BY MEANS OF NATURAL SELECTION. Library
Edition. 2 vols. 12s. ; or popular Edition. 6s.

DESCENT OF MAN, AND SELECTION IN RELATION TO SEX.
Woodcuts. Library Ed. 2 vols. 15s. ; or popular Ed. 7s. 6d.

VARIATION OF ANIMALS AND PLANTS UNDER DOMESTICATION.
Woodcuts. 2 Vols. 15s.

EXPRESSIONS OF THE EMOTIONS IN MAN AND ANIMALS. With
Illustrations. 12s.

VARIOUS CONTRIVANCES BY WHICH ORCHIDS ARE FERTILIZED
BY INSECTS. Woodcuts. 7s. 6d.

MOVEMENTS AND HABITS OF CLIMBING PLANTS. Woodcuts. 6s.

INSECTIVOROUS PLANTS. Woodcuts. 9s.

CROSS AND SELF-FERTILIZATION IN THE VEGETABLE KINGDOM. 9s.

DIFFERENT FORMS OF FLOWERS ON PLANTS OF THE SAME
SPECIES. 7s. 6d.

POWER OF MOVEMENT IN PLANTS. Woodcuts.

THE FORMATION OF VEGETABLE MOULD THROUGH THE ACTION OF
WORMS. Illustrations. Post 8vo. 6s.

FACTS AND ARGUMENTS FOR DARWIN. By FRITZ MULLER.
Woodcuts. Post 8vo. 6s.

DERBY (EARL OF). Iliad of Homer rendered into English
Blank Verse. With Portrait. 2 Vols. Post 8vo. 10s.

DERRY (BISHOP OF). Witness of the Psalms to Christ and Christianity. Crown 8vo. 9s.

DICEY (PROF. A. V.). England's Case against Home Rule.
Crown 8vo. 7s. 6d.

———— Why England Maintains the Union. A popular rendering
of the above. By C. E. S. Fcap. 8vo. 1s.

DOG-BREAKING. [See HUTCHINSON.]

DÖLLINGER (DR.). Studies in European History, being Acade-
mical Addresses. Translated by MARGARET WARRE. Portrait. 8vo. 14s.

DRAKE'S (SIR FRANCIS) Life, Voyages, and Exploits, by Sea and
Land. By JOHN BARROW. Post 8vo. 2s.

DRINKWATER (JOHN). History of the Siege of Gibraltar,
1779-1783. With a Description of that Garrison. Post 8vo. 2s.

DU CHAILLU (PAUL B.). Land of the Midnight Sun; Illustrations. 2 Vols. 8vo. 36s.

———————— The Viking Age. The Early History, Manners,
and Customs of the Ancestors of the English-speaking Nations. With
1,800 Illustrations. 2 Vols. 8vo. 42s.

———————— Equatorial Africa and Ashango Land. Adven-
tures in the Great Forest of Equatorial Africa, and the Country of the
Dwarfs. Popular Edition. With Illustrations. Post 8vo. 7s. 6d.

DUFFERIN (LORD). Letters from High Latitudes ; a Yacht Voyage to Iceland. Woodcuts. Post 8vo. 7s. 6d.

———————— Speeches in India, 1884—8. 8vo. 9s.

———————— (LADY). Our Viceregal Life in India, 1884—1888.
Portrait. Post 8vo. 7s. 6d.

———————— My Canadian Journal, 1872—78. Extracts from
Home Letters written while Ld. Dufferin was Gov.-Gen. Portraits, Map,
and Illustrations. Crown 8vo. 12s. 100 Large Paper Copies, 1l. 1s. each.

DUNCAN (Col.). English in Spain; or, The Story of the War
of Succession, 1834-1840. 8vo. 16s.

DÜRER (Albert); his Life and Work. By Dr. Thausing.
Edited by F. A. Eaton. Illustrations. 2 Vols. Medium 8vo. 42s.

EARLE (Professor John). The Psalter of 1539 : A Landmark
of English Literature. Comprising the Text, in Black Letter Type.
With Notes. Square 8vo.

EASTLAKE (Sir C.). Contributions to the Literature of the
Fine Arts. With Memoir by Lady Eastlake. 2 Vols. 8vo. 24s.

EDWARDS (W. H.). Voyage up the River Amazon, including a
Visit to Para. Post 8vo. 2s.

ELLESMERE (Lord). Two Sieges of Vienna by the Turks.
Post 8vo. 2s.

ELLIOT (Mrs Minto). The Diary of an Idle Woman in Constan-
tin ple Crown 8vo.

ELLIS (W.). Madagascar Revisited. 8vo. 16s.

———— Memoir. By His Son. Portrait. 8vo. 10s. 6d.

———— (Robinson). Poems and Fragments of Catullus. 16mo. 5s.

ELPHINSTONE (Hon. M.). History of India—the Hindoo and
Mahommedan Periods. Edited by Professor Cowell. Map. 8vo. 18s.

———————— Rise of the British Power in the East. A
Continuation of his History of India in the Hindoo and Mahommedan
Periods. Maps. 8vo. 16s.

———————— Life of. [See Colebrooke.]

———————— (H. W.). Patterns for Ornamental Turning.
Illustrations. Small 4to. 15s.

ELTON (Capt.). Adventures among the Lakes and Mountains
of Eastern and Central Africa. Illustrations. 8vo. 21s.

ELWIN (Rev. Warwick). The Minister of Baptism. A History of
Church Op nion from the time of the Apostles, especially with reference to Heretical and Lay Administration. 8vo. 12s.

ENGLAND. [See Arthur—Brewer—Croker—Hume—Markham
—Smith—and Stanhope.]

ESSAYS ON CATHEDRALS. Edited by Dean Howson. 8vo. 12s.

ETON LATIN GRAMMAR. For use in the Upper Forms.
By F. H. Rawlins, M.A., and W. R. Inge, M.A. Crown 8vo. 6s.

———————— ELEMENTARY LATIN GRAMMAR. For use in
the Lower Forms. Compiled by A. C. Ainger, M.A., and H. G.
Wintle, M.A. Crown 8vo. 3s. 6d.

———————— PREPARATORY ETON GRAMMAR. Abridged
from the above Work. By the same Editors. Crown 8vo. 2s.

———————— FIRST LATIN EXERCISE BOOK, adapted to the
Elementary and Preparatory Grammars. By the same Editors.
Crown 8vo. 2s. 6d.

———————— FOURTH FORM OVID. Selections from Ovid and
Tibullus. With Notes by H. G. Wintle. Post 8vo. 2s. 6d.

ETON HORACE. The Odes, Epodes, and Carmen Sæculare.
With Notes. By F. W. Cornish, M.A. Maps. Crown 8vo. 6s.

———————— EXERCISES IN ALGEBRA, by E. P. Rouse, M.A., and
Arthur Cockshott, M.A. Crown 8vo. 3s.

———————— ARITHMETIC. By Rev. T. Dalton, M.A. Crown 8vo. 3s.

EXPLOSIVES. [See Cundill.]

FERGUSSON (James). History of Architecture in all Countries
from the Earliest Times. A New and thoroughly Revised Edition.
With 1,700 Illustrations. 5 Vols. Medium 8vo
Vols. I. & II. Ancient and Mediæval. Edited by James Spiers.
III. Indian & Eastern. 31s. 6d. IV. Modern. 2 vols. 31s. 6d.

FITZGERALD (Bishop). Lectures on Ecclesiastical History, including the origin and progress of the English Reformation, from Wicliffe to the Great Rebellion. With a Memoir. 2 Vols. 8vo. 21s.

FITZPATRICK (WILLIAM J.). The Correspondence of Daniel O'Connell, the Liberator. With Portrait. 2 Vols. 8vo. 36s.

FLEMING (PROFESSOR). Student's Manual of Moral Philosophy. With Quotations and References. Post 8vo. 7s. 6d.

FLOWER GARDEN. By REV. THOS. JAMES. Fcap. 8vo. 1s.

FORD (ISABELLA O.). Miss Blake of Monkshalton. A Novel. Crown 8vo. 5s.

FORD (RICHARD). Gatherings from Spain. Post 8vo. 3s. 6d.

FORSYTH (WILLIAM). Hortensius; an Historical Essay on the Office and Duties of an Advocate. Illustrations. 8vo. 7s. 6d.

FORTIFICATION. [See CLARKE.]

FRANCE (HISTORY OF). [See ARTHUR—MARKHAM—SMITH— STUDENTS'—TOCQUEVILLE.]

FREAM (W.), LL.D. Elements of Agriculture; a text-book prepared under he authority of the Royal Agricul ural Society of England. With 200 Illustrations. Crown 8vo. 2s. 6d.

FRENCH IN ALGIERS; The Soldier of the Foreign Legion— and the Prisoners of Abd-el-Kadir. Post 8vo. 2s.

FRERE (MARY). Old Deccan Days, or Hindoo Fairy Legends current in Southern India, with Introduction by Sir BARTLE FRERE. With Illustrations. Post 8vo. 5s.

GALTON (F.). Art of Travel; or, Hints on the Shifts and Contrivances available in Wild Countries. Woodcuts. Post 8vo. 7s. 6d.

GAMBIER PARRY (T.). The Ministry of Fine Art to the Happiness of Life Revised Edition, with an Index. 8vo. 14s.

———— (MAJOR). The Combat with Suffering. Fcap. 8vo. 3s. 6d.

GARDNER (PROF. PERCY). New Chapters in Greek History. Historical results of recent excavations in Greece and Asia Minor. With Illustrations. 8vo. 5s.

GEOGRAPHY. [See BUNBURY—CROKER—RAMSAY—RICHARDSON —SMITH—STUDENTS'.]

GEOGRAPHICAL SOCIETY'S JOURNAL. (1846 to 1881.)
SUPPLEMENTARY PAPERS. Royal 8vo.
Vol. I., Part i. Travels and Researches in Western China. By E. COLBORNE BABER. Maps. 5s.
    Part ii.—1. Recent Geography of Central Asia; from Russian Sources. By E. DELMAR MORGAN. 2. Progress of Discovery on the Coasts of New Guinea. By C. B. MARKHAM. Bibliographical Appendix, by E. C. Rye. Maps. 5s.
    Part iii.—1. Report on Part of the Ghilzi Country, &c. By Lieut. J. S. BROADFOOT. 2. Journey from Shiraz to Jashk. By J. R. PREECE. 2s. 6d.
    Part iv.—Geographical Education. By J. S. KELTIE. 2s. 6d.
Vol. II., Part i. — 1. Exploration in S. and S. W. China. By A. R. COLQUHOUN. 2. Bibliography and Cartography of Hispaniola. By H. LING ROTH. 3. Explorations in Zanzibar Dominions by Lieut. C. STEWART SMITH, R.N. 2s. 6d.
    Part ii.—A Bibliography of Algeria, from the Expedition of Charles V. in 1541 to 1857. By Sir R. L. PLAYFAIR. 4s.
    Part iii.—1. On the Measurement of Heights by the Barometer. By JOHN BALL, F.R.S. 2. River Entrances. By HUGH ROBERT MILL. 3. Mr. J.F. Nee ham's Jou ney in South Eastern Tibet. Part iv.—1. The Bibliography of the Barbary States. Part i. By Sir R. L. PLAYFAIR. 2. Hu son's Bay and Strait. By Commodore A. H. MARKHAM, R.N.
Vol. III., Part i.—Journey of Carey and Dalgleish in Chinese Turkestan and Northern Tibet; and Gene al Prejevalsky on the Orography of Northern Tibet.

GEORGE (Ernest). The Mosel ; Twenty Etchings. Imperial
4to. 42s.
———— Loire and South of France; Twenty Etchings. Folio. 42s.
GERMANY (History of). [See Markham.]
GIBBON'S History of the Decline and Fall of the Roman Empire.
Edited with notes by Milman, Guizot, and Dr. Wm. Smith. Maps.
8 Vols. 8vo. 60s. Student's Edition. 7s. 6d. (See Student's.)
GIFFARD (Edward). Deeds of Naval Daring; or, Anecdotes of
the British Navy. Fcap. 8vo. 3s. 6d.
GILBERT (Josiah). Landscape in Art : before the days of Claude
and Salvator. With 150 Illustrations. Medium 8vo. 30s.
GILL (Capt.). The River of Golden Sand. A Journey through
China to Burmah. Edited by E. C. Baber. With Memoir by Col.
Yule, C.B. Portrait, Map, and Illustrations. Post 8vo. 7s. 6d.
———— (Mrs.). Six Months in Ascension. An Unscientific Ac-
count of a Scientific Expedition. Map. Crown 8vo. 9s.
GLADSTONE (W. E.). Rome and the Newest Fashions in
Religion. 8vo. 7s. 6d.
———————— Gleanings of Past Years, 1843-78. 7 Vols. Small
8vo. 2s. 6d. each. I. The Throne, the Prince Consort, the Cabinet and
Constitution. II. Personal and Literary. III. Historical and Specu-
lative. IV. Foreign. V. and VI. Ecclesiastical. VII. Miscellaneous.
———————— Special Aspects of the Irish Question ; A Series of
Reflections in and since 1886. Collected from various Sources and
Reprinted. Crown 8vo. 3s. 6d.
GLEIG (G. R.). Campaigns of the British Army at Washington
and New Orleans. Post 8vo. 2s.
———— Story of the Battle of Waterloo. Post 8vo. 3s. 6d.
———— Narrative of Sale's Brigade in Affghanistan. Post 8vo. 2s.
———— Life of Lord Clive. Post 8vo. 3s. 6d.
———————— Sir Thomas Munro. Post 8vo. 3s. 6d.
GOLDSMITH'S (Oliver) Works. Edited with Notes by Peter
Cunningham. Vignettes. 4 Vols. 8vo. 30s.
GOMM (F.M. Sir Wm.). His Letters and Journals. 1799 to
1815. Edited by F. C. Carr Gomm. With Portrait. 8vo. 12s.
GORDON (Sir Alex.). Sketches of German Life, and Scenes
from the War of Liberation. Post 8vo. 3s. 6d.
———— (Lady Duff). The Amber-Witch. Post 8vo. 2s.
———————— The French in Algiers. Post 8vo. 2s.
GORE (Rev. Charles, Edited by). Lux Mundi. A Series of
Studies in the Religion of the Incarnation. By various Writers.
Popular Edition, Crown 8vo. 6s.
———————— The Bampton Lectures, 1891 ; The Incarna-
tion of the Son of God. 8vo. 7s. 6d.
GOULBURN (Dean). Three Counsels of the Divine Master for
the conduct of the Spiritual Life :—The Commencement ; The
Virtues ; The Conflict. Crown 8vo. 9s.
See also Puroon.
GRAMMARS. [See Curtius — Eton—Hall — Hutton—King
Edward—Leathes—Maetzner—Matthiæ—Smith.]
GREECE (History of). [See Grote—Smith—Students'.]
GRIFFITH (Rev. Charles). A History of Struthfieldsaye.
With Illustrations. 4to. 10s. 6d.

GROTE'S (George) WORKS :—

     History of Greece. From the Earliest Times to the Death of Alexander the Great. *New Edition.* Portrait, Map, and Plans. 10 Vols. Post8vo. 5s. each. (*The Volumes may be had Separately.*)

     Plato, and other Companions of Socrates. 3 Vols. 8vo. 45s.; or, New Edition, Edited by Alex. Bain. 4 Vols. Crown 8vo. 5s. each.

     Aristotle. 8vo. 12s.

     Personal Life. Portrait. 8vo. 12s.

     Minor Works. Portrait. 8vo. 14s.

—— (Mrs.). A Sketch. By Lady Eastlake. Crown 8vo. 6s.

GUILLEMARD (F. H.), M.D. The Voyage of the Marchesa to Kamschatka and New Guinea. With Notices of Formosa and the Islands of the Malay Archipelago. New Edition. With Maps and 150 Illustrations. One volume. Medium 8vo. 21s.

HAKE (G. Napier) on Explosives. [See Cundill.]

HALL'S (T. D.) School Manual of English Grammar. With Illustrations and Practical Exercises. 12mo. 3s. 6d.

—— Primary English Grammar for Elementary Schools. With numerous Exercises, and graduated Parsing Lessons. 16mo. 1s.

—— Manual of English Composition. With Copious Illustrations and Practical Exercises. 12mo. 3s. 6d.

—— Child's First Latin Book, comprising a full Practice of Nouns, Pronouns, and Adjectives, with the Verbs. 16mo. 2s.

HALLAM'S (Henry) WORKS :—

     The Constitutional History of England. *Library Edition,* 3 Vols. 8vo. 30s. *Cabinet Edition,* 3 Vols. Post 8vo. 12s. *Student's Edition,* Post 8vo. 7s. 6d.

     History of Europe during the Middle Ages. *Library Edition,* 3 Vols. 8vo. 30s. *Cabinet Edition,* 3 Vols. Post 8vo. 12s. *Student's Edition,* Post 8vo. 7s. 6d.

     Literary History of Europe during the 15th, 16th, and 17th Centuries. *Library Edition,* 3 Vols. 8vo. 36s. *Cabinet Edition,* 4 Vols. Post 8vo. 16s.   [Portrait. Fcap. 8vo. 3s. 6d.

HART'S ARMY LIST. (*Published Quarterly and Annually.*)

HAY (Sir J. H. Drummond). Western Barbary, its Wild Tribes and Savage Animals. Post 8vo. 2s.

HAYWARD (A.). Sketches of Eminent Statesmen and Writers, 2 Vols. 8vo. 28s.

—— The Art of Dining. Post 8vo. 2s.

—— A Selection from his Correspondence. Edited with an Introductory account of Mr. Hayward's Early Life. By H. E. Carlisle. 2 vols. Crown 8vo. 24s.

HEAD'S (Sir Francis) WORKS :—

     The Royal Engineer. Illustrations. 8vo. 12s.

     Life of Sir John Burgoyne. Post 8vo. 1s.

     Rapid Journeys across the Pampas. Post 8vo. 2s.

     Stokers and Pokers ; or, the L. and N. W. R. Post 8vo. 2s.

HEBER'S (Bishop) Journals in India. 2 Vols. Post 8vo. 7s.

—— Poetical Works. Portrait. Fcap. 8vo. 3s. 6d.

HERODOTUS. A New English Version. Edited, with Notes and Essays by Canon Rawlinson, Sir H. Rawlinson and Sir J. G. Wilkinson. Maps and Woodcuts. 4 Vols. 8vo. 48s.

HERRIES (Rt. Hon. John). Memoir of his Public Life. By his Son, Edward Herries, C.B. 2 Vols. 8vo. 24s.

FOREIGN HAND-BOOKS.

HAND-BOOK—TRAVEL-TALK. English, French, German, and
Italian. New and Revised Edition. 18mo. 3s. 6d.
—————— DICTIONARY : English, French, and German.
Containing all the words and idiomatic phrases likely to be required by
a traveller. Bound in leather. 16mo. 6s.
—————— HOLLAND AND BELGIUM. Map and Plans. 6s.
—————— NORTH GERMANY and THE RHINE,—
The Black Forest, the Hartz, Thüringerwald, Saxon Switzerland,
Rügen, the Giant Mountains, Taunus, Odenwald, Elsass, and Loth-
ringen. Map and Plans. Post 8vo. 10s.
—————— SOUTH GERMANY AND AUSTRIA,—Wurtem-
berg, Bavaria, Austria, Tyrol, Styria, Salzburg, the Dolomites, Hungary,
and the Dannbe, from Ulm to the Black Sea. Maps and Plans. Two
Parts. Post 8vo. 12s.
—————— SWITZERLAND, Alps of Savoy, and Piedmont
In Two Parts. Maps and Plans. Post 8vo. 10s.
—————— FRANCE, Part I. Normandy, Brittany, the French
Alps, the Loire, Seine, Garonne, and Pyrenees. Maps and Plans.
7s. 6d.
—————— FRANCE, Part II. Central France, Auvergne, the
Cevennes, Burgundy, the Rhone and Saone, Provence, Nimes, Arles,
Marseilles, the French Alps, Alsace, Lorraine, Champagne, &c. Maps
and Plans. Post 8vo. 7s. 6d.
—————— THE RIVIERA. Provence, Dauphiné. The Alpes
Maritimes, Avignon, Nimes, Arles, Marseilles, Toulon, Cannes,
Grasse, Nice, Menaco, Mentone, Bordighera, San Remo, Alassio,
Savona, &c.; Gren ble, Grande Chartreuse. Maps and Plans. 8vo. 5s.
—————— MEDITERRANEAN — its Principal Islands,
Cities, Seaports, Harbours, and Border Lands. For Travellers and
Yachtsmen, with nearly 50 Maps and Plans. Two Parts. Post 8vo. 21s.
—————— ALGERIA AND TUNIS. Algiers, Constantine,
Oran, Tlemcen Bougie, Tebessa, Biskra, the Atlas Range. Maps and
Plans. Post 8vo. 12s.
—————— PARIS, and Environs. Maps and Plans. 3s. 6d.
—————— SPAIN, Madrid, The Castiles, The Basque Provinces,
Leon, The Asturias, Galicia, Estremadura, Andalusia, Ronda, Granada,
Murcia, Valencia, Catalonia, Aragon, Navarre, The Balearic Islands,
&c. &c. Maps and Plans. Two Parts. Post 8vo. 20s.
—————— PORTUGAL, Lisbon, Oporto, Cintra, Ma'ra,
Madeira, the Azores, Canary Islands, &c. Map and Plan. 12s.
—————— NORTH ITALY, Turin, Milan, Cremona, the
Italian Lakes, Bergamo, Brescia, Verona, Mantua, Vicenza, Padua,
Ferrara, Bologna, Ravenna, Rimini, Piacenza, Genoa, the Riviera,
Venice, Parma, Modena, and Romagna. Maps and Plans. Post 8vo. 10s.
—————— CENTRAL ITALY, Florence, Lucca, Tuscany, The
Marshes, Umbria, &c. Maps and Plans. Two Parts. Post 8vo. 6s.
—————— ROME AND ITS ENVIRONS. 50 Maps and Plans. 10s.
—————— SOUTH ITALY AND SICILY, including Naples
and its Environs, Pompeii, Herculaneum, Vesuvius; Sorrento, Capri;
Amalfi, Paestum, Pozzuoli, Capua, Taranto, Bari; Brindisi and the
Roads from Rome to Naples; Palermo, Messina, Syracuse, Catania
&c. Two Parts. Maps. Post 8vo. 12s
—————— NORWAY, Christiania, Bergen, Trondhjem. The
Fjelds and Fjords. An entirely new Edition. Maps and Plans. 7 . 6d.
—————— SWEDEN, Stockholm, Upsala. Gothenburg, the
Shores of the Baltic, &c. Maps and Plan. Post 8vo. 6s.

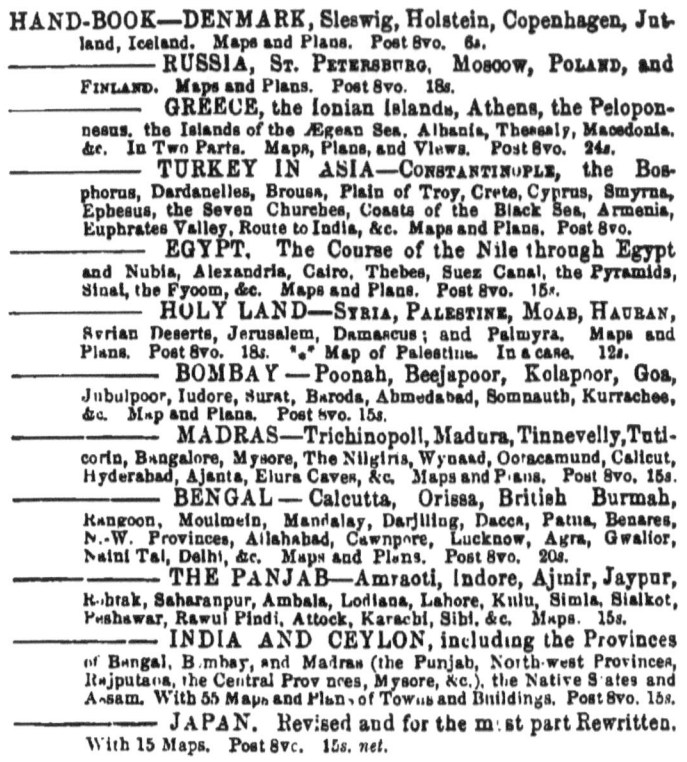

HAND-BOOK—DENMARK, Sleswig, Holstein, Copenhagen, Jutland, Iceland. Maps and Plans. Post 8vo. 6s.

———— RUSSIA, St. Petersburg, Moscow, Poland, and Finland. Maps and Plans. Post 8vo. 18s.

———— GREECE, the Ionian Islands, Athens, the Peloponnesus, the Islands of the Ægean Sea, Albania, Thessaly, Macedonia, &c. In Two Parts. Maps, Plans, and Views. Post 8vo. 24s.

———— TURKEY IN ASIA—Constantinople, the Bosphorus, Dardanelles, Broussa, Plain of Troy, Crete, Cyprus, Smyrna, Ephesus, the Seven Churches, Coasts of the Black Sea, Armenia, Euphrates Valley, Route to India, &c. Maps and Plans. Post 8vo.

———— EGYPT. The Course of the Nile through Egypt and Nubia, Alexandria, Cairo, Thebes, Suez Canal, the Pyramids, Sinai, the Fyoom, &c. Maps and Plans. Post 8vo. 15s.

———— HOLY LAND—Syria, Palestine, Moab, Hauran, Syrian Deserts, Jerusalem, Damascus; and Palmyra. Maps and Plans. Post 8vo. 18s. *⁎* Map of Palestine. In a case. 12s.

———— BOMBAY — Poonah, Beejapoor, Kolapoor, Goa, Jubulpoor, Iudore, Surat, Baroda, Ahmedabad, Somnauth, Kurrachee, &c. Map and Plans. Post 8vo. 15s.

———— MADRAS—Trichinopoll, Madura, Tinnevelly, Tuticorin, Bangalore, Mysore, The Nilgiris, Wynaad, Ooracamund, Calicut, Hyderabad, Ajanta, Elura Caves, &c. Maps and Plans. Post 8vo. 15s.

———— BENGAL — Calcutta, Orissa, British Burmah, Rangoon, Moulmein, Mandalay, Darjiling, Dacca, Patna, Benares, N.-W. Provinces, Allahabad, Cawnpore, Lucknow, Agra, Gwalior, Naini Tal, Delhi, &c. Maps and Plans. Post 8vo. 20s.

———— THE PANJAB—Amraoti, Indore, Ajmir, Jaypur, Rohtak, Saharanpur, Ambala, Lodiana, Lahore, Kulu, Simla, Sialkot, Peshawar, Rawul Pindi, Attock, Karachi, Sibi, &c. Maps. 15s.

———— INDIA AND CEYLON, including the Provinces of Bengal, Bombay, and Madras (the Punjab, North-west Provinces, Rajputana, the Central Provinces, Mysore, &c.), the Native States and Assam. With 55 Maps and Plans of Towns and Buildings. Post 8vo. 15s.

———— JAPAN. Revised and for the most part Rewritten. With 15 Maps. Post 8vo. 15s. net.

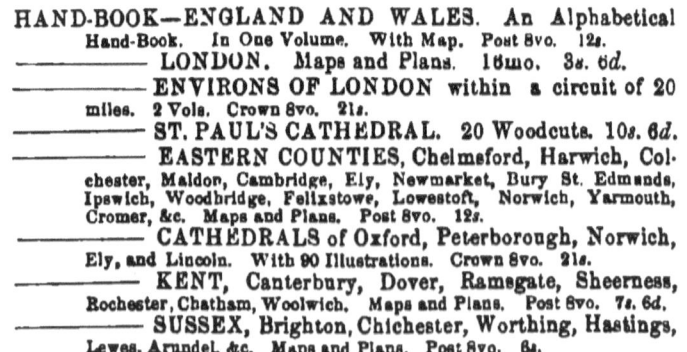

ENGLISH HAND-BOOKS.

HAND-BOOK—ENGLAND AND WALES. An Alphabetical Hand-Book. In One Volume. With Map. Post 8vo. 12s.

———— LONDON. Maps and Plans. 16mo. 3s. 6d.

———— ENVIRONS OF LONDON within a circuit of 20 miles. 2 Vols. Crown 8vo. 21s.

———— ST. PAUL'S CATHEDRAL. 20 Woodcuts. 10s. 6d.

———— EASTERN COUNTIES, Chelmsford, Harwich, Colchester, Maldon, Cambridge, Ely, Newmarket, Bury St. Edmunds, Ipswich, Woodbridge, Felixstowe, Lowestoft, Norwich, Yarmouth, Cromer, &c. Maps and Plans. Post 8vo. 12s.

———— CATHEDRALS of Oxford, Peterborough, Norwich, Ely, and Lincoln. With 90 Illustrations. Crown 8vo. 21s.

———— KENT, Canterbury, Dover, Ramsgate, Sheerness, Rochester, Chatham, Woolwich. Maps and Plans. Post 8vo. 7s. 6d.

———— SUSSEX, Brighton, Chichester, Worthing, Hastings, Lewes, Arundel, &c. Maps and Plans. Post 8vo. 6s.

HAND-BOOK—SURREY AND HANTS, Kingston, Croydon,
Reigate, Guildford, Dorking, Winchester, Southampton. New Forest,
Portsmouth, Isle of Wight, &c. Maps and Plans. Post 8vo. 10s.

——————— BERKS, BUCKS, AND OXON, Windsor, Eton,
Reading, Aylesbury, Uxbridge, Wycombe, Henley, Oxford, Blenheim,
the Thames, &c. Maps and Plans. Post 8vo. 9s.

——————— WILTS, DORSET, AND SOMERSET, Salisbury,
Chippenham, Weymouth, Sherborne, Wells, Bath, Bristol, Taunton,
&c. Map. Post 8vo. 12s.

——————— DEVON, Exeter, Ilfracombe, Linton, Sidmouth,
Dawlish, Teignmouth, Plymouth, Devonport, Torquay. Maps and Plans.
Post 8vo. 7s. 6d.

——————— CORNWALL, Launceston, Penzance, Falmouth,
the Lizard, Land's End, &c. Maps. Post 8vo. 6s.

——————— CATHEDRALS of Winchester, Salisbury, Exeter,
Wells, Chichester, Rochester, Canterbury, and St. Albans. With 130
Illustrations. 2 Vols. Crown 8vo. 36s. St. Albans separately. 6s.

——————— GLOUCESTER, HEREFORD, and WORCESTER,
Cirencester, Cheltenham, Stroud, Tewkesbury, Leominster, Ross, Mal-
vern, Kidderminster, Dudley, Evesham, &c. Map. Post 8vo. 9s.

——————— CATHEDRALS of Bristol, Gloucester, Hereford,
Worcester, and Lichfield. With 50 Illustrations. Crown 8vo. 16s.

——————— NORTH WALES, Bangor, Carnarvon, Beaumaris,
Snowdon, Llanberis, Dolgelly, Conway, &c. Maps. Post 8vo. 7s.

——————— SOUTH WALES, Monmouth, Llandaff, Merthyr,
Vale of Neath, Pembroke, Carmarthen, Tenby, Swansea, The Wye, &c.
Map. Post 8vo. 7s.

——————— CATHEDRALS OF BANGOR, ST. ASAPH,
Llandaff, and St. David's. With Illustrations. Post 8vo. 15s.

——————— NORTHAMPTONSHIRE AND RUTLAND—
Northampton, Peterborough, Towcester, Daventry, Market Har-
borough, Kettering, Wellingborough, Thrapston, Stamford, Upping-
ham, Oakham. Maps. Post 8vo. 7s. 6d.

——————— DERBY, NOTTS, LEICESTER, STAFFORD,
Matlock, Bakewell, Chatsworth, The Peak, Buxton, Hardwick, Dove Dale,
Ashborne, Southwell, Mansfield, Retford, Burton, Belvoir, Melton Mow-
bray, Wolverhampton, Lichfield, Walsall. Tamworth. Map. Post 8vo.

——————— SHROPSHIRE and CHESHIRE, Shrewsbury, Lud-
low, Bridgnorth, Oswestry, Chester, Crewe, Alderley, Stockport,
Birkenhead. Maps and Plans. Post 8vo. 6s.

——————— LANCASHIRE, Warrington, Bury, Manchester,
Liverpool, Burnley, Clitheroe, Bolton, Blackburne, Wigan, Preston, Roch-
dale, Lancaster, Southport, Blackpool, &c. Maps & Plans. Post 8vo. 7s. 6d.

——————— THE ENGLISH LAKES, in Cumberland, West-
moreland, and Lancashire; Lancaster, Furness Abbey, Ambleside,
Kendal, Windermere, Coniton, Keswick, Grasmere, Ulswater,
Carlisle, Cockermouth, Penrith, Appleby, &c. Maps. Post 8vo. 7s. 6d.

——————— YORKSHIRE, Doncaster, Hull, Selby, Beverley,
Scarborough, Whitby, Harrogate, Ripon, Leeds, Wakefield, Bradford,
Halifax, Huddersfield, Sheffield. Map and Plans. Post 8vo. 12s.

——————— CATHEDRALS of York, Ripon, Durham, Carlisle,
Chester, and Manchester. With 60 Illustrations. 2 Vols. Cr. 8vo. 21s.

——————— DURHAM and NORTHUMBERLAND, New-
castle, Darlington, Stockton, Hartlepool, Shields, Berwick-on-Tweed,
Morpeth, Tynemouth, Coldstream, Alnwick, &c. Map. Post 8vo. 10s.

——————— LINCOLNSHIRE, Grantham, Lincoln, Stamford,
Sleaford, Spalding, Gainsborough, Grimsby, Boston. Maps and Plans.
Post 8vo. 7s. 6d.

——————— WARWICKSHIRE. Map. Post 8vo.

——————— HERTS, BEDS and HUNTS.

HAND-BOOK—SCOTLAND, Edinburgh, Melrose, Kelso, Glasgow, Dumfries, Ayr, Stirling, Arran, The Clyde, Oban, Inverary, Loch Lomond, Loch Katrine and Trossachs, Caledonian Canal, Inverness, Perth, Dundee, Aberdeen, Braemar, Skye, Caithness, Ross, Sutherland, &c. Maps and Plans. Post 8vo. 9s.

—————— IRELAND, Dublin, Belfast, the Giant's Causeway, Donegal, Galway, Wexford, Cork, Limerick, Waterford, Killarney, Bantry, Glengariff, &c. Maps and Plans. Post 8vo. 10s.

HICKSON (DR. SYDNEY J.). A Naturalist in North Celebes; a Narrative of Travels in Minahassa, the Sangir and Talaut Islands, with Notices of the Fauna, Flora, and Ethnology of the Districts visited. Map and Illustrations. 8vo. 16s.

HISLOP (STEPHEN). [See SMITH, GEORGE.]

HOBSON (J. A.). [See MUMMERY.]

HOLLWAY (J. G.). A Month in Norway. Fcap. 8vo. 2s.

HONEY BEE. By REV. THOMAS JAMES. Fcap. 8vo. 1s.

HOOK (DEAN). Church Dictionary. A Manual of Reference for Clergymen and Students. New Edition, thoroughly revised. Edited by WALTER HOOK, M.A., and W. R. W. STEPHENS, M.A. Med. 8vo. 21s.

—————— (THEODORE) Life. By J. G. LOCKHART. Fcap. 8vo. 1s.

HOPE (A. J. BERESFORD). Worship in the Church of England. 8vo, 9s.; or, Popular Selections from, 8vo, 2s. 6d.

—————— WORSHIP AND ORDER. 8vo. 9s.

HOPE-SCOTT (JAMES), Memoir. [See ORNSBY.]

HORACE; a New Edition of the Text. Edited by DEAN MILMAN. With 100 Woodcuts. Crown 8vo. 7s. 6d.

—————— [See ETON.]

HOUGHTON'S (LORD) Monographs. Portraits. 10s. 6d.

—————— POETICAL WORKS. Portrait. 2 Vols. 12s.

—————— (ROBERT LORD) Stray Verses, 1889-90. Crown 8vo. 6s.

HOME AND COLONIAL LIBRARY. A Series of Works adapted for all circles and classes of Readers, having been selected for their acknowledged interest, and ability of the Authors. Post 8vo. Published at 2s. and 3s. 6d. each, and arranged under two distinctive heads as follows:—

CLASS A.
HISTORY, BIOGRAPHY, AND HISTORIC TALES.

SIEGE OF GIBRALTAR. By JOHN DRINKWATER. 2s.
THE AMBER-WITCH. By LADY DUFF GORDON. 2s.
CROMWELL AND BUNYAN. By ROBERT SOUTHEY. 2s.
LIFE OF SIR FRANCIS DRAKE. By JOHN BARROW. 2s.
CAMPAIGNS AT WASHINGTON. By REV. G. R. GLEIG. 2s.
THE FRENCH IN ALGIERS. By LADY DUFF GORDON. 2s.
THE FALL OF THE JESUITS. 2s.
LIFE OF CONDÉ. By LORD MAHON. 3s. 6d.
SALE'S BRIGADE. By REV. G. R. GLEIG. 2s.
THE SIEGES OF VIENNA. By LORD ELLESMERE. 2s.

THE WAYSIDE CROSS. By CAPT. MILMAN. 2s.
SKETCHES OF GERMAN LIFE. By SIR A. GORDON. 3s. 6d.
THE BATTLE OF WATERLOO. By REV. G. R. GLEIG. 3s. 6d.
AUTOBIOGRAPHY OF STEFFENS. 2s.
THE BRITISH POETS. By THOMAS CAMPBELL. 3s. 6d.
HISTORICAL ESSAYS. By LORD MAHON. 3s. 6d.
LIFE OF LORD CLIVE. By REV. G. R. GLEIG. 3s. 6d.
NORTH WESTERN RAILWAY. By SIR F. B. HEAD. 2s.
LIFE OF MUNRO. By REV. G. R. GLEIG. 3s. 6d.

CLASS B.
VOYAGES, TRAVELS, AND ADVENTURES.

JOURNALS IN INDIA. By BISHOP HEBER. 2 Vols. 7s.
TRAVELS IN THE HOLY LAND. By IRBY and MANGLES. 2s.
MOROCCO AND THE MOORS. By J. DRUMMOND HAY. 2s.
LETTERS FROM THE BALTIC. By A LADY. 2.
NEW SOUTH WALES. By MRS. MEREDITH. 2s.
THE WEST INDIES. By M. G. LEWIS. 2s.
SKETCHES OF PERSIA. By SIR JOHN MALCOLM. 3s. 6d.
MEMOIRS OF FATHER RIPA. 2s.
TYPEE AND OMOO. By HERMANN MELVILLE. 2 Vols. 7.
MISSIONARY LIFE IN CANADA. By REV. J. ABBOTT. 2s.
LETTERS FROM MADRAS. By A LADY. 2s.

HIGHLAND SPORTS. By CHARLES ST. JOHN. 3s. 6d.
PAMPAS JOURNEYS. By F. B. HEAD. 2s.
GATHERINGS FROM SPAIN. By RICHARD FORD. 3s. 6d.
THE RIVER AMAZON. By W. H. EDWARDS. 2s.
MANNERS & CUSTOMS OF INDIA. By REV. C ACLAND. 2s.
ADVENTURES IN MEXICO. By G. F. RUXTON. 3s. 6d.
PORTUGAL AND GALICIA. By LORD CARNARVON. 3s. 6d.
BUSH LIFE IN AUSTRALIA. By REV. H. W. HAYGARTH. 2s.
THE LIBYAN DESERT. By BAYLE ST. JOHN. 2s.
SIERRA LEONE. By A LADY. 3s. 6d.

. Each work may be had separately.

HUME (The Student's). A History of England, from the Invasion of Julius Cæsar to the Revolution of 1688. New Edition, revised, corrected, and continued to the Treaty of Berlin, 1878. By J. S. BREWER, M.A. With 7 Coloured Maps & 70 Woodcuts. Post 8vo. 7s. 6d.
. Sold also in 3 parts. Price 2s. 6d. each.

HUNNEWELL (JAMES F.). England's Chronicle in Stone; Derived from Personal Observations of the Cathedrals, Churches, Abbeys, Mona-teries, Castles, and Palaces, made in Journeys through the Imperial Island. With Illustrations. Medium 8vo. 24s.

HUTCHINSON (GEN.). Dog Breaking, with Odds and Ends for those who love the Dog and the Gun. With 40 Illustrations. Crown 8vo. 7s. 6d. *.* A Summary of the Rules for Gamekeepers. 1s.

HUTTON (H E.). Principia Græca; an Introduction to the Study of Greek. Comprehending Grammar, Delectus, and Exercise-book, with Vocabularies. Sixth Edition. 12mo. 3s. 6d.

HYMNOLOGY, DICTIONARY OF. [See JULIAN.]

ICELAND. [See COLES—DUFFERIN.]

INDIA. [See BROADFOOT—DUFFERIN—ELPHINSTONE—HAND-BOOK —SMITH—TEMPLE—MONIER WILLIAMS—LYALL.]

**IRBY AND MANGLES' Travels in Egypt, Nubia, Syria, and the Holy Land. Post 8vo. 2s.

JAMES (F. L.). The Wild Tribes of the Soudan : with an account of the route from Wady Halfa to Dongola and Berber. With Chapter on the Soudan, by SIR S. BAKER. Illustrations. Crown 8vo. 7s. 6d.

JAMESON (MRS.). Lives of the Early Italian Painters— and the Progress of Painting in Italy—Cimabue to Bassano. With 50 Portraits. Post 8vo. 12s.

JANNARIS (PROF. A. N.). A Pocket Dictionary of the Modern Greek and English Languages, as actually Written and Spoken. Being a Copious Vocabulary of all Words and Expressions Current in Ordinary Reading and in Everyday Talk, with Especial Illustration by means of Distinctive Signs, of the Colloquial and Popular Greek Language, for the Guidance of Students and Travellers. Fcap. 8vo.

c

JAPAN. [See BIRD—HANDBOOK—REED.]

JENNINGS (L. J.). Field Paths and Green Lanes : or Walks in
Surrey and Sussex. Popular Edition. With Illustrations. Cr. 8vo. 6s.
[See also CROKER.]

JERVIS (REV. W. H.). The Gallican Church, from the Con-
cordat of Bologna, 1516, to the Revolution. With an Introduction.
Portraits. 2 Vols. 8vo. 28s.

JESSE (EDWARD). Gleanings in Natural History. Fcp. 8vo. 3s. 6d.

JOHNSON'S (DR. SAMUEL) Life. [See BOSWELL.]

JULIAN (REV. JOHN J.). A Dictionary of Hymnology. A
Companion to Existing Hymn Books. Setting forth the Origin and
History of the Hymns contained in the Principal Hymnals, with
Notices of their Authors, &c., &c. Medium 8vo. (1636 pp.) 42s.

JUNIUS' HANDWRITING Professionally investigated. Edited by the
Hon. E. TWISLETON. With Facsimiles. Woodcuts. &c. 4to. £3 3s.

KEENE (H. G.). The Literature of France. 220 pp. Crown
8vo. 3s. (University Extension Manuals.)

KENDAL (MRS.) Dramatic Opinions. Post 8vo. 1s.

KERR (ROBT.). The Consulting Architect : Practical Notes on
Administrative Difficulties. Crown 8vo, 9s.

KING EDWARD VITH's Latin Grammar. 12mo. 3s. 6d.
—————————————— First Latin Book. 12mo. 2s. 6d.

KIRKES' Handbook of Physiology. Edited by W. MORRANT
BAKER and V. D. HARRIS. With 500 Illustrations. Post 8vo. 14s.

KNIGHT (PROF.). The Philosophy of the Beautiful. Crown 8vo.
3s. 6d. (University Extension Manuals.)

KUGLER'S HANDBOOK OF PAINTING.—The Italian Schools.
A New Edition, revised. By Sir HENRY LAYARD. With 200 Illustrations. 2 vols. Crown 8vo. 30s.

—————————————— The German, Flemish, and
Dutch Schools. New Edition revised. By Sir J. A. CROWE. With
60 Illustrations. 2 Vols. Crown 8vo. 24s.

LANE (E. W.). Account of the Manners and Customs of Modern
Egyptians. With Illustrations. 2 Vols. Post 8vo. 12s.

LAWLESS (HON. EMILY). Major Lawrence, F.L.S. : a Novel.
3 Vols. Crown 8vo. 31s. 6d. Cheap Edition, 6s.

—————— Plain Frances Mowbray, etc. Crown 8vo. 6s.

LAYARD (SIR A. H.). Nineveh and its Remains. With Illustrations. Post 8vo. 7s. 6d.

—————— Nineveh and Babylon. Illusts. Post 8vo. 7s. 6d.

—————— Early Adventures in Persia, Babylonia, and Susiana,
including a residence among the Bakhtiyari and other wild tribes,
before the discovery of Nineveh. Portrait, Illustrations and Maps.
2 Vols. Crown 8vo. 21s.

LEATHES (STANLEY). Practical Hebrew Grammar. With the
Hebrew Text of Genesis i.—vi., and Psalms i.—vi. Grammatical.
Analysis and Vocabulary. Post 8vo. 7s. 6d.

LENNEP (REV. H. J. VAN). Travels in Asia Minor. With Illustrations of Biblical History and Archæology. 2 Vols. Post 8vo. 24s.

—————— Modern Customs and Manners of Bible Lands, in
Illustration of Scripture. Illustrations. 2 Vols. 8vo. 21s.

LESLIE (C. R.). Handbook for Young Painters. Illustrations.
Post 8vo. 7s. 6d.

LETO (Pomponio). Eight Months at Rome during the Vatican Council. 8vo. 12s.

LETTERS from the Baltic. By Lady Eastlake. Post 8vo. 2s.
———————— Madras. By Mrs. Maitland. Post 8vo. 2s.
———————— Sierra Leone. By Mrs. Melville. 3s. 6d.

LEVI (Leone). History of British Commerce; and Economic Progress of the Nation, from 1763 to 1878. 8vo. 18s.
———————— The Wages and Earnings of the Working Classes in 1883-4. 8vo. 3s. 6d.

LEWIS (T. Hayter). The Holy Places of Jerusalem. Illustrations. 8vo. 10s. 6d.

LEX SALICA; the Ten Texts with the Glosses and the Lex Emendata. Synoptically edited by J. H. Hessels. With Notes on the Frankish Words in the Lex Salica by H. Kern, of Leyden. 4to. 42s.

LIDDELL (Dean). Student's History of Rome, from the earliest Times to the establishment of the Empire. Woodcuts. Post 8vo. 7s. 6d.

LIND (Jenny), The Artist, 1820—1851. Her early Art-life and Dramatic Career. From Original Documents, Letters, Diaries, &c., in the possession of Mr. Goldschmidt. By Canon H. Scott Holland, M.A., and W. S. Rockstro. With Portraits, Illustrations, and Appendix of Music. 2 Vols. 8vo. 32s.

LINDSAY (Lord). Sketches of the History of Christian Art. 2 Vols. Crown 8vo. 21s.

LISPINGS from LOW LATITUDES; or, the Journal of the Hon. Impulsia Gushington. Edited by Lord Dufferin. With 24 Plates. 4to 21s.

LIVINGSTONE (Dr). First Expedition to Africa, 1840-56. Illustrations. Post 8vo. 7s. 6d.
———————— Second Expedition to Africa, 1858-64. Illustrations. Post 8vo. 7s. 6d.
———————— Last Journals in Central Africa, to his Death. By Rev. Horace Waller. Maps and Illustrations. 2 Vols. 8vo. 15s.
———————— Personal Life. By Wm. G. Blaikie, D.D. With Map and Portrait. 8vo. 6s.

LOCKHART (J. G.). Ancient Spanish Ballads. Historical and Romantic. Translated, with Notes. Illustrations. Crown 8vo. 5s.
———————— Life of Theodore Hook. Fcap. 8vo. 1s.

LONDON: Past and Present; its History, Associations, and Traditions. By Henry B. Wheatley, F.S.A. Based on Cunningham's Handbook. Library Edition, on Laid Paper 3 Vols. Medium 8vo. 3l. 3s.

LOUDON (Mrs.). Gardening for Ladies. With Directions and Calendar of Operations for Every Month. Woodcuts. Fcap. 8vo. 3s. 6d.

LUMHOLTZ (Dr. C.). Among Cannibals; An Account of Four Years' Travels in Australia, and of Camp Life among the Aborigines of Queensland. With Maps and 120 Illustrations. Medium 8vo. 21s.

LUTHER (Martin). The First Principles of the Reformation, or the Three Primary Works of Dr. Martin Luther. Portrait. 8vo. 12s.

LYALL (Sir Alfred C.), K.C.B. Asiatic Studies; Religious and Social. 8vo. 12s.

LYELL (Sir Charles). Student's Elements of Geology. A new Edition, entirely revised by Professor P. M. Duncan, F.R.S. With 100 Illustrations. Post 8vo. 9s.
———————— Life, Letters, and Journals. Edited by his sister-in-law, Mrs. Lyell. With Portraits. 2 Vols. 8vo. 30s.

c 2

LYNDHURST (Lord). [See Martin.]

McCLINTOCK (Sir L.). Narrative of the Discovery of the
Fate of Sir John Franklin and his Companions in the Arctic Seas.
With Illustrations. Post 8vo. 7s. 6d.

MACDONALD (A.). Too Late for Gordon and Khartoum.
With Maps and Plans. 8vo. 12s.

MACGREGOR (J.). Rob Roy on the Jordan, Nile, Red Sea, Gen-
nesareth, &c. A Canoe Cruise in Palestine and Egypt and the Waters
of Damascus. With 70 Illustrations Crown 8vo. 7s. 6d.

MACKAY (Thomas). The English Poor. A Sketch of their
S cial and Economic History; and an attempt to estimate the influence of private property on character and habit. Crown 8vo. 7s 6d.

———— A Plea for Liberty : an Argument against Socialism and
Socialistic Legislation. Essays by various Writers. With an Intro-
duction by Herbert Spencer. Third and Popular Edition. With a
New and Original Essay on Self Help and State Pensions by C. J.
Radley. Post 8vo. 2s.

MAHON (Lord). [See Stanhope.]

MAINE (Sir H. Sumner). A Memoir of, by Sir M. E. Grant
Duff. wi h a Selection fr m his Indian Speeche, and Minutes. Edited
by Whitley Stokes. With Portrait. 8vo.

———— Ancient Law: its Connection with the Early History
of Society, and its Relation to Modern Ideas. 8vo. 9s.

———— Village Communities in the East and West. 8vo. 9s.

———— Early History of Institutions. 8vo. 9s.

———— Dissertations on Early Law and Custom. 8vo. 9s.

———— Popular Government. 8vo. 7s. 6d.

———— International Law. 8vo. 7s. 6d.

MALCOLM (Sir John). Sketches of Persia. Post 8vo. 3s. 6d.

MARCO POLO. [See Yule.]

MARKHAM (Mrs.). History of England. From the First Invasion by the Romans, continued down to 1880. Woodcuts. 12mo. 3s. 6d.

———— History of France. From the Conquest of Gaul by
Julius Cæsar, continued down to 1878. Woodcuts. 12mo. 3s. 6d.

———— History of Germany. From its Invasion by Marius
to the completion of Cologne Cathedral. Woodcuts. 12mo. 3s. 6d.

———— (Clements R.). A Popular Account of Peruvian Bark
and its introduction into British India. With Maps. Post 8vo. 14s.

MARSH (G. P.). Student's Manual of the English Language.
Edited with Additions. By Dr. Wm. Smith. Post 8vo. 7s. 6d.

MARTIN (Sir Theodore). Life of Lord Lyndhurst. With
Portraits. 8vo. 16s.

MASTERS in English Theology. Lectures by Eminent Divines.
With Introduction by Canon Barry. Post 8vo. 7s. 6d.

MATTHIÆ'S Greek Grammar. Abridged by Blomfield.
Revised by E. S. Crooke. 12mo. 4s.

MAUREL'S Character, Actions, &c., of Wellington. 1s. 6d.

MELVILLE (Hermann). Marquesas and South Sea Islands.
2 Vols. Post 8vo. 7s.

MEREDITH (Mrs. C.) Notes & Sketches of N. S. Wales. Post 8vo. 2s.

MEXICO. [See Brocklehurst—Ruxton.]

MICHAEL ANGELO, Sculptor, Painter, and Architect. His Life
and Works. By C. Heath Wilson. Illustrations. 8vo. 15s.

MILL (Dr. H. R.) The Realm of Nature: An Outline of Physio-
graphy. With 19 Coloured Maps and 68 Illustrations and Diagrams
(380 pp.). Crown 8vo. 5s. (University Extension Manuals.)

MILLER (Wm.). A Dictionary of English Names of Plants
applied among English speaking People to Plants, Trees, and Shrubs.
In Two Parts. La.in-English and English-Latin. Medium 8vo. 12s.

MILMAN'S (Dean) WORKS:—

HISTORY OF THE JEWS, from the earliest Period down to Modern
Times. 3 Vols. Post 8vo. 12s.

EARLY CHRISTIANITY, from the Birth of Christ to the Abolition of Paganism in the Roman Empire. 3 Vols. Post 8vo. 12s.

LATIN CHRISTIANITY, including that of the Popes to the
Pontificate of Nicholas V. 9 Vols. Post 8vo. 36s.

HANDBOOK TO ST. PAUL'S CATHEDRAL. Woodcuts. 10s. 6d.

QUINTI HORATII FLACCI OPERA. Woodcuts. Sm. 8vo. 7s. 6d.

FALL OF JERUSALEM. Fcap. 8vo. 1s.

———— (BISHOP, D.D.) Life. With a Selection from his
Correspondence and Journals. By his Sister. Map. 8vo. 12s.

MILNE (DAVID, M.A.). A Readable Dictionary of the English
Language. Etymologically arranged. Crown 8vo. 7s. 6d.

MINCHIN (J. G.). The Growth of Freedom in the Balkan
Peninsula. With a Map. Crown 8vo. 10s. 6d.

MISS BLAKE OF MONKSHALTON. By ISABELLA FORD. A
New Novel. Crown 8vo. 6s.

MIVART (ST. GEORGE). Lessons from Nature ; as manifested in
Mind and Matter. 8vo. 15s.

———— The Cat. An Introduction to the Study of Backboned
Animals, especially Mammals. With 200 Illustrations. Medium 8vo. 30s.

MOGGRIDGE (M. W.). Method in Almsgiving. A Handbook
for Helpers. Post 8vo. 3s. 6d.

MOORE (THOMAS). Life and Letters of Lord Byron. [See BYRON.]

MORELLI (GIOVANNI). Italian Painters. Critical Studies of their
Works. The Borghese and Doria Pamphili Galleries in Rome. Trans-
lated from the Ge man by CONSTANCE JOCELYN FFOULKES, with an
Introductory Notice by Sir HENRY LAYARD, G.C.B. 15s.

MOSELEY (PROF. H. N.). Notes by a Naturalist during
the voyage of H.M.S. "Challenger" round the World in the years
1872-76, under the command of Cap'ain sir O. S. Nares and Cap ain
F. T. Th m on. A New and Cheaper Edit., with Portrait, Map, and
numerous Woodcuts. Crown 8vo.

MOTLEY (JOHN LOTHROP). The Correspondence of. With
Portrait. 2 Vols. 8vo 30s.

———————— History of the United Netherlands : from the
Death of William the Silent to the Twelve Years' Truce, 1609. Portraits.
4 Vols. Post 8vo. 6s. each.

——————— Life and Death of John of Barneveld.
Illustrations. 2 Vols. Post 8vo. 12s.

MUIRHEAD (JOHN H.). The Elements of Ethics. Crown 8vo.
3s. (University Ext ns'on Series.)

MUMMERY (A. F.) AND J. A. HOBSON. The Physiology of
Industry : Being an Exposure of certain Fallacies in existing Theories
of Political Economy. Crown 8vo. 6s.

MUNRO'S (GENERAL) Life. By REV. G. R. GLEIG. 3s. 6d.

MUNTHE (AXEL). Letters from a Mourning City. Naples during the Autumn of 1884. Translated by MAUDE VALERIE WHITE.
With a Frontispiece. Crown 8vo. 6s.

MURCHISON (SIR RODERICK). And his Contemporaries. By
ARCHIBALD GEIKIE. Portraits. 2 Vols. 8vo. 30s.

MURRAY (John). A Publisher and his Friends : Memoir and
Correspondence of the late John Murray, with an Account of the Origin
and Progress of the House, 1768—1843. By Samuel Smiles, LL.D.
With Portraits. 2 Vols. 8vo. 32s.

MURRAY (A. S.). A History of Greek Sculpture from the
Earliest Times. With 130 Illustrations. 2 Vols. Medium 8vo. 36s.

———— Handbook of Greek Archæology. Sculpture,
Vases, Bronzes, G, ms, Ter a-co'tas, Architecture, Mural Paintings,
&c. Many Illustrations. Crown 8vo. 18s.

MURRAY'S MAGAZINE. Vol. I. to Vol. X. 8vo.
7s. 6d. each.

NADAILLAC (Marquis de). Prehistoric America. Translated
by N. D'Anvers. With Illustrations. 8vo. 16s.

NAPIER (General Sir Charles). His Life. By the Hon.
Wm. Napier Bruce. With Portrait and Maps. Crown 8vo. 12s.

———— (General Sir George T.). Passages in his Early
Military Life written by himself. Edited by his Son, General Wm.
C. E. Napier. With Portrait. Crown 8vo. 7s. 6d.

———— (Sir Wm.). English Battles and Sieges of the Peninsular
War. Portrait. Post 8vo. 5s.

NASMYTH (James). An Autobiography. Edited by Samuel
Smiles, LL.D., with Portrait, and 70 Illustrations. Post 8vo, 6s. ; or
Large Paper, 16s.

———— The Moon: Considered as a Planet, a World, and a
Satellite. With 26 Plates and numerous Woodcuts. Medium 8vo. 21s.

NEWMAN (Mrs.). Begun in Jest. A New Novel. 3 vols.
Crown 8vo. 31s. 6d.

NEW TESTAMENT. With Short Explanatory Commentary.
By Archdeacon Churton, M.A., and the Bishop of St. David's.
With 110 authentic Views, &c. 2 Vols. Crown 8vo. 21s. bound.

NEWTH (Samuel). First Book of Natural Philosophy ; an Introduction to the Study of Statics, Dynamics, Hydrostatics, Light, Heat,
and Sound, with numerous Examples. Small 8vo. 3s. 6d.

———— Elements of Mechanics, including Hydrostatics,
with numerous Examples. Small 8vo. 8s. 6d.

———— Mathematical Examples. A Graduated Series
of Elementary Examples in Arithmetic, Algebra, Logarithms, Trigo-
nometry, and Mechanics. Small 8vo. 8s. 6d.

NIMROD, On the Chace—Turf—and Road. With Portrait and
Plates. Crown 8vo. 5s. Or with Coloured Plates, 7s. 6d.

NORRIS (W. E.). Marcia. A Novel. Crown 8vo. 6s.

NORTHCOTE'S (Sir John) Notebook in the Long Parliament.
Containing Proceedings during its First Session, 1640. Edited, with
a Memoir, by A. H. A. Hamilton. Crown 8vo. 9s.

OCEAN STEAMSHIPS: A Popular Account of their Construction, Development, Management and Ap, l ances. By Various Writers.
Beautifully Illustrated, with 96 Woodcuts, Maps, &c. Medium 8vo. 12s.

O'CONNELL (Daniel). [See Fitzpatrick.]

ORNSBY (Prof. R.). Memoirs of J. Hope Scott, Q.C. (of
Abbotsford). 2 vols. 8vo. 24s.

OTTER (R. H.). Winters Abroad : Some Information respecting
Places visited by the Author on account of his Health. 7s. 6d.

OVID LESSONS. [See Eton.]

OWEN (Lieut.-Col.). Principles and Practice of Modern Artillery.
With Illustrations. 8vo. 15s.

OXENHAM (Rev. W.). English Notes for Latin Elegiacs ; with
Prefatory Rules of Composition in Elegiac Metre. 12mo. 3s. 6d.

PAGET (LORD GEORGE). The Light Cavalry Brigade in the Crimea. Map. Crown 8vo. 10s. 6d.

PALGRAVE (R. H. I.). Local Taxation of Great Britain and Ireland. 8vo. 6s.

PALLISER (MRS.). Mottoes for Monuments, or Epitaphs selected for General Use and Study. With Illustrations. Crown 8vo. 7s. 6d.

PARKER (C. S.), M.P. [See PEEL.]

PEEL'S (SIR ROBERT) Memoirs. 2 Vols. Post 8vo. 15s.

—— Life of: Early years; as Secretary for Ireland, 1812–18, and Secretary of State. 1822–27. Published by his Trustees, Viscount Hardinge and Right Hon. Arthur Wellesley Peel. Edited by CHARLES STUART PARKER, M.P. With Portrait. 8vo. 18s.

PENN (RICHARD). Maxims and Hints for an Angler and Chess-player. Woodcuts. Fcap. 8vo. 1s.

PERCY (JOHN, M.D.). METALLURGY. Fuel, Wood, Peat, Coal, Charcoal, Coke, Fire-Clays. Illustrations. 8vo. 30s.

—— Lead, including part of Silver. Illustrations. 8vo. 30s.

—— Silver and Gold. Part I. Illustrations. 8vo. 30s.

—— Iron and Steel. A New and Revised Edition, with the Author's Latest Corrections, and brought down to the present time. By H. BAUERMAN, F.G.S. Illustrations. 8vo.

PERRY (REV. CANON). History of the English Church. See STUDENTS' Manuals.

PHILLIPS (SAMUEL). Literary Essays from "The Times." With Portrait. 2 Vols. Fcap. 8vo. 7s.

POLLOCK (C. E.). A Book of Family Prayers. Selected from the Liturgy of the Church of England. 16mo. 3s. 6d.

POPE'S (ALEXANDER) Life and Works. With Introductions and Notes, by J. W. CROKER, REV. W. ELWIN, and W. J. COURTHOPE. 10 Vols. With Portraits. 8vo. 10s. 6d. each.

PORTER (REV. J. L.). Damascus, Palmyra, and Lebanon. Map and Woodcuts. Post 8vo. 7s. 6d.

PRAYER-BOOK (BEAUTIFULLY ILLUSTRATED). With Notes, by REV. THOS. JAMES. Medium 8vo. 18s. cloth.

PRINCESS CHARLOTTE OF WALES. Memoir and Correspondence. By LADY ROSE WEIGALL. With Portrait. 8vo. 8s. 6d.

PRITCHARD (CHARLES, D.D.). Occasional Thoughts of an Astronomer on Nature and Revelation. 8vo. 7s. 6d.

PSALMS OF DAVID. With Notes Explanatory and Critical by Dean Johnson, Canon Elliott, and Canon Cook. Medium 8vo. 10s. 6d.

PUSS IN BOOTS. With 12 Illustrations. By OTTO SPECKTER. 16mo. 1s. 6d. Or coloured, 2s. 6d.

QUARTERLY REVIEW (THE). 8vo. 6s.

QUILL (ALBERT W.). History of P. Cornelius Tacitus. Translated into English, with Introduction and Notes Critical and Explanatory. 2 Vols. 8vo.

RAE (EDWARD). Country of the Moors. A Journey from Tripoli to the Holy City of Kairwan. Etchings. Crown 8vo. 12s.

—— The White Sea Peninsula. Journey to the White Sea, and the Kola Peninsula. Illustrations. Crown 8vo. 15s.

—— (GEORGE). The Country Banker; His Clients, Cares, and Work, from the Experience of Forty Years. Crown 8vo. 7s. 6d.

RAMSAY (PROF. W. M.). The Historical Geography of Asia Minor. With 6 Maps, Tables, &c. 8vo. 18s.

RASSAM (HORMUZD). British Mission to Abyssinia. Illustrations. 2 Vols. 8vo. 28s.

RAWLINSON'S (CANON) **Five Great Monarchies of Chaldæa,** Assyria, Media, Babylonia, and Persia. With Maps and Illustrations. 8 Vols. 8vo. 42s.

———— Herodotus, a new English Version. *See* page 12.

RAWLINSON'S (SIR HENRY) **England and Russia in the East;** a Series of Papers on the Condition of Central Asia. Map. 8vo. 12s.

REJECTED ADDRESSES (THE). BY JAMES AND HORACE SMITH. Woodcuts. Post 8vo. 3s. 6d.; or *Popular Edition*, Fcap. 8vo. 1s.

RICARDO'S (DAVID) **Works.** With a Notice of his Life and Writings. By J. R. M'CULLOCH. 8vo. 16s.

RIPA (FATHER). Residence at the Court of Peking. Post 8vo. 2s.

ROBERTSON (CANON). History of the Christian Church, from the Apostolic Age to the Reformation, 1517. 8 Vols. Post 8vo. 6s. each.

ROBINSON (W.). **English Flower Garden.** An Illustrated Dictionary of all the Plants used, and Directions for their Culture and Arrangement. With numerous Illustrations. Medium 8vo. 15s.

———— The Vegetable Garden; or, the Edible Vegetables, Salads, and Herbs cultivated in Europe and America. By M. VILMORIN-ANDRIEUX. With 750 Illustrations. 8vo. 15s.

———— Sub-Tropical Garden. Illustrations. Small 8vo. 5s.

———— Parks and Gardens of Paris, considered in Relation to other Cities. 350 Illustrations. 8vo. 18s.

———— Wild Garden; or, Our Groves and Gardens made Beautiful by the Naturalization of Hardy Exotic Plants. With 90 Illustrations. 8vo. 10s. 6d.

———— God's Acre Beautiful; or, the Cemeteries of the Future. With 8 Illustrations. 8vo. 7s. 6d.

ROMANS, St. Paul's Epistle to the. With Notes and Commentary by E. H. GIFFORD, D.D. Medium 8vo. 7s. 6d.

ROME (HISTORY OF). [See GIBBON—INGE—LIDDELL—SMITH—STUDENTS'.]

ROMILLY (HUGH H.). The Western Pacific and New Guinea. 2nd Edition. With a Map. Crown 8vo. 7s. 6d.

ROSS (MRS.) The Land of Manfred, Prince of Tarentum and King of Sicily: Rambles in remote parts of S. Italy, with special reference to their Historical associations. Illustrations. Crown 8vo. 10s. 6d.

RUMBOLD (SIR HORACE). The Great Silver River: Notes of a Residence in the Argentine Republic. Second Edition, with Additional Chapter. With Illustrations. 8vo. 12s.

RUXTON (GEO. F.). Travels in Mexico; with Adventures among Wild Tribes and Animals of the Prairies and Rocky Mountains. Post 8vo. 3s. 6d.

ST. JOHN (CHARLES). Wild Sports and Natural History of the Highlands of Scotland. Illustrated Edition. Crown 8vo. 15s. *Cheap Edition*, Post 8vo. 3s. 6d.

———— (BAYLE). Adventures in the Libyan Desert. Post 8vo. 2s.

ST. MAUR (MRS. ALGERNON), LADY SEYMOUR. Impressions of a Tenderfoot, during a Journey in search of Sport in the Far West. With Map and Illustrations. Crown 8vo. 12s.

SALE'S (SIR ROBERT) Brigade in Affghanistan. With an Account of the Defence of Jellalabad. By REV. G. R. GLEIG. Post 8vo. 2s.

SALMON (PROF. GEO., D.D.). An Introduction to the Study of the New Testament, and an Investigation into Modern Biblical Criticism, based on the most recent Sources of Information. Crown 8vo. 9s.

———— Lectures on the Infallibility of the Church. Post 8vo. 9s.

SCEPTICISM IN GEOLOGY; and the Reasons for it. An assemblage of facts from Nature combining to refute the theory of "Causes now in Action." By VERIFIER. Woodcuts. Crow bvo. 6s.

SCHARF (GEORGE). Authentic Portraits of Mary, Queen of Scots. An attempt to distinguish those to be relied upon from others indiscriminately bearing her name, and to dispel the confused ideas that have so long prevailed respecting her personal appearance. With Illustrations. Large 8vo.

SCHLIEMANN (DR. HENRY). Ancient Mycenæ. Illustrations. Medium 8vo. 50s.

———— Ilios ; the City and Country of the Trojans, With an Autobiography. Illustrations. Imperial 8vo. 50s.

———— Troja : Results of the Latest Researches and Discoveries on the site of Homer's Troy, and other sites made in 1882. Illustrations. Medium 8vo. 42s.

———— Tiryns : A Prehistoric Palace of the Kings of Tiryns, discovered by excavations in 1884-5. With Illustrations. Medium 8vo. 42s.

SCHREIBER (LADY CHARLOTTE). English Fans and Fan Leaves. Collected and Described. With 160 Plates. Folio. 7l. 7s.

———————— Foreign Fans and Fan Leaves. French, Italian, and German, chiefly relating to the French Revolution, Collected and Described. 150 Plates. Folio. 7l. 7s.

———————— Playing Cards of Various Ages and Countries, selec ed from the Collection of Lady Charlotte Schreiber. Vol I., English and Scottish ; Dutch and Flemish. With 141 Plaies. Folio.

SCOTT (SIR GILBERT). The Rise and Development of Mediæval Architecture. With 400 Illustrations. 2 Vols. Medium 8vo. 42s.

SHAIRP (PRINCIPAL) AND HIS FRIENDS. By Professor WM. KNIGHT, of St. Andrews. With Portrait. 8vo. 15s.

SHAW (T. B.). Manual of English Literature. Post 8vo. 7s. 6d.

———— Specimens of English Literature. Post 8vo. 5s.

———— (ROBERT). Visit to High Tartary, Yarkand, and Kashgar. With Map and Illustrations. 8vo. 16s.

SHAW (R. NORMAN). [See ARCHITECTURE.]

SMILES' (SAMUEL, LL.D.) WORKS :—

BRITISH ENGINEERS ; from the Earliest Period to the Death of the Stephensons. Illustrations. 5 Vols. Crown 8vo. 7s.6d. each.

GEORGE STEPHENSON. Post 8vo. 2s. 6d.

JAMES NASMYTH. Portrait and Illustrations. Post 8vo. 6s.

JASMIN : Barber, Poet, Philanthropist. Post 8vo. 6s.

SCOTCH NATURALIST (THOS.EDWARD). Illustrations. Post 8vo.6s.

SCOTCH GEOLOGIST (ROBERT DICK). Illustrations. 8vo. 12s.

SELF-HELP. With Illustrations of Conduct and Perseverance. Post 8vo. 6s.

———— In French. 5s.

CHARACTER. A Book of Noble Characteristics. Post 8vo. 6s.

THRIFT. A Book of Domestic Counsel. Post 8vo. 6s.

DUTY. With Illustrations of Courage, Patience, and Endurance. Post 8vo. 6s.

INDUSTRIAL BIOGRAPHY. Iron-Workers and Tool-Makers. 6s.

MEN OF INVENTION. Post 8vo. 6s.

LIFE AND LABOUR ; or, Characteristics of Men of Culture and Genius. Post 8vo. 6s.

SMITH'S (Samuel, LL.D.) Works —*continued.*
  The Huguenots ; Their Settlements, Churches, and Indus-
  tries in England and Ireland. Crown 8vo. 7*s.* 6*d.*
  Boy's Voyage Round the World. Illustrations. Post 8vo. 6*s.*
SIEMENS (Sir Wm.), C.E. Life of. By Wm. Pole, C.E. Portraits.
  8vo. 16*s.*
——— The Scientific Works of: a Collection of Papers and
  Discourses. Edited by E. F. Bamber, C.E. Vol. i.—Heat and
  Metallurgy; ii. — Electricity, &c.; iii. — Addresses and Lectures.
  Plates. 3 Vols. 8vo. 12*s.* each.
——— (Dr. Werner von). Collected Works of. Translated
  by F. F. Bamber. Vol. i.—Scientific Papers and Addresses. ii.—
  Applied Science. With Illustrations. 8vo.
SIERRA LEONE. By Mrs. Melville. Post 8vo. 3*s.* 6*d.*
SIMMONS' Constitution and Practice of Courts-Martial. 15*s.*
SMEDES (Susan Dabney). A Southern Planter. Memoirs of
  Thomas Dabney. Preface by Mr. Gladstone. Post 8vo. 7*s.* 6*d.*
SMITH (Dr. George) Student's Manual of the Geography of British
  India, Physical and Political. Maps. Post 8vo. 7*s.* 6*d.*
——— Life of Dr. Somerville of Glasgow, late Evangelist in India,
  Africa, Australia, Canada, and Chief Countries of Europe (1813—1889).
  Portrait. Post 8vo. 9*s.*
——— Life of Wm. Carey, D.D., 1761—1834. Shoemaker and
  Missionary. Professor of Sanscrit, Bengalee and Marathee at the College
  of Fort William, Calcutta. Illustrations. Post 8vo. 7*s.* 6*d.*
——— Life of Stephen Hislop, Pioneer, Missionary, and Naturalist
  in Central India, 1844—1863. Portrait. Post 8vo. 7*s.* 6*d.*
——— (Philip). History of the Ancient World, from the Creation
  to the Fall of the Roman Empire, A.D. 476 3 Vols. 8vo. 31*s.* 6*d.*
——— (R. Bosworth). Mohammed and Mohammedanism.
  Crown 8vo. 7*s.* 6*d.*
SMITH'S (Dr. Wm.) DICTIONARIES:—
  Dictionary of the Bible; its Antiquities, Biography,
  Geography, and Natural History. Illustrations. 3 Vols. 8vo. 105*s.*
  Concise Bible Dictionary. Illustrations. 8vo. 21*s.*
  Smaller Bible Dictionary. Illustrations. Post 8vo. 7*s.* 6*d.*
  Christian Antiquities. Comprising the History, Insti-
  tutions, and Antiquities of the Christian Church. Illustrations. 2 Vols.
  Medium 8vo. 3*l.* 13*s.* 6*d.*
  Christian Biography, Literature, Sects, and Doctrines;
  from the Times of the Apostles to the Age of Charlemagne. Medium 8vo.
  Now complete in 4 Vols. 6*l.* 16*s.* 6*d.*
  Greek and Roman Antiquities. Including the Laws, Institu-
  tions, Domestic Usages, Painting, Sculpture, Music, the Drama, &c.
  Third Edition, Revised and Enlarged. 2 Vols. Med. 8vo. 31*s.* 6*d.* each.
  Greek and Roman Biography and Mythology. Illustrations.
  3 Vols. Medium 8vo. 4*l.* 4*s.*
  Greek and Roman Geography. 2 Vols. Illustrations.
  Medium 8vo. 56*s.*
  Atlas of Ancient Geography—Biblical and Classical.
  Folio. 6*l.* 6*s.*
  Classical Dictionary of Mythology, Biography, and
  Geography. 1 Vol. With 750 Woodcuts. 8vo. 18*s.*
  Smaller Classical Dict. Woodcuts. Crown 8vo. 7*s.* 6*d.*
  Smaller Dictionary of Greek and Roman Antiquities.
  Woodcuts. Crown 8vo. 7*s.* 6*d.*
  Smaller Latin-English Dictionary. 12mo. 7*s.* 6*d.*

SMITH'S (Dr. Wm.) Dictionaries—*continued.*

Complete Latin-English Dictionary. With Tables of the
Roman Calendar, Measures, Weights, Money, and a Dictionary of
Proper Names. 8vo. 16*s.*

Copious and Critical English-Latin Dict. 8vo. 16*s.*

Smaller English-Latin Dictionary. 12mo. 7*s. 6d.*

SMITH'S (Dr. Wm.) ENGLISH COURSE:—

School Manual of English Grammar,with Copious Exercises,
Appendices and Index. Post 8vo. 3*s. 6d.*

Primary English Grammar, for Elementary Schools, with
carefully graduated Parsing Lessons. 16mo. 1*s.*

Manual of English Composition. With Copious Illustrations and Practical Exercises. 12mo. 3*s. 6d.*

Primary History of Britain. 12mo. 2*s. 6d.*

School Manual of Modern Geography. Post 8vo. 5*s.*

A Smaller Manual of Modern Geography. 16mo. 2*s. 6d.*

SMITH'S (Dr. Wm.) FRENCH COURSE:—

French Principia. Part I. A First Course, containing a
Grammar, Delectus, Exercises, and Vocabularies. 12mo. 3*s. 6d.*

Appendix to French Principia. Part I. Containing additional Exercises, with Examination Papers. 12mo. 2*s. 6d.*

French Principia. Part II. A Reading Book, containing
Fables, Stories, and Anecdotes, Natural History, and Scenes from the
History of France. With Grammatical Questions, Notes and copious
Etymological Dictionary. 12mo. 4*s. 6d.*

French Principia. Part III. Prose Composition, containing
Hints on Translation of English into French, the Principal Rules of
the French Syntax compared with the English, and a Systematic Course
of Exercises on the Syntax. 12mo. 4*s. 6d.* [Post 8vo. 6*s.*

Student's French Grammar. With Introduction by M. Littré.

Smaller Grammar of the French Language. Abridged
from the above. 12mo. 3*s. 6d.*

SMITH'S (Dr. Wm.) GERMAN COURSE:—

German Principia. Part I. A First German Course, containing a Grammar, Delectus, Exercise Book, and Vocabularies. 12mo. 3*s. 6d.*

German Principia. Part II. A Reading Book; containing
Fables, Anecdotes, Natural History, and Scenes from the History of
Germany. With Questions. Notes, and Dictionary. 12mo. 3*s. 6d.*

Practical German Grammar. Post 8vo. 3*s. 6d.*

SMITH'S (Dr. Wm.) ITALIAN COURSE:—

Italian Principia. Part I. An Italian Course, containing a
Grammar, Delectus, Exercise Book, with Vocabularies, and Materials
for Italian Conversation. 12mo. 3*s. 6d.*

Italian Principia. Part II. A First Italian Reading Book,
containing Fables, Anecdotes, History, and Passages from the best
Italian Authors, with Grammatical Questions, Notes, and a Copious
Etymological Dictionary. 12mo. 3*s.* '*d.* [Children).

SMITH'S (Dr. Wm.) Young Beginner's First Latin Course (for

I. A First Latin Book. The Rudiments of Grammar, Easy
Grammatical Que tions and Exercises with Vocabular es. 12mo. 2*s.*

II. A Second Latin Book. An Easy Latin Reading Book,
with an Analysis of the Sentences, Notes, and a Dict onary. 12mo. 2*s.*

III. A Third Latin Book. The Principal Rules of Syntax,
with Easy Ex rcises, Ques.ions, Vocabula ies, and an English-Latin
Dictionary. 2*s.*

IV. A Fourth Latin Book. A Latin Vocabulary for Beginners.
Arrange l acc rding to Subjects and Etymologies. 12mo. 2*s.*

SMITH'S (Dr. Wm.) LATIN COURSE.

PRINCIPIA LATINA. Part I. First Latin Course, containing a Grammar, Delectus, and Exercise Book, with Vocabularies. 12mo. 3s. 6d.
*** In this Edition the Cases of the Nouns, Adjectives, and Pronouns are arranged both as in the ORDINARY GRAMMARS and as in the PUBLIC SCHOOL PRIMER, together with the corresponding Exercises.

APPENDIX TO PRINCIPIA LATINA. Part I.; being Additional Exercises, with Examination Papers 12mo. 2s. 6d.

PRINCIPIA LATINA. Part II. A Reading-book of Mythology, Geography, Roman Antiquities, and History. With Notes and Dictionary. 12mo. 3s. 6d.

PRINCIPIA LATINA. Part III. A Poetry Book. Hexameters and Pentameters; Eclog. Ovidianæ; Latin Prosody. 12mo. 3s. 6d.

PRINCIPIA LATINA. Part IV. Prose Composition. Rules of Syntax, with Examples, Explanations of Synonyms, and Exercises on the Syntax. 12mo. 3s. 6d.

PRINCIPIA LATINA. Part V. Short Tales and Anecdotes for Translation into Latin. A New and Enlarged Edition. 12mo. 3s. 6d.

LATIN-ENGLISH VOCABULARY AND FIRST LATIN-ENGLISH DICTIONARY FOR PHÆDRUS, CORNELIUS NEPOS, AND CÆSAR. 12mo. 3s. 6d.

STUDENT'S LATIN GRAMMAR. For the Higher Forms. A new and thoroughly revised Edition. Post 8vo. 6s.

SMALLER LATIN GRAMMAR. New Edition. 12mo. 3s. 6d.

SMITH'S (Dr. Wm.) GREEK COURSE:—

INITIA GRÆCA. Part I. A First Greek Course, containing a Grammar, Delectus, and Exercise-book. With Vocabularies. 12mo. 3s. 6d.

APPENDIX TO INITIA GRÆCA. Part I. Containing additional Exercises. With Examination Papers. Post 8vo. 2s. 6d.

INITIA GRÆCA. Part II. A Reading Book. Containing Short Tales, Anecdotes, Fables, Mythology, and Grecian History. 12mo. 3s. 6d.

INITIA GRÆCA. Part III. Prose Composition. Containing the Rules of Syntax, with copious Examples and Exercises. 12mo. 3s. 6d.

STUDENT'S GREEK GRAMMAR. For the Higher Forms. Post 8vo. 6s.

SMALLER GREEK GRAMMAR. 12mo. 3s. 6d.

GREEK ACCIDENCE. 12mo. 2s. 6d.

PLATO, Apology of Socrates, &c. With Notes. 12mo. 3s. 6d.

SMITH'S (Dr. Wm.) SMALLER HISTORIES:—

SCRIPTURE HISTORY. Maps and Woodcuts. 16mo. 3s. 6d.

ANCIENT HISTORY. Woodcuts. 16mo. 3s. 6d.

ANCIENT GEOGRAPHY. Woodcuts. 16mo. 3s. 6d.

MODERN GEOGRAPHY. 16mo. 2s. 6d.

GREECE. With Coloured Map and Woodcuts. 16mo. 3s. 6d.

ROME. With Coloured Maps and Woodcuts. 16mo. 3s. 6d.

CLASSICAL MYTHOLOGY. Woodcuts. 16mo. 3s. 6d.

ENGLAND. With Coloured Maps and Woodcuts. 16mo. 3s. 6d.

ENGLISH LITERATURE. 16mo. 3s. 6d.

SPECIMENS OF ENGLISH LITERATURE. 16mo. 3s. 6d.

SOMERVILLE (MARY). Physical Geography. Post 8vo. 9s.

———— Connexion of the Physical Sciences. Post 8vo. 9s.

———— (DR., OF GLASGOW). [See SMITH, GEORGE.]

SOUTH (John F.). Household Surgery ; or, Hints for Emergencies. With Woodcuts. Fcap. 8vo. 3s. 6d.

SOUTHEY (Robt.). Lives of Bunyan and Cromwell. Post 8vo. 2s.

STANHOPE'S (Earl) WORKS :—

History of England from the Reign of Queen Anne to the Peace of Versailles, 1701-83. 9 Vols. Post 8vo. 5s. each.
Life of William Pitt. Portraits. 3 Vols. 8vo. 36s.
Notes of Conversations with the Duke of Wellington. Crown 8vo. 7s. 6d.
Miscellanies. 2 Vols. Post 8vo. 13s.
British India, from its Origin to 1783. Post 8vo. 3s. 6d.
History of "Forty-Five." Post 8vo. 3s.
Historical and Critical Essays. Post 8vo. 3s. 6d.
Retreat from Moscow, and other Essays. Post 8vo. 7s. 6d.
Life of Condé. Post 8vo. 3s. 6d.
Story of Joan of Arc. Fcap. 8vo. 1s.
Addresses on Various Occasions. 16mo. 1s.
[See also Wellington.]

STANLEY'S (Dean) WORKS :—

Sinai and Palestine. Coloured Maps. 8vo. 12s.
Bible in the Holy Land; Extracts from the above Work. Woodcuts. Post 8vo. 3s. 6d.
Eastern Church. Plans. Crown 8vo. 6s.
Jewish Church. From the Earliest Times to the Christian Era. Portrait and Maps. 3 Vols. Crown 8vo. 18s.
Church of Scotland. 8vo. 7s. 6d.
Epistles of St. Paul to the Corinthians. 8vo. 18s.
Life of Dr. Arnold. Portrait. 2 Vols. Cr. 8vo. 12s.
Canterbury. Illustrations. Crown 8vo. 6s.
Westminster Abbey. Illustrations. 8vo. 15s.
Sermons Preached in Westminster Abbey. 8vo. 12s.
Memoir of Edward, Catherine, and Mary Stanley. Cr. 8vo. 9s.
Christian Institutions. Crown 8vo. 6s.
Essays on Church and State ; 1850—1870. Crown 8vo. 6s.
Sermons to Children, including the Beatitudes, the Faithful Servant, &c. Post 8vo. 3s. 6d.
[See also Bradley.]

STEBBING (Wm.). Some Verdicts of History Reviewed. 8vo. 12s.

STEPHENS (Rev. W. R. W.). Life and Times of St. John Chrysostom. A Sketch of the Church and the Empire in the Fourth Century. Portrait. 8vo. 7s. 6d.

STREET (G. E.), R.A. Gothic Architecture in Brick and Marble. With Notes on North of Italy. Illustrations. Royal 8vo. 26s.

—— Memoir of. By Arthur E. Street. Portrait. 8vo. 15s.

STUART (Villiers). Egypt after the War. With Descriptions of the Homes and Habits of the Natives, &c. Coloured Illustrations and Woodcuts. Royal 8vo. 31s. 6d.

—————— Adventures Amidst the Equatorial Forests and Rivers of South America, also in the West Indies and the Wilds of Florida; to which is added " Jamaica Revisited." With Map and Illustrations. Royal 8vo. 21s.

STUDENTS' MANUALS. Post 8vo.   7s. 6d. each Volume :—

Hume's History of England from the Invasion of Julius Cæsar to the Revolution in 1688. Revised, and continued to the Treaty of Berlin, 1878. By J. S. Brewer, M.A. Coloured Maps and Woodcuts. Or in 3 parts, price 2s. 6d. each.
    *** Questions on the above Work, 12mo.   2s.

History of Modern Europe, from the Fall of Constantinople to the Treaty of Berlin, 1878. By R. Lodge, M.A.

Old Testament History ; from the Creation to the Return of the Jews from Captivity. Woodcuts.

New Testament History. With an Introduction connecting the History of the Old and New Testaments. Woodcuts.

Evidences of Christianity. By H. Wace, D.D.   [In the Press.

Ecclesiastical History ; a History of the Christian Church. By Philip Smith, B.A. With numerous Woodcuts. 2 Vols. Part I. A.D. 30—1003. Part II., 1003—1614.

English Church History.   By Canon Perry.   3 Vols. First Peri d, A.D. 596—1509. Second Period, 1509—1717. Third Period. 1717—1884.

Ancient History of the East ; Egypt, Assyria, Babylonia, Media, Persia, Asia Minor, and Phœnicia. By Philip Smith, B.A. Woodcuts.

——— Geography. By Canon Bevan. Woodcuts.

History of Greece ; from the Earliest Times to the Roman Conquest. By Wm. Smith, D.C.L. Woodcuts.
    *** Questions on the above Work, 12mo.   2s.

History of Rome ; from the Earliest Times to the Establishment of the Empire. By Dean Liddell. Woodcuts.

History of the Roman Empire ; from the Establishment of the Empire to the reign of Commodus. By J. B. Bury. With Illustrations.

Gibbon's Decline and Fall of the Roman Empire. Woodcuts.

Hallam's History of Europe during the Middle Ages.

Hallam's History of England ; from the Accession of Henry VII. to the Death of George II.

History of France ; from the Earliest Times to the Fall of the Second Empire. By H. W. Jervis. With Coloured Maps and Woodcuts.

English Language.   By Geo P. Marsh.

English Literature.   By T. B. Shaw, M.A.

Specimens of English Literature.   By T. B. Shaw.   5s.

Modern Geography ; Mathematical, Physical and Descriptive. By Canon Bevan, M.A. Woodcuts.

Geography of British India.   Political and Physical.   By George Smith, LL.D. Maps.

Moral Philosophy. By Wm. Fleming.

STURGIS (Julian).   Comedy of a Country House.   6s.

SUMNER'S (Bishop) Life and Episcopate during 40 Years. By Rev. G. H. Sumner. Portrait. 8vo. 14s.

SWAINSON (Canon).   Nicene and Apostles' Creeds ; Their Literary History ; together with some Account of "The Creed of St. Athanasius." 8vo. 16s.

TACITUS. [See Quill.]

TEMPLE (Sir Richard). India in 1880. With Maps. 8vo. 16s.

——— Men and Events of My Time in India. 8vo. 16s.

TEMPLE (Sir Richard). Oriental Experience. Essays and Addresses delivered on Various Occasions. With Maps and Woodcuts. 8vo. 16s.

THIBAUT'S (Antoine) Purity in Musical Art. With Prefatory Memoir by W. H. Gladstone, M.P. Post 8vo. 7s. 6d.

THOMAS (Sidney Gilchrist), Inventor; Memoir and Letters. Edited by R. W. Burnie. Portraits. Crown 8vo. 9s.

THOMSON (J. Arthur). The Study of Animal Life. With many Illustrations. (University Extension Manuals.)

THORNHILL (Mark). The Personal Adventures and Experiences of a Magistrate during the Indian Mutiny. Crown 8vo. 12s.

TITIAN'S LIFE AND TIMES. By Crowe and Cavalcaselle. Illustrations. 2 Vols. 8vo. 21s.

TOCQUEVILLE'S State of Society in France before the Revolution, 1789, and on the Causes which led to that Event. 8vo. 12s.

TOZER (Rev. H. F.). Highlands of Turkey, with Visits to Mounts Ida, Athos, Olympus, and Pelion. 2 Vols. Crown 8vo. 24s.

———— Lectures on the Geography of Greece. Post 8vo. 9s.

TRISTRAM (Canon). Great Sahara. Illustrations. Crown 8vo. 15s.

———— Land of Moab : Travels and Discoveries on the East Side of the Dead Sea and the Jordan. Illustrations. Crown 8vo. 15s.

TWINING (Rev. Thos.). Recreations and Studies of a Country Clergyman of the Last Century. 2 Vols. Crown 8vo. 9s. each.

———— (Louisa). Symbols and Emblems of Early and Mediæval Christian Art. With 5 0 Illustrations. Crown 8vo. 6s.

TYLOR (E. B.). Researches into the Early History of Mankind, and Development of Civilization. 3rd Edition. 8vo. 12s.

———— Primitive Culture: the Development of Mythology, Philosophy, Religion, Art, and Custom. 2 Vols. 8vo. 3rd Edit. 21s.

UNIVERSITY EXTENSION MANUALS. Edited by Professor Wm. Knight (St. Andrew's). A series of Manuals dealing with Literature, Science, Philosophy, History, Art, &c. Crown 8vo. Prospectus with full particulars will be forwarded on application

VIRCHOW (Professor). The Freedom of Science in the Modern State. Fcap. 8vo. 2s.

WACE (Rev. Henry), D.D. The Principal Facts in the Life of our Lord, and the Authority of the Evangelical Narratives. Post 8vo. 6s.

———— Christianity and Morality. Boyle Lectures for 1874 and 1875. Seventh Edition. Crown 8vo. 6s.

———— The Foundations of Faith, being the Bampton Lectures for 1879. 8vo. 7s. 6d.

WALES (H.R.H. the Prince of). Speeches and Addresses. 1863-1888. Ed ted by Dr. J. Macaulay. With Portrait. 8vo. 12s.

WELLINGTON (Duke of). Notes of Conversations with the late Earl Stanhope. 1831-1851. Crown 8vo. 7s. 6d.

———— Supplementary Despatches, relating to India, Ireland, Denmark, Spanish America, Spain, Portugal, France, Congress of Vienna, Waterloo and Paris. 15 Vols. 8vo. 20s. each.

———— Civil and Political Correspondence. Vols. I. to VIII. 8vo. 20s.

————Speeches in Parliament. 2 Vols. 8vo. 42s.

WESTCOTT (Canon B. F.) The Gospel according to St. John, with Notes and Dissertations (Reprinted from the Speaker's Commentary.) 8vo. 10s. 6d.

WHARTON (Capt. W. J. L.), R.N. Hydrographical Surveying : being a description of the means and methods employed in constructing Marine Charts. With Illustrations. 8vo. 15s.

WHITE (W. H.). Manual of Naval Architecture, for the use of Naval Officers, Shipbuilders, and Yachtsmen, &c. Illustrations. 8vo. 24s.

WHYMPER (Edward). Travels amongst the Great Andes of the Equator. With 140 Original Illustrations, drawn by F. Barnard, A. Corbould, F. Dadd, W. E. Lapworth, W. H. Overend, P. Skelton, E. Wagner, E. Wilson, Joseph Wolf, and others. Engraved by the Author. With Maps and Illustrations. Medium 8vo. 21s. Net. To range with "Scrambles amongst the Alps."

————— Supplementary Appendix to the above. With 61 Figures of New Genera and Species. Illus. Medium 8vo. 21s. Net.

——— ——— How to Use the Aneroid Barometer. With numerous Tables. 2s. 6d. Net.

WILBERFORCE'S (Bishop) Life of William Wilberforce. Portrait. Crown 8vo. 6s.

————————— (Samuel, D.D.), Lord Bishop of Oxford and Winchester; his Life. By Canon Ashwell, and R. G. Wilberforce. Portraits. 3 Vols. 8vo. 15s. each.

WILKINSON (Sir J. G.). Manners and Customs of the Ancient Egyptians, their Private Life, Laws, Arts, Religion, &c. A new edition. Edited by Samuel Birch, LL.D. Illustrations. 3 Vols. 8vo. 84s.

————————— Popular Account of the Ancient Egyptians. With 500 Woodcuts. 2 Vols. Post 8vo. 12s.

WILLIAMS (Sir Monier). Brahmanism and Hinduism, Religious Thought and Life in India as based on the Veda. Enlarged Edit. 18s.

————— Buddhism; its connection with Brahmanism and Hinduism, and in its contrast with Christianity. With Illus. 8vo. 21s.

WINTLE (H. G.). Ovid Lessons. 12mo, 2s. 6d. [See Eton.]

WOOD'S (Captain) Source of the Oxus. With the Geography of the Valley of the Oxus. By Col. Yule. Map. 8vo. 12s.

WOODS (Mrs.). Esther Vanhomrigh. A Novel. Crown 8vo. 6s.

WORDS OF HUMAN WISDOM. Collected and Arranged by E. S. With a Preface by Canon Liddon. Fcap. 8vo. 3s. 6d.

WORDSWORTH (Bishop). Greece ; Pictorial, Descriptive, and Historical. With an Introduction on the Characteristics of Greek Art, by Geo. Scharf. New Edition revised by the Rev. H. F. Tozer, M.A. With 400 Illustrations. Royal 8vo. 31s. 6d.

————————— (Charles), Bishop of St. Andrews. The Collects of the Church of England, together with certain Psalms and Hymns appropriate to the Principal Festivals, rendered into Latin Verse. Crown 8vo, gilt edg s, 5s.

YORK (Archbishop of). Collected Essays. Crown 8vo. 9s.

YORK-GATE LIBRARY (Catalogue of). Formed by Mr. Silver. An Index to the Literature of Geography, Maritime and Inland Discovery, Commerce and Colonisation. Compiled by E. A. Petherick. 2nd Edition. Royal 8vo. 42s.

YOUNGHUSBAND (Capt. G. J.). The Queen's Commission : How to Prepare for it; how to Obtain it, and how to Use it. With Practical Information on the Cost and Prospects of a Military Career, Intended for Cadets, Subalterns, and Parents. Crown 8vo. 6s.

YULE (Colonel). The Book of Ser Marco Polo, the Venetian, concerning the Kingdoms and Marvels of the East. Illustrated by the Light of Oriental Writers and Modern Travels. With Maps and 80 Plates. 2 Vols. Medium 8vo.

————— and A. C. Burnell. A Glossary of Anglo-Indian Colloquial Words and Phrases, and of Kindred Terms; Etymological, Historical, Geographical, and Discursive. Medium 8vo. 36s.

————— (A. F.). The Cretan Insurrection. Post 8vo. 2s. 6d.

BRADBURY, AGNEW, & CO. LD., PRINTERS, WHITEFRIARS.